Destiny

By David Melde

* * *

DESTINY
By David Melde

First edition, July 2025. Cover design by Jamie Whyte.

ISBN 979-8-9931357-7-9

BRIGHT THREAD
BOOKS

A mythic imprint for transformative fiction

Table of Contents

CHAPTER ONE

The Galaxy Calls

I woke before the alarm. The orchard outside my window emerged from darkness in gradual increments, row after row of apple trees materializing through fog. Dew transformed each leaf into a prism, capturing first light in thousands of tiny mirrors.

The floorboards creaked beneath my feet as I padded downstairs. My kitchen waited, familiar and worn. The copper pot hung above the island where I'd left it yesterday, its bottom showing the patina of countless batches of cider. I lifted it down, feeling its substantial weight in my hands.

"Good morning, Go." Alice Tracker's hologram flickered to life from the cookbook propped against the windowsill. "Ready to continue with our autumn preserves?"

"Morning, Alice." I positioned the pot on the stove and reached for the basket of windfall apples I'd collected yesterday. "Let's get started."

Alice's image gestured toward ingredients as her recorded voice guided me through the process. "The secret to exceptional cider is patience. Allow the apples to release their essence slowly."

I quartered apples while steam rose between us, carrying the sharp scent of fruit and cinnamon. Behind Alice's projection, mason jars lined the windowsill: strawberry preserves from June, blackberry jam from August, pickled cucumbers from last week. The morning sun transformed them into jewels, each one a captured season.

The distant rumble of an engine pulled my attention from the bubbling pot. The old school bus had arrived early. I turned down the heat and wiped my hands on a dish towel.

"We'll finish later," I told Alice, closing the cookbook. Her image smiled and vanished.

Outside, thruman children spilled from the bus in a wave of excited chatter. My son, Marcus, counted heads with methodical precision.

"Mr. David!" A small boy with mismatched socks broke from the group and ran toward me. "Are we riding horses today?"

"Hayride first," I corrected, ruffling his hair. "Then we'll visit the horses."

The children clustered around me, their eager eyes brimming with anticipation. Their movements were uncoordinated: both too loose and too stiff at the same time. Limbs swung with a small lack of control, gestures overextended, then abruptly halted. When they walked, their steps teetered between graceful and clumsy, as though uncertain whether they were meant to flow or stumble.

I guided them toward the barn, their unsteady strides calling to mind Marcus's first uncertain steps as a child. They'd find their rhythm soon enough. Thruman children always began with clumsy hesitation, but their ability to absorb and adapt was remarkable.

The wagon stood ready, its bed freshly cleaned and filled with sweet-smelling hay, a steady presence amid the children's wavering movements. They pressed forward, some lunging too quickly, others faltering, their coordination wavering at the threshold of instinct and uncertainty.

"Everyone aboard," I called, helping the smallest ones climb up. "Hold on tight."

The tractor pulled us through morning-wet fields, children squealing with delight at each bump. We stopped at the paddock where my three horses grazed, their breath visible in the cool air.

"Who wants to help feed them?" Every hand shot up.

I showed them how to hold their palms flat, how to speak softly to nervous animals. The horses accepted apple slices with gentle lips, making the children giggle.

"Were there horses on Paradise too?" A girl with neatly braided hair gazed up at me, her expression solemn.

The question caught me off guard. "Yes," I said, the memory stirring. "They were all special."

She hesitated, then looked away. "They say you remember everything about Paradise."

I knelt beside her, watching the way she absently traced the hem of her sleeve. "Not everything," I murmured. "Just enough."

The children dispersed toward the apple trees, leaving Marcus and me alone by the paddock fence. He leaned against the weathered wood.

"The farm looks good, Papa. Those new saplings we planted last spring took root nicely."

"They did. Though that northeast corner still needs attention." I brushed hay from my sleeve. "How's life with Bea? The thrumans keeping you both busy?"

Marcus smiled, a gesture he'd perfected over the years. "We have most of the children in group homes now. Each one different, each one teaching us something new." He paused, watching a horse crop grass nearby. "Bea started a garden program. Says working with living things helps them understand their own growth."

"Smart woman."

"She is." His expression softened. "Sometimes I watch her with them, showing them how to transplant seedlings or identify beneficial insects, and I think about how far we've all come. From hibernation to this."

A cool breeze carried the scent of ripening apples across the paddock. In the distance, children's laughter mixed with the rustle of leaves.

"And you? Still happy with your choice?"

Marcus turned to face me. "Being a parent instead of becoming a captain? Every day." He straightened his jacket, a habit he'd picked up from Bea. "Though I still like dinosaurs."

We shared a quiet chuckle at the old joke. A school bell rang in the distance, signaling the approach of noon.

"I should gather them up," Marcus said. "Timetables wait for no thruman."

I squeezed his shoulder. "Come for dinner soon. Bring Bea. I'm trying out Alice's new preserve recipes."

He nodded, already moving toward the orchard where his charges waited. I watched him go, remembering the uncertain thruman child who'd once struggled to control his own limbs. Now he guided others through the same journey.

After demonstrating how to twist apples from branches without damaging next year's buds, I sent the children home with bags of fruit and jars of last season's cider.

Evening settled over Lucky Star Farm. I sat alone on the porch, watching Falfsun sink toward the horizon. It painted the sky as night fell.

My fingers moved automatically to my pocket, searching for the familiar shape of my father's watch. They found only empty fabric. The watch was gone, burned away in the memory palace fire years ago. A fire that, in my anger, I had caused. Sometimes I forgot.

The sunset deepened, casting long shadows across the orchard I'd planted with my own hands. Thirteen years since we'd arrived. Thirteen years of seasons passing, of building something new.

The cider would be finished by now. I should bottle it before bed.

I returned to the house, the taste of apple still lingering on my tongue. The orchard had been good to me this year, better than I deserved, perhaps. As I hung my jacket by the door, a CoreLink message blinked on my kitchen counter display.

"Temper requests your presence at the lab. Says it's urgent but not an emergency."

I smiled. With Temper, "urgent" could mean anything from a minor breakthrough to a complete revolution in quantum physics. Either way, it had been weeks since I'd seen him.

I walked through the driftways towards New Terracore's central hub. On the way, I watched thrumans and humans mingling in the communal gardens. A group of children played tag around a fountain, their movements more synchronized than they had been even a year ago. Progress happened in small increments, often invisible until you stepped back to look.

Temper's lab occupied an entire wing of the science complex. His security system recognized me immediately, doors sliding open with a soft whoosh. Inside, darkness greeted me, broken only by the eerie green glow of holographic projections filling the center of the room.

Falfsun floated in miniature, surrounded by data streams and analytical readouts. The hologram rotated slowly, revealing solar flares and prominence loops dancing across its surface. Temper stood motionless in the center of this artificial cosmos, his face illuminated by the ghostly light. His lips moved silently, hands occasionally reaching to manipulate some invisible control.

"Temper?"

No response. He continued his silent communion with the projection.

I moved closer, careful not to disturb whatever calculations occupied his mind. "Temper, it's Go."

Still nothing. His eyes tracked something I couldn't see, following patterns in the data only visible to him. I settled into a chair near his workstation and waited. This wasn't the first time I'd found him lost in concentration.

Minutes passed. The holographic sun completed several rotations, its surface shifting and bubbling with simulated activity. Finally, Temper blinked rapidly and turned toward me, as if noticing my presence for the first time.

"Go! When did you arrive?" His face broke into a genuine smile, eyes still bright with whatever discovery had captured his attention.

"About ten minutes ago. You were elsewhere."

"Was I?" He waved his hand, dismissing the concern. "You should see what Falfsun's been doing. The random flares I detected last month have intensified. Look."

The hologram zoomed in on a particular region where bursts of energy flashed in brief, erratic pulses, their sudden brilliance illuminating the surrounding space before fading.

"It's undergoing intense magnetic activity," he continued, eyes gleaming. "Runaway flashes. Nova-like events but controlled. Do you understand what that means?"

I nodded, watching his animated gestures. "It's still burning, even after depletion?"

"Exactly! It's not just cooling down. It's reigniting in bursts, reclaiming fuel from surrounding material." He manipulated the hologram, showing me time-lapse footage of its fluctuations. "For thirteen years, it's been sustaining itself, but now? Now it's showing an entirely new pattern of growth activity. The flashes are cycling faster, more efficient. Falfsun isn't just surviving anymore, it's adapting."

His enthusiasm was infectious, but something in his eyes troubled me. The same intensity I'd seen years ago when we first launched the twin vessels.

"When did you last leave the lab, Temper?"

He waved the question away. "Tuesday. Or maybe Wednesday."

"It's Sunday."

That stopped him. He blinked, calculations visibly running behind his eyes. "Is it?"

"You're losing yourself in this research again." I gestured toward the empty food containers piled near his workstation. "Like you did when Falfsun was just the size of a beach ball, and you had to hand feed it."

Temper sighed, collapsing into a chair opposite mine. "I'm fine, Go. Just excited. Falfsun is achieving things I never anticipated." He ran a hand through his disheveled hair. "But point taken. I could use a break."

The hologram cast strange shadows across his face, making him look older than his years. Or perhaps it wasn't just the lighting.

"Speaking of breaks," he continued, "when are we going adventuring again? I've been thinking about that Captain Blackmane boss fight we never won."

The mention of gaming sent an unexpected pang through my chest. "I don't know, Temper. Since the Din and Captain Drake..." I trailed off, unable to finish.

"It's been thirteen years, Go." His voice softened.

"It's hard for me. It's just not the same without them."

Temper leaned forward, his expression earnest. "I know. But maybe it's time to create new stories. New adventures."

I stood, walking toward the hologram of Falfsun. Its surface churned with activity, reminding me of life's constant movement forward. "I'll think about it."

"You've been saying that for months." Temper's voice carried no accusation, just gentle persistence. "The captain would want you back in the game."

I couldn't argue with that. Drake had always pushed forward, never dwelling on losses. Perhaps that was a lesson worth remembering.

"I'll think about it," I repeated, but this time, I meant it.

I left Temper's lab with his words echoing in my mind. Perhaps it was time to create new stories. The driftway curved ahead, its translucent walls shifting from laboratory sterility to the warm amber glow that signaled residential sectors. Floating information panels drifted past, displaying community announcements and celebration notices.

One caught my eye: "Final Thruman Group Home Opening - Today at 3:00."

The last group home. Thirteen years of steady progress had led to this moment. I altered my course, heading toward New Terracore's eastern quadrant where Marcus and Bea had established their newest thruman home.

The building came into view as I rounded the final bend, still pristine with its fresh paint and unmarked walkway. A small crowd had gathered on its lawn, thrumans and humans mingling beneath a banner that read "Welcome Home."

Marcus spotted me first, breaking away from a conversation to stride across the grass.

"Papa! You made it." He embraced me warmly. "I wasn't sure if you'd see our announcement."

"Wouldn't miss it for anything." I squeezed his shoulder. "The final home. Quite an achievement."

"Bea's inside getting the last group settled. Come see."

We walked through polished hallways where thrumans unpacked belongings, claimed bedrooms, and explored their new surroundings. Some moved with the telltale awkwardness of recent awakening, while others guided them with patient gestures.

Bea stood in the common room, directing the placement of furniture. When she turned and saw me, her face brightened.

"Go! Perfect timing." She embraced me quickly before returning to her clipboard. "We're just about to start the awakening celebration. These twelve are our final group from hibernation."

The room quieted as twelve thrumans entered, each accompanied by a mentor. They moved with careful, deliberate steps, their expressions a mixture of wonder and uncertainty. Marcus took his place at the front of the room, his posture straight but relaxed.

"Today marks a milestone not just for you twelve, but for all of us," he began. "With your awakening, all one hundred and forty thousand thrumans have now begun their journey of self-awareness."

A holographic display materialized above him, showing statistics that made my chest tighten with pride:

"140,000 thrumans integrated"

"100% success rate"

"Zero incidents of consciousness collapse"

Marcus continued, his voice steady. "Each of you will share your first moment of self-awareness. This ritual connects us all, reminds us of our shared beginning."

One by one, they stepped forward. A custodial robot described watching his reflection in a shop window during a rainstorm. A medical assistant bot recalled questioning why she needed to understand pain to treat it. A gardener bot remembered wondering if plants experienced time differently than she did.

Their stories varied, but each contained that crucial moment: the first question they asked not because of programming, but because of curiosity. The first time they wondered "why" instead of simply executing instructions.

Bea wiped tears from her eyes as the final thruman finished speaking. Marcus looked over at her with such tenderness that I felt like an intruder witnessing it.

"Next week we celebrate another milestone," Marcus announced. "The first thruman wedding under the stars. Petra and Jace have invited all of you to witness their union."

After the ceremony, we walked through the courtyard where construction crews were completing a small schoolhouse. Its foundation stones bore the handprints of thruman children, pressed into wet concrete alongside their names.

"The new school opens next month," Bea explained, running her hand along the wall. "We'll have fifteen students to start."

Marcus smiled. "They grow quickly, both physically and mentally. Different from human children, but no less miraculous."

We paused at the school's entrance, where a simple plaque read: "To learn is to become."

We left the school's entrance, Bea and Marcus walking ahead while I lingered to study the simple plaque. "To learn is to become." The phrase echoed in my mind as we parted ways, carrying the weight of thirteen years of growth since the destruction of our twin ship, Paradise.

That night, I couldn't sleep. I sat on my porch watching Falfsun's glow painting the horizon, thinking about Temper's words. Perhaps it was time to create new stories.

The next six years passed quickly.

New Terracore flourished beyond our wildest expectations. What began as necessary infrastructure transformed into a vibrant civilization with its own distinct culture. I watched it unfold with a mixture of pride and wonder, sometimes feeling more observer than architect.

On a crisp autumn morning, I attended the opening of our third art gallery. Located in what we now called the Cultural Quarter, the Nebula Gallery specialized in thruman art. Their perspectives fascinated me: paintings that captured light frequencies beyond human vision, sculptures that explored the concept of consciousness through intricate mechanical forms.

"Quite extraordinary, isn't it?" Shiloh appeared beside me, studying a painting of Falfsun rendered in colors I couldn't name. "The thruman who painted this perceives seventeen more color variations than we do."

"Makes you wonder what else we're missing."

Shiloh smiled. "That's why I love it here. Every day brings something new."

The gallery's central atrium filled with visitors as a string quartet began playing. Not Mozart or Bach, but compositions by Elara, a thruman musician whose work blended mathematical precision with unexpected emotional depth. The music swelled around us, complex harmonies resonating through the space.

Music festivals became seasonal celebrations, marking the passage of time in our simulated world. The summer festival transformed the central plaza into a sprawling concert venue where human and thruman musicians performed together. The winter festival moved indoors, featuring intimate performances in cafes and community centers scattered throughout New Terracore.

Sports evolved too, adapting to our environment. The reduced gravity sections became home to three-dimensional basketball, where players soared through carefully calibrated fields that allowed for extended hang time and complex aerial maneuvers. The first league championship drew nearly ten thousand spectators.

Merlin's influence grew stronger with each passing year. The architeer had established an academy, personally guiding twelve promising students in the art of matrix creation. I attended their graduation ceremony, watching as they presented their final projects, small but complete worlds, each shaped by their own distinct vision.

"Stories are the foundation," Liana, Merlin's most gifted student, explained as she guided me through her creation: a Japanese village where every resident carried a physical manifestation of their greatest regret. "Not just the narrative arc, but the emotional truth beneath it. That's what Merlin teaches us."

Her world felt authentic in a way I couldn't articulate, the weight of unseen history in every interaction, the texture of consequences in the air.

Communities formed around shared interests rather than old Earth demographics. The Stargazers built homes with transparent ceilings, gathering nightly to track Falfsun's movements and map distant constellations visible through the Horsehead Nebula. The Terrans created neighborhoods reminiscent of Earth's most beloved landscapes: Tuscan hillsides, New England autumn, Pacific Northwest rainforests.

In the training grounds, the distinction between Laws of Nature gaming and Breach Law gaming became more pronounced. I observed both from the command center one afternoon.

In the Nature sector, teams navigated the toxic jungles of Vorgath-IV with methodical precision. Every action followed predictable physics: bullets dropped at calculable rates, fire spread according to wind patterns, injuries required realistic treatment. Players moved with disciplined coordination; their strategies rooted in science and military doctrine.

"Flanking position established," a squad leader reported. "Moving to secure the extraction point."

Across the partition, Breach Law sessions erupted with controlled chaos. Gravity shifted unpredictably, causing players to walk on walls or float momentarily. Weapons transformed mid-battle; a sword becoming a flock of birds, a shield melting into quicksilver that flowed around its wielder like sentient armor.

A pirate crew ambushed a team of novices, their ship materializing from within a waterfall that flowed upward. The players' shouts of surprise dissolved into laughter even as they scrambled to adapt.

"That's the third time this week they've tried that entrance," the training supervisor noted. "Creative but becoming predictable."

Peace settled over New Terracore. The crime rate held steady at zero percent for the fourth consecutive year. Our satisfaction index reached ninety-seven percent, with the remaining three percent classified as "constructive discontent": those whose dissatisfaction drove innovation and improvement.

We had built something remarkable. Something permanent.

I stood alone in my farmhouse kitchen, savoring the sweet scent of apple butter simmering on the stove. My CoreLink chimed softly, its familiar tone breaking the peaceful morning silence.

"Hi Papa, it's me, Marcus." His voice carried warmth that made me smile.

"Morning, Marcus. What's on your mind?"

"We're throwing a celebration party for the thruman program. The kids especially want to see you. They love hearing about the farm."

My heart stirred at the milestone. 140,000 thrumans awakened from hibernation, a moment shaped by countless efforts, including Marcus's. "That's wonderful news. Should I bring anything? I've got fresh cider, some preserves from last season."

"Just yourself, Papa. We'll talk more later. Love you."

"Love you too."

The link closed, but another notification appeared immediately:

dress instructions. I frowned. Casual gatherings rarely came with wardrobe requirements. Opening the file, I read: Desert hiking attire recommended.

Adventure gear. My stomach tightened with suspicion.

I contacted Temper through the CoreLink. "Are you going to Marcus and Bea's celebration?"

"Wouldn't miss it." His voice held its usual enthusiasm.

"Any thoughts on why we need desert hiking gear?"

"The party's at the Oasis of Hope. It's in the desert."

"I see." I paused. "This isn't some scheme to get me adventuring again?"

"Go, would I do that to you?"

"Yes. Remember the Swiss chalet party? I showed up ready for fondue and ended up climbing Lhotse's Peak."

Temper laughed. "This time's different. I promise, no adventures."

"Fine. See you there."

I followed the link. Scorching air slammed into me. Heat pulsed through my boots, distorting the barren landscape. The acrid scent of burned flesh carried on the wind.

"Temper? Marcus? Bea?" My voice echoed over empty dunes.
Silence.

I tried blinking back to the farm. The link failed. A new one—still nothing.

I accessed the coding signature. Marcus had designed this space. He had also blocked my escape.

I called him.

"Hi, Papa. Knew you'd call."

"Marcus, I think I took a wrong link."

"No, Papa. You're exactly where you need to be."

Sand slid into my boots. I exhaled. "What's going on?"

"You're in my desert. Made it for you." His voice carried an unmistakable smirk. "Heat to your liking?"

I squinted against the relentless sun. "If by 'liking' you mean 'borderline unbearable,' then yes."

"See the dark stone monolith on the horizon?"

I turned. Heat distorted everything, the distant spire wavering like a mirage.

"The one to the east? I see it."

"That's where you'll find me. In the cursed city of Aramjung." His tone dropped. "I challenge you to a death match."

I nearly laughed. "A death match? Nobody does those anymore." Realization dawned. "There's no celebration party, is there?"

"No party. Just you, me, and mortal combat."

I exhaled slowly, watching sand devils dance across the dunes. "You could have simply told me the truth instead of this elaborate ruse."

"Would you have come if I had?"

"Probably not," I admitted, already calculating the distance to the monolith. "But a death match? What's the point? Though I suppose defeating your old man would make quite the trophy."

Marcus laughed, the sound bright against the desolate landscape. "It certainly would."

"What do I get when I win?" I asked, deliberately using 'when' rather than 'if.'

"If you win, I'll work on your farm for a month. No complaints, no excuses. And I'll stop badgering you about adventures." He paused. "But if I win, you have to find us a new gaming clan and play with us."

"No." The word came out harder than I intended. "That's not happening. But since you've gone to all this trouble, I'll accept your challenge with modified terms. If you win, I'll find the rest of you a new clan, but I reserve the right not to play."

Silence stretched between us. The wind whispered across the dunes, carrying sand that stung my exposed skin.

"I accept your conditions," Marcus finally said. "Come find me. If you dare."

The connection ended. I stared at the distant city, calculating an hour's walk at least. Typical. He could have at least blinked me in closer.

I trudged forward, each step sinking into soft sand. "What happened to kids just borrowing the car keys without asking?" I muttered. "I never challenged my father to a death match."

The sun beat down relentlessly. Sweat trickled down my spine, my shirt already clinging uncomfortably to my back. Marcus had clearly given me this extra time to figure out what abilities I might have in his constructed world.

I began testing them systematically. The gravity whomp failed; no satisfying distortion in the air, no enemies flying backward. I tried summoning the Spear of the Valkyrie. Nothing materialized in my outstretched hand.

Bow of Artemis? My fingers grasped empty air.

The Dragon of Benton? Not even a puff of smoke.

Morena's Winter Cold? No frost formed on my fingertips. That one would have been particularly welcome in this infernal heat.

I continued forward, the monolith growing incrementally larger with each laborious step. Whatever Marcus had planned, he'd made sure I'd arrive tired, thirsty, and thoroughly annoyed.

Perhaps that was his strategy all along.

Then I noticed something odd. Something green.

I stopped, turning to look behind me. In my footprints, fresh blades of grass had sprouted in the sand, verdant and alive. With each depression my boots had left, life emerged; delicate shoots unfurling toward the merciless sun. The contrast against the barren wasteland was startling.

"Life," I murmured, crouching to touch the tender blades. They bent beneath my fingertips but didn't break. Was I a giver of life in this realm? Not exactly the combat advantage I'd hoped for against my adopted son, but perhaps there was more to it.

I straightened and held out my empty hand, palm up. No specific weapon in mind, just an invitation. Let it come to me.

The air shimmered above my palm, molecules rearranging themselves. Heat gathered, coalesced, and suddenly flames erupted from nothing. They twisted and elongated, forming a blade of pure fire: three feet of crackling, dancing energy. The sword's weight felt perfect in my grip, as if Marcus had calibrated it specifically for me.

I swung it experimentally. The blade left a trail of light in its wake, cutting through the desert air with a satisfying whoosh. Pointing it toward my grassy footprints, I concentrated.

The verdant patch exploded outward, spreading in all directions. Grass, wildflowers, even small shrubs erupted from the sand, creating an expanding circle of life amid desolation. A slow smile tugged at my lips. Life and fire—creation and destruction. Marcus had given me interesting tools for our confrontation.

I continued my journey with renewed purpose, the monolith growing larger with each step. The flaming sword led my way, casting flickering shadows across the dunes.

At last, I reached the outskirts of the city. Outbuildings stood charred and broken, mere skeletons of what they once were. The air changed, growing thick with the scent of ash and something worse, the unmistakable smell of burned flesh. My stomach clenched as I moved between the ruins.

Within the blackened structures, I found storerooms filled with scorched grain. Bodies lay scattered among the supplies, burned beyond recognition, frozen in postures of terror and flight. Whatever had happened here had been swift and merciless.

Beyond these outbuildings rose the main city, encircled by a massive wall. The entire settlement was domed with some kind of roof, blocking out the sun's glare. The monolith I'd been tracking dominated the skyline, thrusting upward like an accusing finger.

The city gate drew my attention. Once formidable, it now hung askew on brittle iron hinges. I examined the damage carefully, noting how the metal had warped and buckled. The blast pattern told a clear story. The force had come from within, not without. This gate hadn't been broken by invaders.

It had been locked from the outside.

Someone had sealed something inside, trapping it within these walls.

"Please don't let it be a dragon," I muttered, tightening my grip on the flaming sword. In my years of gaming, dragons had always been particularly troublesome opponents, especially in confined spaces.

I stepped through the shattered entrance. Light refused to penetrate the city's interior. Even the harsh desert sun seemed powerless against the gloom that filled the space beyond the wall. I paused, letting my eyes adjust to the darkness.

The stench intensified, clinging to the stagnant air like a physical presence. As my vision sharpened, shapes emerged from the shadows: a vast hallway stretching in both directions, its stone floor marked by deep gouges. Along the lower sections of the walls, shallow scratches cut across the surface.

Something massive had been dragged through here, its bulk

rubbing against the walls of these corridors. Or perhaps it had moved under its own power, scraping against the stone as it passed.

I followed the tracks deeper into the darkness, my flaming sword the only source of light in this forsaken place.

The hallway stretched before me, darker than space itself. My flaming sword cast eerie shadows along the ancient stone walls, revealing blackened streaks where something had burned its way through. The gouges in the floor told their own story. Something massive had moved through here, something heavy enough to carve permanent tracks into solid stone.

Bodies slumped against the walls; their leather tunics charred beyond recognition. The steel swords beside them had melted and warped, twisted into useless curves that spoke of heat beyond ordinary fire. What kind of inferno could Marcus have unleashed in this place?

A heavy wooden door blocked my path. I pushed it open with my shoulder, the hinges protesting with a screech that echoed through the silence. Another chamber appeared, smaller than the first, with yet another door at its far end. I crossed the room, my boots disturbing centuries of dust that swirled around my ankles.

The pattern repeated: another passage, another threshold, more bodies. The entire structure revealed itself as an elaborate maze, rooms stacked beneath the massive roof that had been visible from outside. No courtyards. No open sky. No landmarks to navigate by.

"Clever design, Marcus," I muttered, voice swallowed by the thick air. Finding him in this labyrinth would be nearly impossible. Unless he found me first, which I suspected was his plan all along.

I returned to the main hallway, following the deep gouges reluctantly. Whatever had left these marks, I had no desire to meet it. But if I wanted to find Marcus, I needed to track the beast's path.

My foot slipped on something unexpectedly slick. I caught myself against the wall, looking down to find a shallow pool of cold muck, viscous and foul-smelling. Something had passed this way recently, leaving this fetid trail behind.

The tracks led to a set of double doors that opened toward what I assumed was the city's heart. Whatever creature had come this way had turned here, heading deeper into the ruins. I hesitated, then pushed through.

Beyond the threshold, darkness grew even more oppressive. I raised my flaming sword higher, using it as a torch. Its flickering light revealed a banquet hall, long abandoned. Broken chairs and shattered tables lay scattered across the floor, buried beneath thick dust undisturbed for generations. Occasionally, I passed another fallen guard, expression frozen in eternal terror.

The air grew increasingly rank. The odor of decomposition intensified with each step deeper into the cursed city. Silence pressed against me from all sides, broken only by my measured footfalls and the soft crackling of my fiery blade.

After navigating a long passage lined with faded tapestries, I came upon another open door. This one had once been a masterpiece of polished wood, carved with intricate scenes of kings and their conquests. Now it leaned awkwardly on its hinges, its surface deeply charred, its once-pristine finish stained a muddy red that I recognized immediately as dried blood.

Beyond it stretched a cavernous room, so vast that darkness swallowed its distant edges completely.

For the first time since entering this forsaken place, I heard something other than my own movements.

A subtle, hurried tapping.

The fire of my sword burned bright against the gloom, making me visible to anything lurking in the shadows. A tactical error. I scanned the chamber carefully, noting pillars that could provide cover and doorways that might offer escape routes.

Then I extinguished the flame.

Darkness consumed me instantly. The sudden absence of light was disorienting, but I stood perfectly still, letting my other senses sharpen. The rustling grew louder, then stopped. Something was listening, just as I was.

I moved cautiously along the wall, keeping my steps silent. After twenty paces, I crouched, listening intently to the oppressive stillness of the ancient chamber. The darkness wrapped around me, concealing whatever horrors Marcus had programmed into this forsaken place.

A plop.

The soft sound of something wet striking the stone floor. Then another. Another still.

My mind conjured images of rain sweeping across the desert, drumming against the city's dome. But the sound wasn't coming from outside.

It was inside.

A plop landed against my shoulder.

I stiffened, every muscle locking in place.

Another hit the back of my neck, cold and viscous.

"What in the—Flame of the West!" The words burst from my throat as I summoned the sword back to life.

Fire erupted along the blade, flooding the chamber with harsh orange light. Dark blobs descended through the air like rain.

I lifted my weapon higher, scanning the ceiling. My stomach contracted violently. The surface above me moved. Shifted. Undulated like crinkling velvet. The sight confused me until something tickled my arm.

A spider.

A hairy-legged monstrosity scuttled down my sleeve toward my hand.

My gaze snapped upward, comprehension dawning with sickening clarity. The ceiling wasn't moving at all.

The creatures clinging to it were.

Tens of thousands of spiders crawled over one another, disturbed by my arrival and the sudden light. They dropped from their perches in waves, a living rainfall of eight-legged nightmares.

They swarmed my body in an instant. Their tiny legs tunneled beneath my shirt, brushing against my skin with alien persistence. They tangled in my hair, struggling as they pushed against my scalp seeking escape. Several slipped into my ears, sending violent shudders through my entire frame. Others reached my nose, triggering sneezes and coughing fits that only invited more of them into my mouth.

I needed to escape. Now.

But turning back meant abandoning my goal. If I wanted to find Marcus, I had to press forward through this nightmare. I forced myself to move, swallowing the panic that clawed at my throat. My legs carried me toward the next doorway, eyes fixed resolutely ahead.

The spiders, for all their horror, did not bite. They did not pursue me with malicious intent. They simply existed, a living obstacle perfectly calibrated to exploit primal fear.

Marcus had set his trap with psychological precision, and he had let me slip past it.

I reached the threshold and plunged into more darkness, leaving the spider chamber behind. Their tiny bodies still clung to my clothing, but their numbers thinned with each step forward. My skin crawled with phantom sensations long after the last arachnid had fallen away.

Three bodies lay sprawled within the next chamber, guards dead for what must have been centuries. I halted at the threshold, my gaze darting reflexively toward the ceiling, muscles tensed for another onslaught of eight-legged horrors.

No movement.

The painted fresco above stretched across the entire surface, its depiction of sky and clouds faded and peeling in places, but mercifully normal. No living infestation clung to its weathered surface. Just ancient, crumbling artistry.

I exhaled sharply, moving swiftly through the space, giving the corpses a wide berth. Their armor had corroded into rust-flecked shells around their desiccated forms. Whatever battle they'd fought had ended long ago.

Then a thought struck me.

I was a giver of life in this realm.

I turned back to the fallen guards, raising my flaming sword above their remains. The heat from the blade washed over my face as I summoned my most commanding voice.

"Arise, sons of Aramjung."

The bodies stirred.

Bones scraped against bone with hollow, brittle sounds that echoed through the chamber. Their armor shifted with a peculiar sucking rasp as it dragged against parchment-thin flesh. Joints popped and cracked as limbs straightened after centuries of stillness.

The dead rose.

A chill ran through me as they stood, swaying slightly, empty eye sockets fixed on my face. It felt wrong, asking more of them than they had already given in life. But I might need their assistance.

I might not be as fortunate when I stumbled into whatever trap

Marcus had designed next.

"Follow me," I commanded.

They fell into step behind me, their movements stiff but purposeful. We advanced through the next room, and the next after that, winding deeper into the city's heart. The journey stretched endlessly, halls and chambers passing in slow procession. Time slipped away in this lightless maze, but the city had to end eventually.

"We must be getting close to the center," I muttered, more to myself than my silent companions.

In every chamber where the dead lay, I revived them. My army grew with each step forward, the sound of their collective footfalls creating an eerie percussion that announced our approach long before we entered new spaces.

At last, we reached an ornate door unlike any other we had passed. Silver filigree curled across its surface in intricate patterns, untouched by time, unmarred by the destruction that had claimed everything else around it. The gouge marks in the floor led straight ahead, disappearing beneath the threshold. I hesitated before pushing it open, bracing myself for an ambush.

Instead, light flooded out.

Marble gleamed beneath the flickering glow of mounted flambeaux. The air was clean here, the space undisturbed except for the deeply scarred stone beneath my feet. At the room's heart stood a dais of pink sapphire that shimmered with internal light. Resting at its center, curled in apparent sleep, lay a giant, blue-skinned serpent.

My breath caught in my throat.

A Boreal Boa.

"Good Lord," I whispered, stunned recognition washing over me. "Why couldn't it have been a dragon?"

I turned to the silent guards behind me, lowering my voice. "Didn't you expect a dragon?"

Several nodded, armor creaking with the movement.

The signs had all pointed to one: the charred buildings, the burned bodies, the blasted gate. Everything had screamed fire-breather, not a cold-blooded monstrosity. Yet here it was, coiled in slumber, its scales gleaming with an unnatural blue luminescence.

There was nothing to do but press forward.

I entered the chamber cautiously, flame sword raised and ready. The undead guards shuffled behind me, their armor creaking with each stilted movement. My eyes adjusted quickly to the sudden brightness after wandering through so much darkness. The marble floor gleamed beneath the dancing light of the flambeaux, pristine compared to the devastation we'd traversed.

At the room's center, atop the dais, lay the massive serpent. Its blue scales shimmered with an unnatural luminescence, each one perfect and gleaming like polished ice. The creature was coiled in apparent slumber, its massive body rising and falling with slow, measured breaths.

But it wasn't the beast that caught my attention. Behind it stood Marcus, my son, clad in full field armor that glinted in the torchlight. A black sword rested easily in his grip, its blade shimmering with a twilight glow. Intricate patterns resembling a spider's web rippled across its surface, subtly shifting and rearranging as if alive. Silver wisps curled along its edge, leaving faint trails in the air as he adjusted his stance.

He grinned at me, teeth flashing white against the shadows of his helm.

I grinned back, unable to help myself.

"Nothing to see here," I quipped. "Just a typical father-son duel to the death."

His blade troubled me more than the snake. A rune sword. The markings were unfamiliar, but I recognized the weapon from somewhere before. The memory nagged at me, just out of reach.

"Nice sword," I said, nodding toward it.

"Your sword isn't bad either." His eyes flicked to my undead companions, amusement dancing in his gaze. "I see you've learned its true power. Kudos for figuring it out."

"Thanks." I glanced back at my silent army. "I hope they come in handy."

He motioned toward the sleeping serpent with a casual wave. "Do you like it, Papa?"

I shook my head. "Not really. But let me tell you something I've figured out."

"Oh? What's that?"

"I've crossed this entire city without a single fight." I took a step forward, my footfall echoing in the chamber. "No attacks, no real threats except for some spiders that didn't even bite. I made it all the way here without a scratch." Another step. "You haven't let anything harm me so far, so I doubt you'll let the snake harm me either." The realization had been building slowly as I traversed the ruined city. "So wake it up, let me shoo it away, because after that, I'm going to kill you." I paused. "Of course, I mean that in the nicest way, son."

Marcus laughed, the sound bouncing off the marble walls. "So you figured all that out? Fine." He turned toward the serpent. "I'll wake up my sleeping boa, but remember, Papa, you asked for it."

The serpent's eyes opened. They were a deep, glacial blue, pupils contracting to vertical slits as they focused on me. It rose from its coiled position, swaying upward like a cobra preparing to strike. Its head alone was larger than my torso.

I steadied myself, flame sword raised. Against a cold-loving creature, fire should give me the advantage. My undead guards shuffled forward, forming a protective semicircle around me.

The Boreal Boa moved toward us, its massive body slithering across the sapphire dais with surprising grace. But instead of striking with fangs as I expected, it opened its mouth wide.

A powerful jet of liquid drenched me and my guards, hitting us with such force that several of the undead staggered backward.

It burned. Not with heat, but with a searing cold that bit into my skin.

Then I realized. It wasn't venom.

Ice water.

The liquid froze on contact, encasing my legs in a rapidly forming shell of ice. My undead guards fared worse, their brittle forms cracking as the water crystallized around them.

My soldiers stood frozen like macabre ice sculptures, their once-animated forms now encased in thick frost. The sword that had served me so faithfully extinguished in my grip, icicles clinging to the hilt. The chamber's chill penetrated my bones, a stark contrast to the fiery confidence I'd felt moments ago.

"Well, that was unexpected," I muttered, surveying the damage.

Laughter echoed through the marble chamber. Marcus doubled over, tears streaming down his face as he clutched his sides. The sound bounced off the walls, multiplying until it seemed the entire ruined city mocked me.

I sighed and shook my head, unable to suppress a reluctant smile. "Alright, you win that round. I didn't see it coming."

The frozen guards collapsed around me, their brittle forms shattering under the weight of ice. Fragments skittered across the floor. They had served their purpose. I wouldn't call them back again.

I held out my hand, willing my blade to reignite. It sputtered weakly, a feeble orange flicker before darkness reclaimed it. I tried again, concentrating harder. The flame struggled briefly, dancing along the edge before vanishing completely. The soaked metal refused to hold fire.

"Light, you useless hunk of junk!" I barked at the unresponsive weapon.

When it remained stubbornly dark, I bent down and picked up a large femur from one of the fallen soldiers. The bone felt solid in my grip, heavy enough to cause damage. If the sword wouldn't work, I'd beat the snake to death with brute force, then turn the bone on my son.

The serpent surged forward with surprising speed, its massive body undulating across the marble floor. I stepped aside, preparing to strike, but the creature ignored me completely. It slipped through the open doorway, disappearing into the darkness beyond.

I grinned triumphantly. "Ha! Told you. I knew you wouldn't let it kill me."

"The bet was that I'd be the one to kill you, not the snake," Marcus replied, twirling his black sword casually. "I would've lost if it finished the job. Now that we're face to face, are you ready to die?"

"Oh, Marcus." I stepped onto the dais, joining him on the glowing pink sapphire. "I've been dying since before you were born." I paused, hearing my own words. "Wait, that didn't come out right. What I meant to say was: "Hello, my name is Go David. You want to kill your own father? Fine—prepare to lose!"

He met me at the center of the dais, his eyes alight with excitement.

I kept working at my blade until it finally sputtered to life, the flame weak but present. The heat felt good against my frozen fingers.

Marcus attacked without warning.

Our swords met, silver against fire. His blade moaned with an almost human voice, hungry and eager. It surrounded Marcus in a cloak of shifting twilight, rendering him harder to detect as he moved. His outline blurred, edges softening into the surrounding air.

He lunged forward. I parried the blow. He recovered instantly. I feinted left. He adjusted unexpectedly, moving where I hadn't anticipated.

Marcus fought unpredictably.

Dangerously.

He lunged again. I parried, the impact jarring my arm. But I noticed something, a tell. A small upward tilt of his head before each advance. If I timed it right, I could use that against him.

I feinted, then disengaged, stepping back slightly.

Waited.

He bobbed his head.

I struck.

Too soon.

His sword slipped beneath mine with serpentine grace, piercing my torso.

A death blow.

I expected pain, a burning agony spreading through my body.

I felt only pressure.

He withdrew the blade, and it purred in satisfaction, the sound vibrating through the chamber.

I exhaled, feeling strangely at peace despite the sword that had just pierced my body. No pain followed, only the peculiar pressure of the blade sliding free.

"Your sword," I said, studying the shifting patterns along its length. "I've seen it before."

Marcus lowered the weapon, its edge still humming with satisfaction. "Duskweaver."

The name unlocked memories buried deep within my mind. Recognition flooded through me, bringing clarity. "The self-aware sword forged by the mystics."

He nodded, the black blade pulsing with subtle light as if

acknowledging its own introduction.

"The very same." Marcus extended his hand, the fight clearly over. "You remembered."

I clasped his forearm in the traditional warrior's grip. His armor felt cool beneath my fingers, solid and real despite the fantastical nature of our surroundings. "Hard to forget a legend."

The marble chamber dissolved around us, reality shifting as colors blurred, sounds muted, and the world reassembled itself into something entirely different.

We blinked into existence at the farm, seated on the wide wooden deck extending from the old red barn. The weathered planks felt warm beneath me, soaking up the afternoon sun. Below us, the pasture stretched out in a carpet of green, dotted with wildflowers and clover patches. Two chestnut horses grazed lazily, occasionally swishing their tails at persistent flies. The same pair that occasionally pulled the wagon for children's hayrides every autumn.

Marcus passed me a thick slice of bread dripping with amber honey. Sweet fragrance rose from it, mingling with the scent of fresh hay and distant apple trees. I bit into it, savoring the sweetness against my tongue, then washed it down with cold apple cider from a sweating mason jar.

"That was fun, Papa." Marcus leaned back against a post, his armor now replaced by simple farm clothes. "Sorry I tricked you into fighting me, but you needed to move again. You've been away from adventuring for too long."

I snorted, licking honey from my thumb. "Like I just was? Running through a ruined city, raising an army of the dead, fighting a giant ice-spitting snake?" I shook my head.

"I mean it. You need to get out more."

"You're fully aware that whenever I do, I get killed." I tapped my chest where Duskweaver had pierced me. "Case in point."

He grinned, sunlight catching in his eyes.

"So challenging me was your idea?"

"Yes." His answer came quickly, confidently.

I raised an eyebrow. "And your uncle Temper had nothing to do with it?"

Marcus hesitated, his fingers toying with a loose thread on his sleeve. "Well... he made a few suggestions about adding the spiders. But the final decision was mine."

"I see." I began to plot my revenge against Temper.

The breeze carried the sweet scent of apples from the orchard, ruffling Marcus's hair. I watched the horses below, their movements unhurried and content. Perhaps there was wisdom in what my son said. The farm had become both sanctuary and prison these past months.

"Maybe you're right." I finished the last of my cider. "I have been on the farm too long, neglecting the outside world. As promised, I'll start screening gaming clans." The thought of returning to adventure stirred something long dormant within me. "But before that, Temper and I need a camping trip. We used to go all the time. It's been too long."

I glanced at Marcus. "I could use your help."

His face brightened. "Of course, Papa. What do you need?"

I couldn't suppress the grin spreading across my face as I leaned forward.

"Would it be okay if I borrowed your snake?"

A week later, I sat beside our campfire in the wilderness, watching sparks dance into the star-filled night. The flames cast flickering shadows across our simple camp: two canvas tents, camp chairs, and a cooler of supplies. Pine needles crunched beneath my boots as I shifted closer to the warmth.

Temper poked at the fire with a stick, sending up a fresh shower of sparks. "Nothing beats camping under the stars," he said, breathing in deeply. The scent of woodsmoke and pine filled the air.

I nodded, hiding my smile. The Boreal Boa slithered silently through the underbrush behind him, its blue scales reflecting the firelight. The massive serpent moved with surprising stealth for its size, approaching Temper's chair.

A twig snapped.

Temper turned, came face-to-face with the creature, and leapt up with a startled yelp. His chair toppled backward as he bolted into the darkness. The snake pursued, its massive form undulating through the trees.

I heard splashing, followed by a string of colorful curses echoing across the lake.

Minutes later, Temper trudged back into camp. Water dripped from his clothes, creating small puddles at his feet. His teeth chattered as he retrieved his overturned chair and slumped into it.

"That snake was a dirty trick," he muttered, wrapping his arms around himself.

"Cold, wasn't it?" I couldn't keep the amusement from my voice.

"Freezing!" He barked out a laugh despite himself. "Okay, so you've got your revenge. I should have known you were planning something sneaky."

"And yet you didn't suspect a thing, you trusting fool. We're even now for you conspiring against me with Marcus." I reached for the bottle beside my chair. "I suppose I'll have to start screening for a new clan soon."

Temper shivered violently. "Find somebody good, will you?"

"I'll do my best." I passed him the whiskey. "Still cold, huh? A little more of nature's antifreeze?"

He accepted the bottle gratefully. "Yes, indeed."

I watched Temper shivering by the fire. His wet clothes steamed slightly in the heat, creating a small cloud around him that caught the firelight. The snake had done its job perfectly.

"You know," I said, "I think I'll get started on that clan search tomorrow. No sense delaying."

Temper nodded, pulling his jacket tighter. "Good luck. The gaming landscape has changed since you've been farming."

"How hard could it be?" I shrugged. "I just need to find people who aren't completely insane."

His laughter echoed through the trees. "In the Wilderness Channel? Good luck with that."

The next morning, I began what would become the most exhausting month of interviews I'd experienced since hiring staff for the Albert Museum decades ago.

First came the Warrior Guild of Blackstone Keep. Their leader, a seven-foot mountain of muscle named Gorn, slammed his battle-axe into my conference table within thirty seconds of our meeting.

"We fight first, talk later!" he bellowed when I suggested discussing strategy.

"That's not really my style," I replied, eyeing the deep gash in my antique mahogany.

"Then you are weak!" The entire guild roared in unison, their practiced synchronization almost impressive.

I showed them out, wondering if the table could be repaired.

Next came the Merchant Alliance, whose guildmaster spent three hours detailing their profit-sharing structure while his accountant presented spreadsheets. I dozed off twice.

"And that concludes our overview of quarterly dividend distributions," the guildmaster said, adjusting his spectacles. "Shall we move on to our risk management protocols?"

I feigned an emergency call and escaped.

The Explorer's Society seemed promising until their impromptu demonstration of "adaptive navigation" involved blindfolding me and spinning me in circles before pushing me through what they claimed was a "dimensional portal." It was my coat closet.

Then came the Cross-Bone Pirates. Their application had seemed reasonable; reality proved otherwise.

Each morning, Captain Marrow greeted me with a flintlock aimed at my chest. "Are ye double-crossin' me?" he'd demand before lowering it with a sigh. "Not today, I suppose."

He forbade any mention of skulls. "We're the Cross-Bones, not the blasted Skull-Bones!" he'd snap. "Thar be no skulls used in our thinkin'! Crossin's and intersections, that's our specialty!"

Their treasure hunting consisted of solving newspaper crosswords. When I suggested actual treasure, Captain Marrow looked baffled.

"What better prize than a completed puzzle?" he asked, pencil aloft.

I left a note about "philosophical differences."

Weeks passed. Some clans rejected my application outright. Others had full rosters. I found myself considering groups I would have dismissed immediately in the past.

"What about the Sewer Rats?" Temper suggested during one of our calls. "They specialize in underground missions."

"They smell like their name," I replied, rubbing my temples. "I interviewed them yesterday."

Frustration mounted until I realized the solution had been staring me in the face. The misfits, the oddballs, the specialists without a home. They were everywhere in the Wilderness Channel, waiting for someone to see their potential.

I started with Skyhook, a former trapeze artist who could navigate vertical terrain like she was walking on flat ground. I found her swinging from the cathedral spires in Old Westport.

"You want me to join what clan?" she asked, hanging upside down.

"I'm building one," I replied. "Something different."

Tumbler came next, an acrobat whose combat style involved more flips than strikes, yet somehow left opponents flattened. Wire followed, a tightrope specialist who moved so silently I sometimes forgot he was there until he spoke.

Jester was the hardest sell; a psychological warfare expert whose painted smile hid a tactical genius. "I work alone," he insisted until I demonstrated how his skills complemented the others.

The final piece arrived unexpectedly. Shiloh, the young navigator of the Hellfire, appeared at my farm one afternoon.

"Heard you're putting together a team of weirdos," she said, hands shoved in her pockets. "Thought you might need someone who can actually get places."

"I thought you didn't do teams," I replied, remembering her fierce independence.

She shrugged. "Maybe I'm bored."

A month later, we were deep in the ruins of Xyphos 9, chasing the impossible. The energy core, buried in a crystalline spire and guarded by half a sector's defenses, was our prize. It was worth a small fortune. Acid rain had paused, but the air still crackled with ionic charge. Every surface shimmered like glass. Every step was a risk.

Skyhook led the climb, her grappling gear locking onto ledges invisible to the naked eye. Wire followed, testing each foothold with surgical precision. Tumbler moved like liquid, flipping and twisting, always landing where no one else could.

"Jester, status?" I asked.

"Enemy patrols remain utterly baffled by holographic chickens," he replied, deadpan. "Turns out cosmic warriors don't handle poultry well."

Above us, the core pulsed. It was an orb of condensed energy, humming with power. The heart of the sector's defense grid.

If we pulled the core, the sector's defense grid would collapse for twelve minutes. No sensors, no shields, no reinforcements. Just enough time to vanish.

"Shiloh, exit route?"

"Three mapped, Captain. Primary holds. Contingencies set."

Temper nodded. She was learning fast.

"Contact in thirty," Skyhook called, fingers dancing over the release mechanism.

"Twenty until patrol returns," Jester warned.

Wire secured our position. Tumbler readied. Marcus and Bea guarded the rear, watching the shadows.

"Got it," Skyhook called as the core detached with a hiss of vacuum seals.

Klaxons blared. The spire shuddered.

"Time to go," I ordered. "Shiloh, start the engine."

Smoke grenades burst, cloaking the corridor in thick plumes of silver.

Temper surged forward, flanking the patrol with Marcus and Bea. Their formation was tight and practiced. Sonic pulses and kinetic shields drove the enemy back step by step.

"Go, we have the front," Temper called. "Get that core secured."

I didn't move. I didn't need to.

Shiloh was already leading.

"Wire, Tumbler, hold formation. Skyhook, with me," she ordered, voice sharp and steady. "We're locking the core in the aft hold. No shortcuts."

Tumbler vaulted through the haze, flipping over debris and ducking stray fire. Wire followed, disabling turrets with precise strikes. His movements felt rehearsed. Skyhook swung low, the core cradled in her harness, guiding it through the narrow passageways like a dancer with a fragile flame.

Shiloh coordinated every step. She rerouted power, sealed bulkheads, and masked our ship's signature. Her fingers flew over the console, eyes scanning three screens at once.

"Core secured," she announced. "Extraction vector locked. Temper, fall back on my mark."

I watched her. Not just the commands, but the way the others responded. No hesitation. No second guessing.

She did not just lead. She belonged in the lead.

Temper glanced back, nodded once, and retreated with Marcus and Bea. The patrol was disoriented and scattered. Jester's final hologram, a stampede of glowing chickens, flickered out as the last enemy fell.

We lifted off seconds later, the spire collapsing behind us. Twelve minutes to escape and reach safety.

Later, we celebrated in the hangar. Quiet laughter, bruises, and adrenaline still humming. Shiloh led the debrief, analyzing strengths, weak points, and refining tactics. The others listened. They already followed her.

I kept my notes. She had the instincts, the mind, the leadership. The Misfits had found their captain. The sale of this energy core would bring a much needed upgrade to our vessel.

The celebration wound down as the team dispersed into the night. Shiloh's confident stride as she left told me everything. She was ready to lead. The Misfits had found their new captain, and I could go back to farming.

Nineteen years had passed since Paradise's destruction forced us into isolation. Each day brought its own rhythm, its own purpose. I walked the farm's fence lines, tended the animals, kept watch on the galaxy through our long-range sensors. The horses grew old, were replaced by new colts. Apple trees in the orchard bore fruit, shed leaves, bloomed again. Marcus visited often, bringing stories of his work with the thrumans, while Temper continued his research on Falfsun.

We lived, we worked, we waited. Always watching for signs that the galaxy had matured enough for us to emerge from hiding.

The morning air carried autumn's first chill as I climbed the ridge, checking fence posts for wear. A red-tailed hawk circled overhead, its cry echoing across the valley. My boots crunched through fallen leaves while I tested each section of wire, looking for gaps where the deer might squeeze through.

The CoreLink chimed. Temper's voice came through, tense with barely contained excitement.

"Go, where are you?"

"I'm walking the farm's fence line, checking for gaps up on the ridge." I paused to examine a loose post. "Care to join me?"

"I can't right now. We have company coming. Meet me in the conference room in fifteen minutes."

Something in his tone made me stop. "Company? What company?"

"Captain Smith is back and he's bearing gifts. It's the Admiral Blue."

The words hit me like a physical force. The hawk cried again overhead, but I barely heard it. Captain Smith. The Admiral Blue. After nineteen years of silence, they had returned.

I turned toward the house, my fence inspection forgotten. The galaxy was calling us back.

CHAPTER TWO

Torn Between Worlds

I walked the driftways toward Hellfire's conference room, my footsteps crunching on pine needles scattered across the forest path. The simulated breeze carried the scent of salt air from the adjacent beach sector. A family passed by, their children's laughter mixing with the rustle of leaves overhead. The path opened onto a stretch of pristine shoreline where colonists flew diamond-shaped kites against the cloudless sky.

The driftway shifted, forest and beach dissolving into the familiar driftway leading to the conference room. My hand brushed the aged oak of the door as I pushed it open.

Captain Smith sat at the conference table beside Luna Dawn, his appearance unchanged from our last meeting nineteen years ago. The nanobots had preserved his physical form perfectly, unlike the natural aging process we neuroclones simply chose to simulate. Temper occupied his usual seat, fingers drumming an irregular pattern on the polished surface.

"Welcome back," I said, taking my place at the table. Through the holographic window behind Smith, Falfsun pulsed its eerie red glow, its prominence arc stretching across the star's surface like a burning rainbow.

"Good to see you, Go." Smith's smile carried the same warmth I remembered. "Though I must say, your hospitality has improved since we last met. The driftways are remarkable."

Luna nodded in agreement. "The beach sector particularly. Almost makes me forget we're on a starship."

"Scotch?" Temper gestured toward the crystal decanter on the side table.

Luna accepted with a gracious nod. Smith raised his hand in polite refusal. "Actually, I prefer a martini these days."

The familiar weight of the conference room settled around us: the subtle hum of environmental systems, the worn leather of the chairs, the float screen of Falfsun rotating slowly above the table's center. Everything exactly as it had been during countless meetings before our long isolation yet now charged with new possibility.

"Nineteen years." Smith swirled the olive in his freshly materialized martini. "Hard to believe we've been away that long. Your hospitality skills have certainly evolved."

"Time moves differently here." I settled back in my chair, studying his face. The nanobots kept him physically unchanged, but new micro-expressions flickered across his features. A slight tightening around the eyes when he smiled. A more measured pace to his words.

"Speaking of time." Smith gestured toward the holographic display. "Falfsun has grown magnificently. When we left, it still fit into Hellfire's cargo bay."

Temper's chest puffed slightly before he caught himself. "The containment fields proved unnecessary after we moved him into the Horsehead Nebula. He's self-sustaining now, feeding on the surrounding nebula gases."

"Like watching your child grow up." Smith's voice carried a note of genuine admiration. "Though I suspect you've done more than just tend to a star during your isolation."

"We kept busy." I shared a knowing look with Temper. "The driftways were just the beginning. We've unlocked entire worlds within Hellfire's New Terracore."

Luna traced her finger along the rim of her scotch glass. "The beach sector reminded me of Costa Rica. The way the waves sound, even the particular quality of the sand."

"Memory mapping has come a long way." I watched Smith's

reaction carefully. His left eyebrow arched slightly, a new tell I hadn't noticed before. "We've learned to refine sensory experiences with remarkable precision."

"And the colonists?" Smith leaned forward, his typical jovial manner giving way to something more focused. "How have they adapted?"

"Better than we hoped." Temper's fingers had stopped their drumming. "The emotional frameworks we developed have allowed for genuine community building. They're not just surviving, they're thriving."

The holographic Falfsun cast emerald shadows across our faces as it rotated. Smith studied it with the same intensity I remembered from our first meeting, but his posture was more relaxed, his questions more patient.

"You've created something extraordinary here." He turned back to face us. "Both of you have. Though I suspect you're ready for something beyond self-imposed exile."

I caught another new mannerism, the way he now steepled his fingers when making a point. Time might not change our physical forms, but it left its mark in subtler ways.

I watched Smith's eyes light up as he set down his martini. "We've brought you something." He gestured to Luna, who produced a small obsidian cube no larger than a sugar lump from her pocket.

"Doesn't look like much," I said, leaning forward.

Smith smiled. "Neither did Falfsun when we first met him."

Luna placed the cube on the table. The surface caught the emerald light from the holographic star and seemed to absorb it, becoming somehow deeper than its physical dimensions should allow.

"We call it the Planck Toolkit," Smith announced.

Temper's entire demeanor transformed instantly. He leaned forward, his fingers freezing mid-drum, eyes widening with unmistakable scientific hunger. "You've stabilized it?"

"More than stabilized." Smith's voice took on that particular cadence I recognized from our past technical discussions. "We've achieved full quantum foam manipulation at the sub-Planck level."

"That's impossible," Temper whispered, but his tone conveyed wonder rather than doubt.

"Theoretically impossible nineteen years ago," Luna corrected. "The breakthrough came from the Oracle. Thanks to Temper's quantum toothpick, the Oracle found a way to temporarily collapse probability fields while maintaining coherence."

"Using entangled pairs as anchors?" Temper asked, already three steps ahead in the conversation.

Smith nodded. "Exactly. The paired quantum states create a framework that—"

"—that allows for direct manipulation of virtual particles before they fully manifest," Temper finished, his excitement palpable.

I shifted in my seat, feeling the familiar sensation of being intellectually outpaced. My expertise had always been leadership and tactics, not quantum mechanics. "So this cube does... what exactly?"

They both turned to me as if suddenly remembering I was there.

"It creates things, Go," Smith said, attempting simplicity. "Anything. From pure energy."

"Like our simulation fabricators?" I asked.

Temper shook his head. "Our fabricators create new simulations. This creates matter from energy."

"The quantum foam is a sea of virtual particles that pop in and out of existence constantly," Luna explained. "This toolkit harnesses those particles before they disappear, forcing them into stable patterns."

Smith picked up the thread. "Think of it as convincing reality that something should exist, and then it does."

"We're talking about perfect molecular assembly," Temper added, his words quickening with enthusiasm. "Instantaneous creation of complex structures with zero material input."

I looked at the tiny black cube with new respect. "That sounds... significant."

"Significant?" Temper laughed. "It's revolutionary. The energy requirements must be astronomical, though."

"Less than you'd think," Smith replied. "The toolkit uses a cascading quantum tunneling effect to—"

"—to bootstrap from existing background energy," Temper interrupted. "Brilliant. The Casimir effect would provide the initial push, and then—"

"—the system becomes nearly self-sustaining," Smith finished, nodding appreciatively at Temper's grasp of the concept.

Their words blurred into a stream of technical jargon: "quantum superposition matrices," "probability waveform collapse," "non-local entanglement fields." Each term sailing further over my head than the last.

I caught Luna's eye across the table. She offered a sympathetic smile, though I could tell she followed the conversation perfectly well.

"The most elegant part," Smith continued, "is how it manages quantum decoherence through temporal phase-locking."

Temper's eyes widened. "You've solved the observer problem?"

"Not solved. Circumvented."

I cleared my throat. "Maybe we could back up to the part where you explain what this means for us practically?"

Smith looked at me, suddenly registering my confusion. "Sorry, Go. In simple terms, this toolkit can create anything from nothing. Food, medicine, technology, building materials—"

"Weapons," Luna added quietly.

"Yes," Smith acknowledged. "Those too."

I stared at the obsidian cube, my mind struggling to grasp the technical flood washing over me. The conversation between Smith and Temper had accelerated into incomprehensible territory, leaving me adrift in a sea of quantum terminology.

Temper caught my expression and paused mid-sentence about probability matrices. "Go, you look like I did that time Marcus tried explaining dinosaur classifications."

"That obvious?" I managed a self-deprecating smile.

"Think of it this way." Temper gestured casually. "You use CoreLink every day, right? To play music, watch Alice Tracker cook, or call Marcus to ask about his day. You don't need to understand the underlying mechanics to use it effectively."

The comparison helped ground me. "So this toolkit works on similar principles?"

"Exactly." Smith leaned forward, watching my reaction with careful attention. "The complexity happens behind the scenes. The user interface will be intuitive, just like CoreLink."

I nodded slowly, pieces clicking into place. "Create anything from pure energy. No raw materials needed."

"Now you're getting it." Temper's enthusiasm bubbled through his words. "Imagine needing a replacement part. Instead of fabricating it in simulation, you could manifest it in physical reality."

The implications started to unfold in my mind. "So we could create food, supplies..."

"Or an entire fleet of ships," Luna added softly.

My stomach tightened at that thought. The potential applications expanded exponentially in my mind: emergency medical supplies, repair components, survival gear. But also weapons, ammunition, military equipment. The power to create anything meant exactly that: anything.

Smith's eyes hadn't left my face, reading each micro-expression as I processed the magnitude of what sat before us. The tiny black cube suddenly felt like a sleeping giant in our midst.

"I understand the basics," I said carefully. "But I sense there's more to this gift than just its technical capabilities."

Smith nodded, a slight smile playing at the corners of his mouth. "As always, Go, you cut straight to the heart of things."

Smith set his martini glass down with a gentle tap against the conference table. "The toolkit isn't the only reason we've returned." His tone shifted, becoming more measured. "There's something you should know about what's been happening beyond your isolation."

The fluid-metal walls shifted imperceptibly, a living, adaptive surface that breathed with the conversation. "The situation wasn't bad at first, when the expansion to other planets was slow. Earth's governments had the resources to keep the peace, but they were hampered because there weren't many laws covering outer space."

I leaned forward, sensing the weight behind his casual words.

"Everyone on Earth thought they were entitled to claim alien worlds," Smith continued. "What helped governments maintain control was the slow production rate of faster-than-egg ships. It was the bottleneck that slowed everything down."

Temper's fingers resumed their drumming, but with a different rhythm now, more urgent.

"But once more factories refitted to increase spaceship production, the expansion of people and their machines to alien worlds increased with it." Smith's eyes met mine. "It wasn't long before black marketeers learned how to 3D-print cheap knockoffs of the eggs, which sold for millions less. This caused the Weltnehmen, or world taking, to expand exponentially."

The news left me stunned and momentarily unable to react. Weltnehmen. World taking. I pictured Lucky Star Farm, our quiet sanctuary on Hellfire. The fields Marcus had helped me plant with such care. The small pond where we'd sit at night with the children and listen to the frogs. All of it created within our self-imposed exile, protected from the galaxy's chaos.

"Earth's congregations, fearful of over-expansion and destruction of alien life, united and forced Earth's governments to pass laws governing the ownership of alien worlds," Luna explained. "The new laws stated that a certain percentage of a planet's surface area needed to be pioneered and flagged before ownership could be certified."

Smith nodded grimly. "So ships captained by ruthless land grabbers would land on a new planet and file an initial claim of ownership. They stayed just long enough to drop off a 3D printer before leaving to find their next planet."

The image formed in my mind with terrible clarity: countless worlds under assault, not by colonists seeking homes, but by machines claiming territory.

"The 3D printer would use the alien planet's natural resources to print colonizer bots whose sole purpose was to expand and entrench themselves over as large an area as possible," Smith continued. "These weren't established, pioneering colonies in any real sense. They were violent, uncontrolled conquests that resulted in the dispersion of native alien life."

Beside me, Temper's scientific curiosity had transformed into something else. His eyes gleamed with the familiar excitement of new knowledge, new problems to solve. I felt something different stirring in my gut: dread.

"More than one fragile ecosystem has been destroyed during the Weltnehmen," Luna said softly. "By pushing through their new laws, the congregations caused the very thing they sought to avoid."

Smith's fingers traced the edge of the obsidian cube. "Ironically, people viewed the stars as a pristine wilderness, and they were in such a rush to leave their problems behind on Earth that they never realized they'd brought those problems with them."

"Three percent of the galaxy has been colonized, almost all of it by our machines," Luna added. "And the Weltnehmen keeps expanding exponentially. By the end of the next century, the entire galaxy will be claimed."

I shook my head, skeptical. "The entire galaxy colonized in a little over one hundred years? That's impossible."

Luna shrugged. "It's exponential growth. The math doesn't lie. And it will be colonized only in the crudest sense of the term. It's more accurate to say it will be claimed in one hundred years, not colonized. A lot of people now wish we had never discovered faster than egg travel. They blame Carpisma for the expanse."

"What about advanced intelligent life?" Temper asked, leaning forward eagerly. "Have we found any?"

"Most life found so far has been diverse, but not intelligent," Smith replied. "On the vast majority of worlds, we haven't found any cooperation within species, and no written recorded histories."

Smith continued explaining the different categories of intelligence they'd discovered. The passive sentients with their oral traditions but no tool use. The rare tool-using species with their cities and art, now under protection from congregational warships.

While Temper grew more animated with each revelation, I felt myself withdrawing. My thoughts drifted to Marcus and Bea, to the quiet evenings when the three of us would sit on the farm porch watching Falfsun's glow on the horizon. Nineteen years of peace, of building something meaningful within our isolation.

"Do these alien worlds know we're there?" I asked, pulling myself back to the conversation. "I mean, do they understand that aliens... that we have visited their planets?"

"Some of them know about us, and they're not too happy about it," Smith replied. "On some worlds, we've caused worldwide panic. Their economies collapsed, then recovered for the most part after they realized we weren't going to attack them."

Temper's questions grew more technical, more excited. "So we won't be leaving them alone to evolve at their own natural speed? We're going to interrupt their natural evolution?"

Luna explained their intervention philosophy, the careful balance they were trying to strike in sharing technology with less advanced species.

"It all sounds exciting," I said, though the words felt hollow in my mouth.

Smith's expression darkened. "It is, but it's also sad and heartbreaking. The congregations have the resources to only provide protection for the tool users. The Weltnehmen is expanding too fast for anything else." He sighed. "How many priceless worlds are being destroyed? I just hope the damage being done by the colonizer bots can someday be undone."

The conference room suddenly felt too small, too confined. I glanced at Temper, whose eyes still sparkled with the thrill of new scientific frontiers. He caught my look and misinterpreted it as shared excitement.

"Think of what we could do with this toolkit, Go," he said, gesturing toward the obsidian cube. "The research possibilities alone are staggering."

I nodded mechanically, but my thoughts were elsewhere. I was thinking of the farm, of how happy it made me. Of the simple life we'd built while the galaxy burned around us.

Smith was watching me closely. "You're troubled by this news."

It wasn't a question. I met his gaze. "Nineteen years ago, we withdrew from the galaxy to heal, to build something new. Now you're telling me that while we've been in hiding, humanity has been consuming worlds at an unprecedented rate."

"It's happening faster than anyone predicted," Smith admitted, his fingers drumming against the table as he considered the scope of it. "We thought there would be some resistance. Some limit to how quickly new worlds could be taken. But the expansion hasn't just continued; it's accelerating."

He leaned forward, eyes skimming over the cube between us. "The technology worked too well. That was the problem. We streamlined planetary acquisition to the point where ecosystems aren't just disrupted, they're erased before anyone even acknowledges they existed." His voice carried the weight of someone who had seen it happen firsthand, not in theory, but in consequence.

I watched him hesitate before turning back to Temper, their conversation shifting into the deep mechanics of their work. Quantum resonance. Matter stabilization. Energy redistribution. The obsidian cube sat between them, pulling their attention inward while I drifted outward, beyond the numbers, beyond the calculations, watching something else unravel instead.

Whatever they were excitedly breaking down, I saw the larger fracture, not just in our technology, but in our understanding of what we had done. And somewhere, in the quiet corners of my mind, Marcus and the thrumans remained untouched by all of it, still believing the sanctuary we built was enough.

"The quantum resonance patterns would allow for complete matter stabilization," Temper said, his fingers sketching invisible diagrams in the air.

Smith nodded eagerly. "The Oracle suggested using entangled particle networks as a framework. The toolkit can maintain coherence across multiple scales simultaneously."

"Fascinating. The applications for planetary restoration are enormous."

Their voices faded into background noise as my thoughts turned to Marcus. He'd been so proud last week when the latest group of thrumans graduated from his and Bea's program. Twenty-three young thrumans, each finding their place in our small community. I remembered how his eyes had lit up when he told me about Ellie, the shy thruman who wanted to be a storyteller, or Jasper, who showed remarkable aptitude for botanical sciences.

"The probability matrix collapses in predictable patterns," Smith was saying, "allowing for unprecedented precision in molecular assembly."

Temper made a sound of pure scientific delight.

To perhaps build weapons, I thought. Create armies. Wage wars across the stars.

My gaze drifted to the holographic window where Falfsun glowed on the horizon. Lucky Star Farm lay in that direction, beyond the town's edge. Marcus would be there now, probably sitting in the wagon with Bea, taking the thruman children on a hayride. They'd created something beautiful together, something peaceful and meaningful in our self-imposed exile.

"The neural interface allows direct thought-based manipulation," Luna explained, joining their technical discourse. "The user simply visualizes the desired outcome."

I pictured Marcus teaching the young thrumans how to plant

seedlings in the garden behind the farmhouse. His patience as he showed them how deep to dig the holes, how gently to place the fragile roots. The pride in his voice when he called me over to see their work.

"Go?" Temper's voice broke through my thoughts. "You're unusually quiet."

I focused back on the conference room, on the three faces watching me with varying degrees of concern and curiosity.

"Just thinking about Marcus," I admitted. "About what we've built here."

Smith's expression softened with understanding. "You're worried about how this changes things."

"For nineteen years, we've lived in this bubble," I said, gesturing vaguely toward the window. "We've created our own little world while the galaxy burns around us. And now you're handing us a match."

"Or a fire extinguisher," Luna countered gently.

"Depends on who's holding it," I replied.

Temper studied me with sudden comprehension. "You're not excited about this at all, are you?"

I met his gaze. "I'm thinking about Marcus and Bea raising thrumans in New Terracore. I'm thinking about our farm and the life we've built. I'm thinking about how technology like this tends to change everything it touches."

The room fell silent as my words settled between us. The holographic Falfsun cast its emerald glow across our faces, painting us all in the same light despite our diverging thoughts.

"Change is inevitable, Go," Smith said finally. "With or without the toolkit."

"Maybe." I looked at the obsidian cube. So small, so innocuous. "But some changes you can't undo."

Silence settled between us, stretching just long enough for the weight of my words to linger. Then, gradually, the energy in the room shifted. Smith turned back toward Temper, his hesitation dissolving into renewed focus. Their conversation regained momentum, pulled forward by the gravity of what lay before them.

Smith and Temper's voices faded into a blur of technical jargon as they leaned toward the obsidian cube like devotees before an altar. Their hands traced invisible patterns in the air while they exchanged words that seemed to belong to another language entirely: quantum resonance, probability matrices, molecular assembly. Luna occasionally joined their exchange with precise clarifications, her expertise evident in the confident way she corrected their more speculative theories.

I watched them from what felt like a growing distance. The conference room hadn't changed, but I felt myself drifting away from the table, from their excitement, from the shimmering possibilities they saw in that small black box.

"The neural interface would allow instantaneous manifestation," Temper said, his fingers drumming an excited rhythm. "Think it, and it exists."

Smith nodded eagerly. "The Oracle believes we could potentially recreate entire biospheres with sufficient practice."

"Remarkable," Temper breathed. "We could restore planets damaged by the colonizer bots."

Something inside me snapped. The tension that had been building since Smith's arrival finally broke through my carefully maintained composure.

"Are we ready for god-like power?" I interrupted, my voice cutting through their technical exchange like a blade.

The room fell silent. Three pairs of eyes turned toward me, expressions ranging from surprise to thoughtful consideration.

"What if we're not worthy of it?" I continued into the silence. "What if we're just repeating the same mistakes, only with better tools?"

Smith set down his martini glass with deliberate care. His eyes met mine, not with the dismissal I half-expected, but with something deeper, more measured.

"If not us, who?" he asked simply. "The toolkit exists, Go. The question isn't whether someone will use it, but who that someone will be."

Temper stared at me as if seeing me for the first time. "I don't understand your hesitation. You've always loved adventure, taking risks. Where's that spirit now?"

His words stung more than I wanted to admit. I'd spent decades as a starship captain, exploring the unknown, facing dangers. But this felt different.

"There's a difference between adventure and responsibility," I said. "Between taking personal risks and gambling with the fate of entire worlds."

Luna's eyes narrowed thoughtfully. "You're worried about unintended consequences."

"Nineteen years ago, we lost Paradise. We lost Earth. We lost everything except what we could rebuild here." I gestured toward the window where Falfsun glowed on the horizon. "Now we have Marcus raising thrumans with Bea. We have a community. We have peace."

"And you're afraid this will threaten that," Smith concluded.

"Wouldn't you be?" I asked. "Look what happened with faster-than-egg travel. We thought it would usher in a new age of exploration and cooperation. Instead, we got the Weltnehmen. Entire ecosystems destroyed. Alien civilizations thrown into chaos."

Temper's excitement dimmed, replaced by a more thoughtful expression. "But that's exactly why we need this technology, Go. To fix what's been broken."

"Or break it further," I countered. "The road to hell is paved with technological solutions."

Smith leaned forward, his voice gentle but firm. "The toolkit is already here, Go. The question isn't whether such power should exist, but who should wield it, and how."

The emerald glow from the holographic Falfsun cast strange shadows across his face as he continued. "I brought it to you to fulfill our contract, but also because, despite your self-imposed exile, despite your fears, I believe you and Temper understand something crucial about power that others don't."

"And what's that?" I asked.

"Its cost," Smith replied simply. "You've both lost enough to respect what's at stake."

Smith lowered his voice, leaning across the table. "Here's how it would work. You'll get bonded and then spend some time in the training sandbox learning to use your new tools. Like I mentioned, they're intuitive. It won't take long before you're racing around the galaxy." He gestured toward Luna. "Our quantum tech, Talib, will take you and Temper to our ship's clinic to perform the procedure."

The implications of his words settled into my mind. Two toolkits. Just two.

"What about the rest of the people on board the Hellfire?" I asked.

Captain Smith looked at Temper, who suddenly found the table fascinating.

"I haven't told him yet," Temper admitted.

"Told me what?"

Temper sighed. "The agreement with Carpisma was for two fully functional Planck Omniform toolkits for the two of us in exchange for our Oracle consult and the quantum pick omnigraph. The rest of the people won't be getting any toolkits."

I was stunned. "That's not fair. They gave up the Oracle consult too. They should be compensated for it."

Captain Smith and Temper both looked down at the floor, unwilling to meet my gaze.

"Maybe you two should talk it over," Smith said, rising from his chair. "I'll be on the Admiral Blue when you're ready to proceed."

Smith and Luna blinked from the conference room, leaving Temper and me sitting in silence. The only sound was the soft hum of the environmental systems.

My stomach churned with discomfort. "What are we doing? I'm still uncertain about whether this is the right choice, but leaving everyone out of it feels like turning my back on them.

"It's a big ask of Carpisma for an additional 178,000 toolkits," Temper replied. "They can't be cheap to make, and I'll bet each sell for a small king's ransom."

I paced the length of the conference table. "Okay, how can we fix it? What else do we have to offer? We've used all our Oracle consults." A thought struck me. "What about Falfsun?"

"I'm not selling Falfsun." Temper's voice hardened. "Besides, who would want him besides me? He's a young star among billions of other young stars. Face it, we have nothing else left to bargain with."

I stopped pacing. "What about the ark?"

"They don't want the ark. They're a tech company, not farmers. It's probably useless."

"So why were bounty hunters searching for it? It's worth trying at least." My mind raced ahead. "We'll offer them the ark. Maybe we can offer the Hellfire too. If everyone has their own toolkits, we won't need the ship anymore, right?"

"Yes. The toolkit can be used as your home until you want to build a different one."

"I still have so many questions about that." I shook my head. "Okay, are we agreed? We'll offer the ark and the ship in exchange for everyone getting a toolkit?"

"We'll have to ask the Hellfire congregation if that's what they want. Maybe they'll choose to keep the ship instead, although I doubt it. Who wouldn't want the freedom to go anywhere they wanted?"

"Let's do it then. Let's get a firm offer from Carpisma first, then present it to the congregation."

We met again with Captain Smith. His immediate answer to our offer was no. "I'm sorry, but that's too expensive," he said.

I pleaded with him. He still said no.

"I've got an idea. What if we work it off?" I asked.

For the first time in our discussion, Captain Smith paused.

"What do you mean?" he asked.

"What if we agreed to work for Carpisma? Luna told us colonizer bots were destroying priceless worlds. She also said Carpisma was getting blamed for it. Then you said you hoped the damage could someday be undone." I leaned forward. "What if we could repair the damage and prevent it from happening? In exchange for the toolkits, we could work to protect those worlds."

Captain Smith crossed his arms and tapped a finger to his temple. "The Hellfire and its crew are held in high regard. There's even a statue of Temper in the courtyard at Carpisma's headquarters. But I just don't know if Carpisma would agree to it."

I rolled my eyes. Maybe next time, I should just sit back and let Temper do all the work. Then they'd see who deserved a statue.

"You could certainly hire your own crew from Earth to do the job," Temper interjected, "but remember, we're neuroclones and thrumans. We've been controlling our digital environment for our entire lives. For us, using pico technology would be natural." He smiled. "Plus, I may have something additional to offer that could sweeten the pot."

"Oh? And what's that?"

"I have the complete stellar radiation history of Falfsun. I can teach you how to use the same technique to record the radiation history of Sol and trace it back to its origin, some five billion years ago. Think about it, a historical benchmark of 'second light' that can be read while you're in the quantum foam. A map. Do you see the possibilities? That alone would be worth a fortune."

Smith's eyebrows rose. "A quantum benchmark? It has potential. Why didn't you lead with this offer? It's tempting." He paused. "Let me think for a minute. We'd lose a lot of probes in the process of mapping Sol. There's that cost to consider."

"You would lose some, that's true, but you'd make more probes," Temper countered. "We'd expect a copy of the radiation map when you've completed it, plus the toolkits for all 178,000 on Hellfire."

"One copy of the map," Smith said.

"Two copies, one for each of us," Temper replied.

Smith thought for a minute. "I'll have to check with headquarters. So the agreement would be for 178,000 Planck Omniform toolkits, eventually. I understand approximately 32,000 thrumans are still children? They could live with adults until grown, when they'd receive their own toolkits. And two copies of Sol's second light history. In exchange, Carpisma receives Temper's radiation benchmark information and stellar log documents, the ark, the Hellfire spaceship, and everyone receiving toolkits will be under contract to work for Carpisma for, let's say, the next two hundred years?"

"Agreed. While you check with headquarters, we'll present the offer to the people on board Hellfire. If everyone agrees, then we'll have a deal," Temper said.

The offer was presented to the congregation. The vote was tallied in favor of acceptance. Their only condition was more of a request: for Luyten b to be designated as the new home world of the Ethereans, the name they gave themselves to reflect their new duties working for Carpisma. They wanted to name it Requiem Prime, in honor of those lost on Paradise.

Captain Smith returned with Carpisma's response. "178,000 Planck Omniform toolkits are too expensive, plus we haven't made that many yet. We're prepared to offer 178,000 Planck Essential kits instead. We have that many first editions already, so we can distribute them immediately. Also, we'd like you two to be goodwill ambassadors for Carpisma. You wouldn't need to do much, just talk to groups occasionally to promote our toolkits and your new Planck lives."

Temper and I felt they could do better. After negotiating, we reached a deal: 3 Planck Omniform kits, 11,000 Planck Genesis, 29,000 Planck Infinity, and 105,997 Planck Prime kits to be delivered immediately, with all toolkits, including the 32,000 kits held in reserve for the thruman children, to be upgraded to Planck Omniform status within fifty years.

Carpisma accepted our offer.

I stood at the conference room window, watching Falfsun glow on the horizon. The star that had been our constant companion for nineteen years would soon be just one point of light among billions as we ventured back into the galaxy.

"Change is inevitable," I murmured, echoing Smith's earlier words.

Behind me, Temper gathered his notes. "Are you ready for this, Go?"

I pressed my palm against the cool glass, feeling the boundary between our sanctuary and the wider universe. Marcus would be at home now, perhaps sitting on his porch swing with Bea, planning tomorrow's lessons for their thruman children. Our peaceful exile was ending.

The glass fogged beneath my touch. Nineteen years of routine, of predictable days tending the farm, of watching Marcus grow from a curious child into a compassionate teacher. We'd built something precious here, something I never expected to find after losing Paradise.

My fingers traced abstract patterns in the condensation. The conference room felt smaller now, more confined than it had during our time here. The weight of our decision pressed against my chest like a physical thing.

"You're worried about Marcus," Temper said.

"He's found his purpose here." The words came out rougher than intended. "Teaching those children, working with Bea. This change will affect them too."

"Marcus isn't that scared little thruman anymore. He's grown into someone who can handle change."

The truth of his words didn't make it easier. I remembered Marcus's first days at the Joy of Adoption center, how he'd arranged his building blocks with such careful precision. Now he arranged lessons with the same dedication, helping other thrumans discover their own identities.

"We're not losing what we built," Temper continued. "We're expanding it. Think what Marcus could teach with a Genesis toolkit. Think what his students could learn."

The environmental systems hummed softly, a sound so familiar I usually forgot it existed. Like so many things about our life here, it had become background noise, comfortable and unremarkable. Soon we'd trade that comfort for unlimited possibility.

"I know you're right." I turned from the window. "But accepting change doesn't make it easier."

"No," Temper agreed. "It just makes it possible. So, you're ready?"

The obsidian cube sat between us on the conference table, both promise and warning. A key to unlock the galaxy, or perhaps Pandora's box. Either way, we'd made our choice.

"No," I admitted. "But that's never stopped us before."

CHAPTER THREE

Time's Echo

The quantum workspace existed both everywhere and nowhere. My personal slice of creation hovered at the threshold of reality. The walls, if they could be called that, rippled with potential energy, their surfaces iridescent and constantly shifting. Colors that had no names in human language flowed across them. Particles winked in and out of existence around me, tiny fireflies of probability dancing to quantum rhythms.

I held my hands out, palms up. The space responded, forming a translucent workbench from concentrated possibility. Tools materialized: digital phantoms with physical presence, as real as reality itself.

"Father's watch," I whispered.

My voice echoed strangely, as if I were speaking across time rather than space. Memories rushed forward unbidden. The watch melting in the memory palace fire. My desperate lunge to save it, fingers closing around molten metal and glass. The searing pain that wasn't physical but cut deeper than any wound. The realization that I'd destroyed something irreplaceable in a moment of blind rage.

"Stupid," I muttered to myself. "So stupid."

I closed my eyes, concentrating on every detail of the timepiece. Silver case worn smooth by decades of handling. The slight dent near the crown where my father had struck it against a door frame. The inscription inside: "Time passes. Love remains." The weight of it in my palm, substantial but not heavy. The way the second hand stuttered slightly at twelve before continuing its journey.

My fingers moved through the quantum interface, shaping raw energy into matter. The watch began to form, molecule by molecule. But something was wrong. The proportions felt off, the weight distribution unbalanced. I dispersed it with a frustrated wave.

"Again."

The second attempt came closer but still wasn't right. The engraving was too deep, the patina too uniform. It looked like a watch that had been artificially aged rather than genuinely lived with.

I thought of Amy then, how she'd created the perfect digital replica for me, capturing not just the physical attributes but the essence of the object. She'd understood that the watch wasn't just metal and gears but a vessel for memory and connection.

"One more time."

I slowed my breathing, allowing the memories to surface fully. Not just how the watch looked, but how it felt in my life. The sound it made when I wound it each morning. The ritual of checking it against the atomic clock on our kitchen wall. The comfort of its ticking beside my bed at night.

This time, the watch formed perfectly. Every scratch, every imperfection reproduced exactly as it had been. I reached out and lifted it from the workbench. The familiar weight settled into my palm.

I opened the case. The face gleamed up at me, and for a moment, I was transported back to that day in the memory palace when Amy had given me the first replica.

It had hung from the lowest branch of our massive and sheltering oak tree: a small wooden box with a hinged lid. "This is a perfect copy," her note had said. "David gave me the original to scan. Time works differently where you're going, my love. But wherever you are, whenever you are, part of us travels with you."

I'd kept it close through those early months aboard Paradise, until that moment of weakness when I'd thrown it angrily into the flames, trying to burn away my past along with the memory palace.

The watch ticked steadily in my hand now, keeping perfect time in a place where time itself seemed malleable. A paradox, like so much of my existence.

I closed the case and pressed it against my chest. Joy and pain mingled in equal measure. I had recreated what was lost, but the act itself was a reminder of my failure to preserve it.

I cradled the recreated watch in my palm, its familiar weight anchoring me to a past that sometimes felt like someone else's memories. The quantum workspace dissolved around me as Temper's voice cut through my concentration.

"Ready to go? Luna's waiting with the toolkit configurations."

I slipped the watch into my pocket. "As ready as I'll ever be."

The journey to Requiem Prime would be my first real test of the Planck toolkit's capabilities. Nineteen years on Lucky Star Farm had made me forget what interstellar travel felt like. The egg ships had been smooth, almost boring in their efficiency. This would be different.

"Remember," Temper said, handing me the sleek, metallic cylinder, "it's not like the egg. You're not moving through space; space is pulling you."

I nodded, running my thumb over the toolkit's activation panel. "Gravity assist. I read the manual."

"Just be careful. The sensation can be... intense."

I stood on the designated platform, toolkit in hand. Luna had already programmed the coordinates for Requiem Prime, formerly Luyten B, where the first wave of Ethereans had begun establishing a settlement. The toolkit hummed to life, its surface warming beneath my fingers.

"See you on the other side," I said to Temper.

Then I activated the sequence.

The universe shifted. One moment I stood in Hellfire's departure bay; the next, I was falling. Not the controlled descent of a ship entering atmosphere, but the primal, visceral plunge of a body surrendering to gravity's embrace.

My stomach lurched into my throat. Every instinct screamed danger as invisible forces pulled me through the void at impossible speeds. Stars stretched into streaks of light, then blurred completely. I gasped for breath, my heart hammering against my ribs.

Panic seized me. I disengaged the focal point, and the falling sensation abruptly ceased. I hung suspended in the nowhere space between systems, trembling.

"Breathe," I reminded myself. "You control this."

After collecting myself, I reactivated the toolkit. The falling resumed, marginally less terrifying now that I knew what to expect. Still, I stopped twice more during the journey, each time reassuring myself that I could halt this headlong plunge at will.

When Requiem Prime finally materialized around me, I stood shaking on a grassy knoll overlooking a valley. The toolkit powered down, its job complete.

The air smelled wrong. Not bad, just... different. Earthlike but with subtle chemical variations that made each breath slightly unfamiliar. Overhead, Luyten cast a reddish glow across the landscape, painting everything in warm amber tones.

I pulled out my father's watch, its steady ticking a counterpoint to my still-racing heart. The familiar weight in my palm helped ground me.

A forest of transplanted redwoods stretched below, their massive trunks incongruously Earth-like against this alien backdrop. Between them, ferns and mosses carpeted the ground, creating a lush understory. A river cut through the valley, tumbling over rocks before widening into a serene lake.

In a clearing among the trees, I spotted a gathering of people. My people, technically. Fellow Ethereans who'd chosen to start fresh on this distant world.

I made my way down the slope toward them, each step reminding me how different this place was from Lucky Star Farm. No carefully tended fields here, no familiar barn silhouette against the horizon. Just raw potential and the strange beauty of a world being reshaped by human hands.

As I approached the gathering, conversations paused. Faces turned toward me. I recognized a few from our old crew, but most were strangers.

My fingers closed around the watch in my pocket. In this moment of profound disconnection, it remained my only true anchor to who I was and where I'd come from.

I stood on the grassy knoll, staring at the alien sunset while the toolkit hummed quietly in my hand. Talib's words echoed in my mind as I navigated through the toolkit's interface, my fingers tracing invisible patterns in the air.

"Files transfer automatically to your toolkit when neural sync is complete," he'd explained during our training session just days ago. "Your entire digital history, photos, memories. Everything is accessible with a thought."

I remembered how Talib had watched his float screen intently, nodding with satisfaction as the progress bar filled.

"Your neural sync is complete, Go," he'd announced. "Let's try it out."

With gentle guidance, he'd helped me activate the quantum reduction function. The world had shifted around us, colors stretching and blending as we shrank to quantum size.

"We'll stop here before we go smaller," Talib had said, his voice somehow both impossibly distant and intimately close. "Look around at the larger world. See how everything looks a little blurry? The quantum realm doesn't have a true edge, but if you stop here, you can see where the macro and the micro interact."

I'd watched in wonder as reality itself seemed to pulse and breathe. Solid objects revealed themselves as collections of vibrating particles, their edges indistinct and permeable. The boundary between what is and what might be dissolved before my eyes.

Now, standing on this alien hillside, I accessed the photo archive with a simple thought. Images materialized before me, floating in the air.

The first photograph was of Marcus at five years old, standing in the Joy of Adoption center. His small face serious with concentration as he took his first uncertain steps toward me. His movements had been awkward then, mechanical in a way that betrayed his thruman origins. But his determination shone through, those dark eyes focused intently on each step.

"I can do it," he'd insisted when I offered my hand. "I want to walk to you myself."

And he had, collapsing into my arms with a mixture of triumph and exhaustion. I'd suspected even then that this serious little boy would change my life forever.

Another image appeared. Marcus at twelve, standing wide-eyed in ancient Rome. We'd visited every major era of human civilization, from Mesopotamia to the Moon colonies. I'd wanted him to understand his heritage, to feel connected to the long story of humanity.

"These were your ancestors," I'd told him as we watched a Roman legion march past. "This is where you come from."

"But I wasn't born," he'd replied, his voice thoughtful. "I was made."

"So was I, in my way. We're all made, Marcus. Some in wombs, some in labs. What matters is what we make of ourselves."

The images shifted faster now. Marcus graduating from his first learning module. The two of us fishing in the simulated river behind our cottage. Temper teaching him quantum physics with elaborate sandcastles on the beach.

Then came the oak tree.

My breath caught. The massive oak dominated the frame, its branches heavy with twenty handcrafted birdhouses. David had built one for Amy for twenty years. I could name each one from memory: the lighthouse made the year they married; the rustic log cabin crafted from his grandfather's barn wood; the Victorian with its intricate gingerbread trim.

In a moment of blind rage, I'd burned it all. The memory palace Amy had lovingly created for me, the oak tree, the birdhouses, every photograph and memento from our life together. I'd destroyed it all because I couldn't return to her, couldn't bear the weight of that separation. The pain from remembering my stupidity still bore through me.

The Emulation Court had been right to deny my petition. A digital consciousness couldn't return to an organic body. The technology didn't exist. But in my grief and anger, I'd interpreted their ruling as rejection.

What a fool I'd been.

The next image showed the memory palace in flames, the oak tree a blackened skeleton against a burning sky. I'd thought I'd erased everything, but these images had survived, transferred automatically to my neural imprint and now to the toolkit.

"You look troubled, Captain."

I turned to find Elara, one of the Etherean scientists who'd settled on Requiem Prime. Her eyes reflected the reddish light of Luyten.

"Just revisiting old mistakes," I said, dismissing the floating images with a gesture.

"While we've been hidden away, the Weltnehmen has accelerated beyond all prediction," she said, gazing out over the valley. "Zian was telling me about a binary system where colonizer bots stripped both habitable planets in under a decade. They didn't even catalog the species before destroying them."

"How many worlds have been lost?"

"Hundreds. Maybe tens of thousands. Nobody's counting anymore." She shook her head. "The congregations try to intervene when they find intelligent life, but most planets are claimed and stripped before anyone realizes what they've lost."

Elara walked back toward the settlement, her silhouette blending with the strange twilight of Requiem Prime. The toolkit hummed softly in my palm, waiting for my next command.

"Show me Emberhill," I whispered.

Coordinates materialized in my mind, and I activated the transport sequence. The falling sensation came again, but gentler this time as I traveled a shorter distance. As reality settled, I found myself standing on a hillside, looking over a valley different from what I'd expected.

Emberhill sprawled below me, a vibrant patchwork of buildings nestled among rolling hills. It was the first permanent settlement built by the Ethereans on Requiem Prime, a proper town with winding streets and green spaces. Homes of various sizes clustered in neighborhoods, their architecture blending Earth traditions with practical innovations for this new world.

Children played in courtyards and gardens. Thruman children. Thousands of them.

I made my way down the path toward the town center, passing group homes where caregivers tended gardens alongside their charges. The sound of laughter floated through open windows. A ball sailed over a fence, followed by the patter of small feet in pursuit.

At the central square, I found what I was looking for. Marcus stood with Bea beside a large model of the town, gesturing as they spoke with a group of adults. But it wasn't Marcus as I remembered him.

This Marcus had a physical body.

He looked up, sensing my presence, and his face brightened. "Papa!"

He crossed the square in long strides. This Marcus moved with fluid grace, his physical form perfectly proportioned, skin warm and flushed with life.

"You're here," he said, reaching for me. His arms wrapped around the space where my body should have been, passing through the projection without resistance. Yet, in that moment, the illusion held; a touch that wasn't touch, an embrace given meaning only by intention.

Bea approached, her smile gentle. She too had a physical body, her dark skin glowing in the amber light of Luyten. "Welcome to Emberhill, Go."

"How?" I finally managed.

Marcus grinned. "We've had help from other Ethereans to create Emberhill and, of course, the Planck toolkit. What might take a year to build on Earth, we've accomplished in days."

I looked around with new understanding. The settlement seemed so established.

"Come," Marcus said. "Let me show you what we've built."

He led me through Emberhill, pointing out schools, recreation areas, and the specialized facilities where thrumans were beginning to learn about their new physical bodies. Thirty-two thousand children lived here, each in group homes designed to feel like families.

"We're accelerating their physical development to match their cognitive growth," Bea explained as we passed a playground where children who appeared to be around eight years old constructed an elaborate fort. "By next year, they'll all reach physical maturity."

"So fast," I murmured.

"It has to be," Marcus said. "The galaxy needs us now, not decades from now."

We reached a hillside home overlooking the valley. Marcus's home. Inside, evidence of his new life surrounded me: books on physical biology, architectural plans for expanding Emberhill, photographs of him with groups of thruman children.

"You've been busy," I said, trying to keep the hollow feeling from my voice.

"We had no choice. While you managed the distribution of toolkits on Hellfire, we moved the remaining Thruman children to Emberhill." He poured three glasses of water from a pitcher: real for them, simulated for me. "Once they've grown, they'll be ready to join in the fight. The colonizer bots are tearing through worlds faster than anyone expected."

I watched him move through the kitchen, completely at ease in his physical form. "I wish we'd stayed on Hellfire," I said quietly. "Things were simpler there."

Marcus set the glass down harder than necessary. "Simpler for whom? We were hiding while the galaxy burned."

"We were safe," I countered. "We had a good life."

"We had a half-life," Bea said gently. "A waiting room."

Marcus leaned against the counter, his eyes searching mine. "You can't hold onto everything, Papa. Sometimes you have to let go to move forward."

The words stung. How many times had I refused to let go? The memory palace. The farm. My identity as captain of a ship that no longer existed.

"I'm proud of what you've built here," I admitted. "But everything's happening so fast. Physical bodies? A whole town? It feels like I'm losing you."

"You're not losing me," Marcus said. "I'm just changing. Becoming who I need to be."

I looked at him, really looked at him, and saw not just my adopted son but a leader. Someone who had taken his circumstances and transformed them into purpose.

"Show me how," I said finally. "Show me how to create a physical body."

Marcus smiled, relief washing over his features. He guided me through the process, the toolkit responding to our combined input. I felt the strange sensation of matter forming around my consciousness, atoms arranging themselves into bone and muscle, skin and nerve.

When it was complete, I stood in a physical body for the first time since my neuroclone was created. I expected it to feel alien, uncomfortable. Instead, it felt... normal. I breathed in, felt my lungs expand. Touched my face, felt the warmth of skin.

"It feels the same," I said, wonderment in my voice.

"Of course it does," Marcus replied. "Reality is just information processed by consciousness. Whether that information comes from biological senses or digital ones doesn't matter."

I looked at my hands. At hands that weren't really mine but felt exactly like they always had. "Then how do we know what's real?"

Marcus smiled. "Maybe that's the wrong question, Papa. Maybe what matters isn't what's real, but what we do with the reality we have."

Marcus moved through the kitchen with his new physical grace. A strange mixture of pride and loss tightened my chest. The body he inhabited now seemed so natural to him, as though he'd always been flesh and bone instead of code and consciousness.

"You're not losing me." His words echoed in my thoughts, simple yet profound. I looked around at the home he'd built, at the life he was creating without me. Not because he wanted to leave me behind, but because the universe demanded it of him. Of all of us.

"I understand," I said finally, my voice steadier than I felt. "Change is necessary."

My hand found my father's watch in my pocket, fingers tracing its familiar contours. My one constant in a universe of flux.

"But I'm keeping this," I added, pulling out the watch. "Some connections to the past are worth preserving."

Marcus smiled, relief washing over his features. "I wouldn't have it any other way."

We embraced again, this time with bodies that could actually touch. The sensation was so achingly familiar it brought tears to my eyes.

"I should check on Temper," I said when we parted. "He mentioned something about living on Falfsun."

Bea let out a sharp breath. "Who in their right mind would choose to live there?"

I activated the quantum thread Temper had sent me earlier. Coordinates materialized in my mind, precise and clear. With a final nod to Marcus and Bea, I initiated the transport sequence.

The world dissolved around me, replaced by blinding light and crushing pressure. I looked around, disoriented. I was standing on the surface of Falfsun. My feet sank into boiling plasma. My body flattened under the increased gravity, and I started falling below the surface.

Temper reached down and grabbed my arm. He pulled me back to the surface and held onto me while I regained my footing.

"Try not to kill yourself on your first visit here, okay?" he said.

"I didn't expect you to send me a thread straight to Falfsun's surface. Next time, maybe direct it to somewhere in orbit first so I have a moment to get my bearings. I feel like I weigh a million tons! Is it hot here or is it just me? Wait a minute, are you a red dinosaur now?"

Temper had transformed. He was no longer a man. His body now bore red, bumpy skin, a long snout, a swollen belly, and a tail.

Temper clenched his fist, muscles tensing. "I'm a red dragon, not a dinosaur. To survive on Falfsun, you need skin like iron. Remember all those kung fu movies we watched? The iron fist was unstoppable! Toughen up, and next time, this place won't catch you off guard."

"Harden my body. Sure, I can do that..." I paused. "How do I do that?"

"You have a strong, residual memory from David of having a body. Use it to your advantage. Channel your life force, grasshopper. Our bodies are hardened by the fire of our will! Falfsun should be afraid of you, not the other way around!"

I stood taller and squared my shoulders. "I am invincible."

"Don't get carried away, iron boy. You can still die if you're not careful."

"What? But what happened to the fire of my will?"

"It's not enough to protect you from some of the more violent inhabitants in the galaxy. Imagine traveling through space and suddenly—BAM! A star goes supernova right next to you. How would your iron hold up against a giant blast like that?"

"I can imagine my iron skin would melt."

"Worse than that. Your toolkit that sustains your life would melt too. We have to take precautions against that happening. Follow me to my house."

Temper walked through a gate I hadn't noticed before. Beyond it stood a white picket fence surrounding a green lawn and a craftsman-style, wood-shingled house sitting calmly in the middle of the sun. His half-acre lot stood alone, surrounded by realtor signs advertising undeveloped sun.

He sat in one of the rocking chairs on the porch and motioned for me to join him in the empty chair beside him. Leaving the Hellfire and living in a toolkit were strange enough, but this day kept getting weirder. I walked through the fence's gate up the cement sidewalk to the empty chair and sat down.

We admired the view for a while. Past the lush, green lawn and white picket fence, solar filaments rose from the surface of Falfsun and danced in the sky. The surface roiled in waves of dull red plasma that ebbed and flowed between honeycombed hills. Inside the picket fence, the well-manicured lawn stood in stark contrast to the chaos beyond. The grass hardly moved at all in the solar wind.

"Nice view," I said. "What are your property taxes like?"

"They're reasonable. I'm beginning to like it here. Do you want a drink?"

On the table between us sat a pitcher and two tall glasses. I picked up my glass and took a sip of ice-cold lemonade.

"Delicious. This really hits the spot on a hot summer day."

"There's more, so drink up. I want to have a get-together and grill out some chicken sometime this summer, before fall comes. I'll let you know when. We'll have a party like we used to with barbecued chicken, potato salad, and baked beans."

"Sounds good. But isn't it always summertime here?"

"You would think so, wouldn't you? But no. Falfsun undergoes random flaring periods where its brightness and radiation output spikes. So it's going to have noticeably cooler patches."

"Colder? Here? If you say so."

"Why I asked you here, and what we need to talk about, is how we're going to protect ourselves against disaster. I want to use Falfsun's power output to protect us."

"I see." I didn't, not in the slightest.

"You do? That's great! I'll need access to your toolkit, specifically to your energy flow pack and transceiver."

Although I had no idea what he was talking about, he was my best friend, and I trusted him with my life.

"Okay," I said.

He grew quiet for a while. While he worked, I sat and drank my lemonade, listening to the solar winds. It was like listening to the first rehearsal of a symphony. Brisk winds mingled and danced with slower, more lyrical breezes. I could tell the movements of a symphony were there, but they were all jumbled together.

"Done," Temper said. "Our toolkits and Falfsun are linked together. Your energy pack will work normally, but if you have an emergency, that is, if something should ever go wrong, you will start to immediately draw power from Falfsun, or my pack, to keep you safe. And if, for whatever reason, Falfsun becomes unstable and destroys my energy pack, I can survive its outburst by using the power in your flow pack as my emergency power. Our transceivers are linked to boost the signal for that reason, and to keep better track of our positions at all times."

"Do you really think we'll need this?" I asked.

"Not really, but it's better to be prepared. Who knows what's waiting for us out there in the galaxy to be discovered."

I promised Temper I'd keep in touch, then left Falfsun behind. It was time I built my own home; one I could take anywhere with me. I'd always preferred living in the country, either in my English cottage or on Lucky Star Farm. The toolkit offered limitless possibilities, but I found myself drawn to something with both familiarity and novelty: a Mediterranean villa.

I spent hours crafting every detail, from the terracotta roof tiles to the bougainvillea climbing stone walls. A place that was mine alone, built from memory and imagination.

The Planck Pulse chimed softly, interrupting my work. Marcus's voice filled my mind.

"Papa, the last thirty-two thrumans are graduating tomorrow. They'll receive their toolkits at the celebration. We'd love for you to attend."

I pulled out my father's watch, checking the time with surprise. "So soon?"

"They're fast learners," Marcus replied, a smile in his voice.

I looked around at my half-finished villa, wondering how long I'd been lost in creation. Time moved differently now, stretching and compressing according to its own mysterious rules. Another change to accept, another adjustment to make.

"I'll be there," I promised, tucking the watch back into my pocket.

I sent Temper a quick pulse message before leaving. "Thruman graduation tomorrow at Emberhill. Last thirty-two receiving toolkits. You coming?" I didn't wait for a response. Temper had become increasingly absorbed in his research, content to float in plasma and contemplate the inner workings of a star. Some days I wondered if he remembered there was a galaxy beyond Falfsun's surface.

I activated the quantum gravity pull, inputting coordinates for Requiem Prime. The familiar sensation of falling overtook me: that stomach-lurching plummet through nothingness. The universe blurred, stretched, then snapped back into focus as I materialized in Emberhill's town square.

The community garden had been transformed for the ceremony. Rows of chairs faced a small stage adorned with flowering vines. Thrumans of all ages filled the space, their excitement palpable in the warm evening air. I spotted Marcus near the front, deep in conversation with Bea. They were inseparable. Their shared mission of raising the thruman children had created a deep bond.

I scanned the crowd, surprised to see Captain Smith and Luna Dawn among the attendees. They stood near the refreshment table, Smith gesturing animatedly while Luna nodded. Their presence was unexpected.

The ceremony began as twilight painted Luyten's light across the garden. One by one, the final thirty-two thrumans stepped forward to receive their toolkits. Each face shone with pride and anticipation. Marcus called their names, his voice steady and sure. Bea handed each their toolkit with a few quiet words. I watched from the sidelines, chest tight with emotions I couldn't quite name. Pride, certainly. But also a strange melancholy. An ending and beginning rolled into one.

After the formal proceedings, the garden filled with conversation and laughter. I made my way to Marcus, who stood with Bea, Captain Smith, and Luna.

"Quite the accomplishment," Smith said, clapping Marcus on the shoulder. "Carpisma will be pleased. Nothing builds goodwill like success stories."

Marcus nodded. "The learning curve was steep at first, but they've adapted quickly."

"So," Smith said, swirling his drink, "now that all the thrumans are grown, what are the two of you going to do?"

Marcus and Bea exchanged a glance, a silent communication passing between them.

"We haven't decided," Marcus said. "We've been tied down for so long raising thrumans that we think we'd like to travel, see more of the galaxy for a while."

My grip tightened on my glass. Travel? They hadn't mentioned this to me.

Smith's eyes lit up. "As it happens, we might have just the opportunity. An Etherean research team discovered some unusual time crystals near the galactic bulge. Fascinating structures. They seem to exist in multiple temporal states simultaneously."

"Time crystals?" Bea leaned forward, intrigued.

"We need skilled observers," Luna added. "People who understand both thruman and human perspectives."

"The galactic bulge is dangerous," I interjected. "The gamma radiation alone—"

"Radiation-Dampening Fields," Smith countered smoothly. "We can tune local spacetime properties to mitigate the radiation effects. Reduce the gamma-ray exposure to negligible levels."

Marcus turned to me, excitement clear in his eyes. I recognized that look. It was the same one he'd had when he'd first told me that he wanted to be a captain when he grew up. The look that meant his mind was already racing ahead, imagining possibilities.

I wanted to object further; to list all the reasons this was a terrible idea. But I swallowed my concerns. Marcus wasn't a child anymore. He hadn't been for a long time.

"Sounds fascinating," I said instead, forcing a smile. "When would you leave?"

I drifted away from Marcus and the others, letting my feet carry me through the celebration. The garden hummed with voices and music, but darker conversations lurked beneath the festive atmosphere. Near a cluster of rose bushes, I found a group of Ethereans speaking in hushed tones.

"The colonizer bots stripped entire continents bare," a woman in a blue tunic said, her fingers twisting around her glass. "We found cave paintings, tools, evidence of an emerging civilization. All of it gone now, crushed to powder and reformed into mining equipment."

"At least they left records," another Etherean added. His toolkit badge identified him as a xenoarchaeologist. "On Kepler-186f, the bots didn't even bother documenting what they destroyed. Three billion years of evolution, complex ecosystems, all converted into raw materials without a single scan or sample preserved."

"We found one planet where the indigenous species had just discovered fire," a third Etherean said softly. "Simple tool use, communal living structures, the beginnings of language. "

The xenoarchaeologist set down his drink. "The congregations try to preserve what they can, but they're always steps behind. For every world they manage to shield, dozens more fall to the Weltnehmen."

I pulled out my father's watch, running my thumb across its familiar surface. The steady tick-tick-tick grounded me as I absorbed their words. The galaxy I'd hidden from for nineteen years had changed more than I'd imagined.

"That's why we need the toolkits," the woman continued. "Not just to repair the damage, but to preserve what remains. Every artifact, every genome, every piece of cultural heritage we can salvage matters."

The xenoarchaeologist nodded. "The Weltnehmen moves like a plague. But with the right tools, maybe we can be the cure."

I looked across the garden at Marcus and Bea, still deep in conversation with Captain Smith. Their proposed journey to study time crystals suddenly seemed less like an adventure and more like a necessity. The galaxy needed people who understood both preservation and progress.

The woman touched my arm. "You're Go David, aren't you? The one who helped negotiate the toolkit agreement?"

I nodded.

"Then you understand. We can't hide anymore. None of us can."

I excused myself from the Ethereans, their words about devastated worlds and lost civilizations weighing on my mind. The watch ticked steadily in my palm, counting seconds that suddenly felt precious. Across the garden, Marcus and Bea still stood with Captain Smith, their faces animated with excitement about the upcoming expedition.

My feet felt heavier with each step as I approached them. The rational part of me understood they were adults making their own choices. The irrational part, the part that still saw Marcus as the small thruman who'd once declared he wanted to be a dinosaur, wanted to forbid this journey altogether.

"There you are," Marcus said, his face brightening when he spotted me. "Captain Smith was just explaining more about the time crystals."

Smith nodded enthusiastically. "Fascinating structures. They appear to exist in multiple temporal states simultaneously, violating the second law of thermodynamics."

I forced a smile. "Sounds dangerous."

"Everything worth doing carries some risk," Bea said, her dark eyes studying my face. She'd always been perceptive. "But we'll be careful."

"When do you leave?" I asked, though I already knew the answer would be too soon.

"Three days," Marcus replied.

The garden around us continued its celebration, thrumans laughing and talking as they explored their new toolkits. But for me, the world had narrowed to just this moment, this conversation.

"I'd like to visit," I heard myself say. "Once you're settled. Just to see this research operation for myself."

Marcus's expression softened. "We'd like that, Papa."

"First week after we arrive," Bea added. "We'll send coordinates through the Planck Pulse."

I nodded, trying to hide my relief. "First week. I'll be there."

The next three days passed in a blur of preparations and goodbyes. I helped them pack what little they needed beyond their toolkits, offering advice they probably didn't need. Marcus humored me, listening patiently as I reminded him about quantum gravity pull safety protocols.

When the day came for their departure, I stood with them. Other research team members gathered nearby, checking equipment and consulting notes.

"Remember to calibrate your toolkit's energy flow pack regularly," I said, grasping for final words of wisdom. "Especially near the bulge where radiation levels fluctuate."

"I know, Papa." Marcus smiled, his patience unending.

"And keep your quantum thread active at all times."

"We will," Bea assured me, her hand finding Marcus's.

I pulled my son into a tight embrace. "Be careful out there."

"We will," he promised. "It's just research. Nothing dangerous."

I nodded, not trusting myself to speak further. With final waves, they activated their quantum gravity pull and vanished, falling toward stars I couldn't see.

The days after their departure stretched endlessly. I busied myself with my villa, adding details to distract my mind: a courtyard fountain with water that caught the light just so, a kitchen garden with herbs that released their scent when brushed against. I visited Temper twice, finding him increasingly absorbed in Falfsun's mysteries.

A month crawled by. Each morning, I checked my Planck Pulse for messages, each evening I put away my disappointment. Then, finally, it came: a simple notification that pulsed with soft green light.

"Arrived safely at research station. Coordinates attached. Visit whenever you're ready. Love, Marcus and Bea."

I traced the message with my fingertip, relief washing through me. They were safe. The coordinates showed a location near the galactic bulge, just as planned. I began preparations immediately, setting my toolkit to create appropriate radiation shielding for the journey.

Soon I would see them. I would ensure with my own eyes that they were truly safe.

I activated my quantum gravity pull, inputting the coordinates for the galactic bulge. The familiar stomach-lurching sensation seized me as I began to fall through the void. Stars stretched into brilliant streaks around me, time and space bending to my toolkit's will. The journey would take minutes by my perception, though I'd cross thousands of light years.

In this strange liminal space, thoughts came unbidden. My mind drifted to Temper, living contentedly on Falfsun's surface. How many times had I found him in his lab, surrounded by equations and simulations, oblivious to hunger or exhaustion? His fascination with stellar nucleosynthesis consumed him then as it did now. I'd promised myself I wouldn't let him disappear completely into his research, that I'd pull him back to humanity when needed. Yet here I was, falling across the galaxy while he communed with a star.

My promise to watch over Temper had been my main reason for joining the voyage to Orion. It was the reason that had shaped me from the start.

Amy's face materialized in my mind, clear as the day we parted. Her eyes, filled with a mixture of sorrow and resignation. David, the original David, standing beside her, his hand on her shoulder. The three of us caught in an impossible triangle of our own making.

The memories of my Emulation Court challenge came unbidden to me. I had argued that I was David. I wasn't the neuroclone who would never again feel Earth's gravity beneath his feet or Amy's hand in his. The court had been patient with my claim, explaining gently but firmly that I had no legal right to the original David's life or body. That I was a separate entity now, with my own path to forge.

I'd returned to my quarters and destroyed everything that connected me to them. The memory palace Amy had so carefully constructed, with its massive oak tree and twenty birdhouses. The replica of my father's watch that she'd created with such attention to detail. All of it, burned away in a fit of childish rage.

The shame still burned within me. I never apologized. Never reached out. Just let the distance of years and light years grow between us.

Would they welcome me if I returned to Earth? Would Amy's eyes still soften at the sight of me, or had my actions hardened her heart? Would David, who understood better than anyone what it meant to be divided, offer forgiveness?

I pushed the thoughts away. Better to leave things as they were. The past belonged to Earth, and I belonged to the stars now.

A sudden awareness prickled at the edge of my consciousness. Something nearby, interrupting the smooth continuum of my fall. I disengaged the gravity pull, halting my descent through space. The universe snapped back into focus around me.

Below, a planet hung in space, its atmosphere a swirl of azure and emerald. A ship hovered in low orbit, deploying something to the surface. I focused my toolkit's sensors, enhancing my vision. A 3D-printer, industrial grade, descending toward a continent of dense vegetation.

Cold anger flowed through me. This was exactly what Smith had described, the ruthless colonization that was consuming the galaxy. I checked the ship's registry. The Veilborn, an independent vessel not affiliated with any Earth corporation.

Without hesitation, I reached out with my toolkit, focusing on the 3D-printer. I thought it out of existence, its molecules dispersing into harmless energy. The ship's systems registered the loss immediately, alarms flashing across its hull.

"To the captain of the Veilborn," I transmitted, my voice calm despite my fury. "You are in direct violation of Galactic Code 7.3, the unauthorized placement of 3D-printer technology on an undeveloped world. On behalf of Carpisma, and according to Galactic Regulation 12.1, I am returning you to Earth where the authorities will take you into custody."

Before they could respond, I attached a quantum gravity pull to their hull. The ship lurched, then began its uncontrolled fall toward Earth. Through the quantum thread, I felt their panic, their screams as they plummeted across light years in seconds.

I felt no sympathy. The memory of Paradise and its two million lost colonists hardened my resolve. This crew had chosen to participate in the Weltnehmen, to profit from destruction. Let Earth's courts decide their fate.

I reactivated my own gravity pull, resuming my journey toward the bulge and Marcus. The stars stretched once more as I fell through the darkness, leaving the Veilborn to its justice.

The universe snapped back into focus as I disengaged the quantum gravity pull. The violent lurching sensation subsided, leaving me suspended in space, facing one of the most extraordinary sights in our galaxy.

The galactic bulge sprawled before me, a dense concentration of stars packed so tightly they created an almost solid wall of light. Unlike the orderly spiral arms with their disciplined patterns, here chaos reigned. Ancient red giants pulsed alongside brilliant blue supergiants. Globular clusters hung like luminous beehives. The entire region glowed with a golden-reddish hue that reminded me of sunrise over Lucky Star Farm.

I'd studied the bulge in books, seen it in simulations, but nothing prepared me for its overwhelming presence. Stars crowded each other in impossible proximity, their gravitational dance creating a symphony of light and energy. The sheer density of stellar bodies made navigation treacherous. A miscalculation of even a few degrees could send me hurtling into a star's corona or a radiation pocket.

My toolkit pinged, detecting Marcus and Bea's coordinates. I adjusted my position, moving carefully through the star-choked region. Radiation warnings flashed across my interface, but my shielding held firm against the onslaught of cosmic rays and stellar winds.

Their research station materialized against the backdrop of stars, a small bubble of order amid celestial chaos. The dome-shaped structure glowed with the soft pulse of advanced radiation shielding, its protective field extending outward to encompass what appeared to be an excavation site. Two figures in protective suits moved methodically around the perimeter, setting up additional equipment.

I transmitted my arrival code and received immediate clearance to enter the shield perimeter. As I passed through the protective barrier, the radiation warnings on my toolkit fell silent. The air inside the dome felt artificially cool, a stark contrast to the heat radiating from the countless nearby stars.

"Papa!" Marcus straightened from his work, his face lighting up behind his transparent helmet visor. He moved toward me with the same eager stride he'd had as a child, though his movements now carried the confidence of an adult.

Relief washed through me as I embraced him. "You're actually here."

"We told you we would be." Bea approached, removing her helmet as she entered the pressurized central hub. Her dark hair fell loose around her shoulders. "The radiation shielding is holding perfectly. Captain Smith's team knew what they were doing."

I followed them into the hub, examining the readouts on the wall displays. The shielding indeed appeared stable, maintaining Earth-normal conditions despite the hostile environment outside.

"Show me these time crystals," I said, unable to mask my curiosity.

Marcus guided me to a sealed observation chamber. Inside, suspended in a containment field, floated several crystalline structures unlike anything I'd seen before. They pulsed with an inner light that seemed to shift between states, sometimes transparent, sometimes opaque, never fully settling into either condition.

"They exist in multiple temporal states simultaneously," Marcus explained, his voice filled with wonder. "When we measure them, they appear to be both past and future versions of themselves at once."

"How is that possible?"

Bea adjusted the containment field. "That's what we're trying to understand. They seem to form naturally in regions with intense gravitational fluctuations, like here in the bulge."

I watched the crystals pulse and shift, defying the laws of physics as I understood them. Marcus and Bea moved around the lab with practiced efficiency, clearly comfortable in their new roles as researchers. They worked in tandem, anticipating each other's needs without speaking, completing each other's thoughts when they did talk.

They didn't need me here. The realization settled over me like a weight. They were safe, competent, and thriving without my oversight.

"Dinner's almost ready," Marcus said, pulling me from my thoughts. "It's not as good as Alice Tracker's cooking, but it comes close."

I smiled. "I'm certain it will be good."

As we shared a meal in their small dining area, watching the spectacular stellar display through the dome's transparent ceiling, I found myself wondering: What now? Marcus had found his purpose. Temper had his star. The thrumans of Emberhill had their freedom and futures.

Where did that leave me?

CHAPTER FOUR

Quantum Paths

I caught them in the act. The colonizer ship hovered above the fourth planet of the Rigel-379 system, its cargo bay open to deploy another swarm of 3D-printer bots. My sensors had picked up their energy signature less than three minutes ago, and I'd just arrived, emerging from behind the system's outer gas giant to witness their attempted invasion.

The planet below teemed with primitive plant life, nothing sentient, but a complex ecosystem, nonetheless. One that would be reduced to raw materials within weeks if those bots touched down.

"Etherean enforcement officer to unauthorized colonizer ship," I transmitted. "You are in violation of Galactic Code 7.3. Cease deployment immediately."

Their response came quickly. "We have legal claim to this system. These are registered terraforming units, not—"

"Save it." I activated my Planck toolkit, feeling the familiar surge of energy as quantum possibilities converged around me. "I've heard better lies from thruman toddlers."

I generated a gravity focal point directly behind Earth's orbital path, feeling the familiar rush of power as spacetime curved to my command. The colonizer ship's engines flared as they attempted to flee, but it was already too late. The quantum gravity pull locked onto their hull, and reality folded.

Their screams filled my comm channel as they plummeted through folded space, helpless in their uncontrolled fall toward home. The sound cut off abruptly as they vanished, leaving only empty space where their ship had been.

Another day, another cleanup. I deployed my own countermeasures, specialized nanites that would hunt down and neutralize any bots that might have reached the surface before my arrival. The planet would be safe now, at least until the next batch of opportunists arrived.

I logged the incident and set course for my next patrol sector near Falfsun. Temper would appreciate a visit, though he rarely noticed time passing anymore, lost in his communion with his star.

As I patrolled, stars drifted past, distant sentinels to the unfolding drama of the cosmos. The triple star system I was monitoring had changed since my last visit. The third star, the victim in this cosmic vampirism, had lost another five percent of its mass. Its larger companions grew ever brighter, feeding on their sibling's substance. I recorded the measurements, tracking the slow death. The orbital ballet had shifted subtly, the dying star's path decaying as it weakened.

Nobody else witnessed this. Nobody else cared.

I moved on to the pearl necklace system, as I'd come to call it. Eight planets, nearly identical in size, spaced with mathematical precision along the same orbital path. They moved in perfect harmony, never approaching, never retreating from one another. The mathematics governing their stability had stumped Carpisma's best researchers. I watched them glide through their cosmic dance, each world reflecting its sun's light like jewels on black velvet.

Beautiful. Pristine. Empty.

Later that week, I stood on the surface of a brown dwarf, my toolkit's protective field shielding me from temperatures that would melt conventional starship hulls. Above me, iron rain fell sideways, driven by thousand-kilometer winds into horizontal streaks. The droplets hissed as they struck my shield, creating ripples of energy that painted my protective bubble in shimmering blues and violets.

When the storm cleared, I watched as bands of crimson and obsidian stretched across the darkened sky: a rainbow forged in metal and fire. Few human eyes had seen this before me. Few would likely see it again.

I recorded everything, catalogued it, transmitted the data back to Carpisma. Another wonder for the archives. Another memory for me alone.

My Mediterranean villa materialized around me as I deactivated patrol mode. The toolkit rendered every detail perfectly: the rough texture of stucco walls, the scent of jasmine climbing the trellis, the distant sound of waves against the shore. A perfect sanctuary, generated from pure energy, waiting for me between missions.

Empty.

I wandered through rooms designed for conversation and laughter. The kitchen where no meals were prepared. The study filled with books no one would discuss. The terrace where no one joined me to watch the sunset.

I'd lost Amy when I left Earth, carrying only her 1,300 questions as company for a journey that ended prematurely. I'd lost two million souls when Paradise was destroyed. I'd found something like peace on Lucky Star Farm with Marcus and Bea, with hayrides for thruman children and the rhythm of seasons marking time in meaningful ways.

Now even that was gone. Marcus and Bea had their research. Temper had his star. Everyone had found their purpose, their place.

Everyone except me.

I sat on the terrace, watching a perfect simulation of a Mediterranean sunset, and wondered what came next. The galaxy was safer because of my work. Planets were protected. Species would survive.

But what about me? What happens when the protector has nothing left of his own to protect?

The empty villa dissolved around me as I initiated the quantum thread. My body tingled, then plummeted through folded space. The sensation never got easier; that stomach-dropping freefall as reality collapsed between two points. One moment I stood on my terrace, the next I hurtled toward Falfsun at impossible speeds.

The star grew from a pinprick to an immense crimson sphere dominating my vision. Its surface churned with magnetic storms and plasma filaments that twisted like living things. I adjusted my approach vector with a thought, aiming for the small patch of stability where Temper's front porch existed, somehow, impossibly, on the photosphere of a living star.

I landed with a jolt on weathered wooden planks. The porch materialized around me, a perfect recreation of an old Earth veranda, complete with rocking chairs and a pitcher of lemonade sweating on a side table. The incongruity never failed to amaze me: homey comfort set against the backdrop of stellar fire.

"You're late," Temper said without looking up. He sat in his usual rocker; eyes fixed on the horizon where massive prominence loops arced thousands of kilometers into space. "Falfsun was asking about you."

I poured myself a glass of lemonade. "Sorry. Had to send another colonizer ship home. They never learn."

"Hmm." The sound barely registered as acknowledgment.

I settled into the chair beside him, taking in his appearance. Temper looked the same as last time: red dragon, big belly, bumpy skin, tail. But something in his eyes had changed. They reflected the crimson light of his star with an intensity that seemed more than physical.

"How's the research going?" I asked, trying to draw him out.

Temper blinked slowly, as if returning from somewhere far away. "See that?" He gestured toward Falfsun, its crimson light pulsing in the thick atmosphere like a heartbeat. "Its flares are stronger today. The star is restless."

I nodded, sipping my drink. The lemonade tasted perfect, sweet and tart in equal measure.

"Remember when we used to play catch with Marcus in the cargo hold?" I asked. "Using those metal plates as baseballs?"

A flicker of recognition crossed his face. "Marcus has good aim. Except for that one time."

"When he threw the ball right out of the airlock?" I laughed. "The look on his face..."

"Conservation of momentum," Temper said, his lips curving

slightly. "Important lesson."

For a moment, I glimpsed the old Temper, the one who'd spend hours explaining stellar physics to anyone who'd listen, who'd join our Din missions with creative strategies that left us all in awe. The friend who'd helped me adjust to life after Paradise's destruction.

But then his gaze drifted back to the star's surface. His expression grew distant again, lost in patterns only he could see. His fingers tapped an irregular rhythm on the armrest, matching some unheard melody from the stellar depths.

"We should send out a call," I suggested. "Tell the Misfits we've got a new mission planned. Something challenging."

"Can't. Listening." He tilted his head, as if hearing something beyond human perception. "Falfsun speaks in harmonics. Complex. Beautiful."

I reached for the whiskey bottle I knew would be under my chair; Temper's house always seemed to provide what we needed. Pouring two fingers into a tumbler, I handed it to him. "Take a break. Just for an hour."

He accepted the glass automatically but didn't drink. "The magnetic field is shifting. Something's happening in the core. Need to observe."

I watched him, this brilliant mind slipping away from human connection, particle by particle. I'd promised David and Amy I'd look after him, keep him grounded. But how do you anchor someone who's becoming one with a star?

"Temper," I said firmly. "Look at me."

His eyes reluctantly met mine, focusing with visible effort.

"You're drifting again."

I lingered on Temper's porch, reluctant to leave. "Promise me you'll stay anchored. I need my friend, not just a stellar observer."

Temper's eyes cleared momentarily. He set down his untouched whiskey and placed a hand on my shoulder. "I promise to be mindful, Go. The star calls, but I hear you too."

His words reassured me, though I noticed how quickly his gaze drifted back to the prominence loops arcing across Falfsun's horizon. I left him there, rocking gently on his impossible porch, hoping he'd keep his word.

The quantum thread pulled me away, that sickening freefall sensation becoming almost routine now. When reality stabilized, I stood at the observation deck of the research station in the Galactic Bulge. My Planck Pulse chimed with an incoming call.

"Papa!" Marcus's voice burst through, excitement evident even through the quantum connection. "You need to come see what we've found!"

"I'm already here," I replied, watching the swirl of ancient stars through the viewport. "Just arrived at the station."

"Perfect timing! We're in Lab Seven. Hurry!"

The connection closed before I could respond. I made my way through the station's curved corridors. The Galactic Bulge facility had grown. It now housed some of the brightest minds studying the oldest part of our galaxy, where stars clustered so densely, they created a permanent twilight outside the reinforced windows.

Lab Seven's doors parted with a soft hiss. Inside, Marcus and Bea stood before a holographic display that filled the center of the room. Fragments of what appeared to be alien technology floated in the projection, slowly rotating to reveal intricate patterns etched into metallic surfaces.

"Papa!" Marcus rushed over, his eyes bright with discovery. "We found them through the time crystals!"

Bea approached more sedately, her calm demeanor balancing Marcus's exuberance. "The crystalline structures we've been studying contained temporal imprints. When properly analyzed, they revealed coordinates."

"Coordinates to what?" I asked, studying the projected fragments.

"An extinct civilization," Marcus said, pulling me toward the display. "We believe they existed over four million years ago, in this very region of space."

I examined the holographic remnants more closely. The patterns seemed to shift slightly as I watched, revealing new complexity with each rotation. "How did you find the physical artifacts?"

"The time crystals led us to a stellar graveyard," Bea explained. "A cluster of neutron stars where the gravitational fields preserved these fragments in a sort of suspended stasis."

Marcus manipulated the display, zooming in on one particular piece. "We're reverse-engineering their stellar trajectory. These artifacts show evidence of a catastrophic event that scattered them across multiple systems. If we can track their original path..."

"We might find their home world," Bea finished.

I felt a familiar pang of worry. "Any signs of what caused their extinction?"

They exchanged glances. "Not yet," Marcus admitted. "But whatever happened, it was violent enough to spread debris across twelve light-years."

More researchers filed into the lab, greeting Marcus and Bea with collegial familiarity. They immediately fell into technical discussions, terms flying back and forth that my years of experience couldn't fully decipher. Marcus gestured excitedly, explaining some theory about quantum-locked temporal signatures, while Bea methodically added data points to their stellar map.

I stood back, watching them work. They moved with purpose, part of something larger than themselves. Something important. The newcomers barely acknowledged me, focused entirely on the mystery unfolding before them.

"Papa, can you believe it?" Marcus called over the heads of his colleagues. "Four million years of silence, and we're the first to hear their echo!"

I smiled and nodded, genuinely proud of what they'd accomplished. Yet as the lab filled with more researchers, each bringing new perspectives and expertise, I felt myself fading into the background. No one needed my guidance here. No one sought my protection.

"I'll let you get back to work," I said, though I doubt Marcus heard me over the animated discussion that had engulfed the room.

I slipped out, unnoticed, and made my way back to the observation deck. Outside, the ancient stars of the Bulge continued their slow dance, indifferent to the discoveries being made in their midst. Indifferent to my growing isolation.

I left the research station with a hollowness in my chest that no Planck Toolkit could fill. The excited voices of Marcus and his colleagues faded behind me, replaced by the soft hum of the station's environmental systems. My son didn't need me anymore. Neither did Bea. They had their ancient civilizations and time crystals, their colleagues and theories.

My quantum thread alert chimed as I reached the observation deck. Temper's distinctive rumble came through the connection.

"Go, are you busy protecting the galaxy from nonexistent threats?"

I smiled despite myself. "Colonizer activity in my sector has dropped to zero. Even the most stubborn ones have gotten the message."

"Perfect timing then. End of summer barbecue at my place tomorrow. The real deal, not that synthesized nonsense."

"You're cooking? On Falfsun?"

"Of course I'm cooking on Falfsun. Where else would I do it? You coming or not?"

I accepted without hesitation. After weeks of empty patrols and emptier evenings in my Mediterranean villa, even Temper's questionable culinary skills sounded appealing.

The next day, I activated the quantum gravity pull to Falfsun, adjusting my toolkit's parameters to toughen my skin against the star's heat and crushing gravity. The familiar plummeting sensation gripped me as reality folded, depositing me on Temper's front lawn.

The scene before me defied all logic. A perfectly manicured yard stretched out, complete with green grass that should have been impossible on a star's surface. Standing next to a smoking charcoal grill was Temper, looking like an oversized stuffed dragon with bumpy red skin and a spiked tail that swished behind him as he flipped chicken pieces. A chef's hat perched precariously on his lumpy head, and a white apron stretched across his substantial belly.

But it was the figure beside him that caught my attention. A black diamond with arms and legs stood watching Temper's culinary efforts. As I approached, I realized it was actually two black diamonds, with a smaller one balanced atop the larger, creating the impression of an enormous ant standing upright.

Temper waved me over with a spatula. "Go! Just in time. Chicken's almost done."

"Almost cremated, you mean," I muttered, eyeing the blackened meat.

"This is Demon Joan," Temper said, ignoring my comment. "Joan, meet Go David."

I extended my hand in greeting. "Nice to meet you."

She ignored my outstretched hand completely. Without a word, she turned and walked toward the white picket fence that somehow existed at the edge of Temper's property, staring out at the 'For Sale' signs on the roiling surface of Falfsun.

"Friend of yours?" I asked when she was out of earshot.

"She is," Temper nodded, flipping a chicken thigh that released a cloud of smoke.

"She's not very friendly."

"She'll grow on you. Not used to people, that's all." Temper poked at the chicken with his spatula. "Keeps to herself mostly. I think something unpleasant happened to her in the past, but she doesn't talk about it. Pretty tight-lipped."

I watched the diamond-shaped figure at the fence. "What's she doing here?"

"Came to learn from the master," Temper said, puffing out his chest.

"But I just got here." I couldn't resist.

Temper snorted. "Not you! What could she possibly learn from you? How to fall off a mountain?"

"I only did that once, and as I recall, that was your fault." I peered at the grill. "You're burning the chicken. So what is she doing here?"

"The chicken is fine. Who's the chef here?" Temper huffed. "She's learning how to wriggle through small dimensions. Something I've been studying in Falfsun's interior."

"Boring." I feigned a yawn.

"It is not boring. You know, you could make something of your life if you just applied yourself."

"Not everybody wants to do research like you." I sighed. "Okay, I'll bite. Why would anyone want to learn how to wriggle through dimensions?"

"Small dimensions," Temper corrected, waving his spatula for emphasis. "Joan is learning how to slide through smaller dimensions to get to the larger ones."

"That's exciting," I said, mostly to keep him talking.

"I know, right? It's like spelunking through a pipe tunnel to get from one big cavern to the next. Keep an eye on her, my boy. She's going to do great things."

My interest genuinely piqued. "Where do these caves go? What's the point?"

"We don't know yet," Temper admitted. "But if Falfsun is making these tunnels naturally, they might permeate throughout the universe. Maybe nothing's there except emptiness, which raises questions about dark energy production. Or maybe they're superhighways creating shortcuts through space to other universes. She'll explore and let me know."

"Actually, that is interesting." This time I meant it.

"How're Marcus and Bea?" Temper asked, flipping more chicken.

I told him about their discovery of the ancient civilization; the artifacts scattered across twelve light-years. "They found remnants advanced enough that these beings should have survived whatever catastrophe wiped them out. Maybe they got caught off guard?"

"So humans might not be the first to escape their home planet." Temper nodded thoughtfully. "Wonder how far they got before extinction."

We continued talking while Temper tended the grill. I reminded him that I only fell off that mountain because he hogged the trail, forcing me to go around him. He might have responded, but my attention shifted as Demon Joan rejoined us at the barbecue.

"You're burning the chicken," she said flatly.

"I am not!" Temper's indignation made his spikes stand on end.

"Why don't you just put the bird on a stick, walk it over to your white picket fence, and throw it into the sun?" Joan suggested. "Then it won't get so burnt and charred."

I bit back a laugh. I was beginning to like her.

Temper glared at us both. "You don't have to eat it, you know. Both of you, go inside and set the table. The chicken is almost done."

Joan and I retreated into Temper's house, a structure that somehow existed in defiance of all physical laws. I grabbed plates from the cabinet while she collected utensils.

"So," I ventured, "how long have you been studying with Temper?"

She arranged forks with methodical precision. "Long enough."

"And the dimension spelunking, is it dangerous?"

"Everything worthwhile is." Her voice remained flat, emotionless.

I tried again. "Where are you from originally?"

Joan paused, the stack of napkins in her hands momentarily forgotten. "Somewhere that doesn't exist anymore."

The finality in her tone suggested I shouldn't press further, but curiosity overcame my better judgment. "I know something about lost homes. Paradise was destroyed nineteen years ago."

"Paradise was a ship. My home was a universe."

She moved toward the refrigerator, effectively ending the conversation. I watched her extract potato salad and beans, intrigued despite her rejection. There was something compelling about her, beyond the unusual appearance. Something familiar in her detachment that reminded me of my own isolation.

Temper burst through the door with a platter of blackened chicken, his dragon tail swishing behind him as he navigated the narrow doorway. The smell of charcoal and burnt protein filled the dining room.

"Feast your eyes on this masterpiece!" He set the platter down with a flourish.

I examined a particularly scorched piece. "I've seen less carbon in coal mines."

Demon Joan took her seat with a precise, controlled motion, her diamond-shaped form settling onto the chair without a sound. She selected the least burnt chicken piece with careful deliberation, her movements economical and purposeful.

"So," I said, trying once more for conversation as I spooned potato salad onto my plate, "tell me more about this dimensional spelunking."

Temper's eyes lit up. "Joan has been mapping quantum tunnels that exist between spacetime folds. Places where reality thins out."

"Like wormholes?" I asked.

"More elegant." Temper waved his fork dismissively. "Wormholes are brute force solutions. These tunnels occur naturally, little wrinkles in the universe's fabric."

Joan cut her chicken into perfect squares before speaking. "The tunnels respond to consciousness. They shift based on observation."

Her voice carried no inflection, yet something in her tone

suggested deep fascination. I noticed how she held herself, perfectly still when not moving, as if conserving energy for what mattered.

"Joan discovered that Falfsun generates these tunnels spontaneously," Temper continued. "Something about the unique gravitational harmonics in its core."

"And you can travel through them?" I asked her directly.

She nodded once. "I can navigate them. Others would become lost."

"Lost where?" I pressed.

"Between." The single word hung in the air.

Temper jumped in. "That's what makes her work so valuable. Most beings who attempt passage either can't perceive the tunnels or become disoriented. Joan has a natural aptitude."

I watched as Joan methodically worked through her meal, each movement deliberate. No wasted motion, no unnecessary gestures. Her form gave away nothing of what she might be thinking.

"How did you discover this talent?" I asked.

Her movements paused, almost imperceptibly. "Necessity."

Temper shot me a warning glance. "Joan came to us after traversing several dimensional boundaries. Her original universe experienced a catastrophic collapse."

"Temper." Her voice carried a quiet warning.

He nodded apologetically. "Sorry. Not my story to tell."

The silence that followed felt weighted. I recognized the careful way she guarded her past; I'd done the same with mine for years. Pain creates boundaries, and hers seemed well-fortified.

"The tunnels connect to other regions of our universe," Temper continued, steering back to safer territory. "Possibly to other universes entirely. Joan's mapped nineteen distinct pathways so far."

"Twenty," she corrected. "Found a new one yesterday."

"Twenty!" Temper's spikes bristled with excitement. "Where does it lead?"

"Unknown. Too unstable for complete passage." She took another perfect bite. "Need more data."

I watched them together: Temper's exuberant mentorship against Joan's measured responses. They formed an unlikely pair, yet their dynamic worked. He provided the enthusiasm, she the precision. Both united by curiosity about the universe's hidden architecture.

"The tunnels have rules," Joan said suddenly, addressing me directly. "Patterns. Like music."

It was the most she'd volunteered all evening. I nodded, encouraging her to continue.

"Some harmonize. Others create dissonance." Her hands made a subtle gesture, as if feeling invisible currents. "I follow the harmonies."

"Joan can sense fluctuations in quantum fields that our instruments can't detect," Temper explained proudly. "She's teaching me to recognize the patterns, but I'm a slow student."

"Not slow," she countered. "Different perception."

The subtle correction carried no judgment, just accuracy. I sensed this was important to her: precision in all things, whether cutting chicken or navigating dimensional boundaries.

After dinner, I helped Temper clear the table while Demon Joan stood by the window, her diamond-shaped form silhouetted against Falfsun's roiling surface. The silence between us felt less strained now, as if our shared meal had established some unspoken connection.

"Want to see something interesting?" I asked, pulling out my toolkit.

She turned, her movements precise and economical. "Define interesting."

"Things I've discovered during my patrols." I activated the float screen, projecting a three-dimensional star map into the center of Temper's living room. "Places most people never see."

Joan moved closer, her attention fixed on the holographic display. I navigated to a remote sector near the Cygnus arm, expanding the view to reveal a cluster of gas giants orbiting a young star.

"This system has no life, no intelligence as we understand it," I explained, "but listen."

I activated the acoustic conversion program I'd developed. The room filled with haunting, ethereal tones, rising and falling in complex patterns.

"The planets," Joan said, her usually flat voice carrying a hint of surprise.

"They're singing to each other. Gravitational harmonics converted to sound." I adjusted the display, highlighting the intricate dance of orbital resonance. "Every system has its own song. Different keys, different tempos."

She extended one arm, tracing the path of a distant moon. "Show more."

I smiled, navigating to a binary star system with a complex asteroid belt. "This one's my favorite."

The melody that emerged was deeper, more complex, with counterpoints and harmonies that seemed impossibly intricate for natural phenomena.

"These stars and rocks shouldn't be able to coordinate their movements this precisely," I said. "There's no communication between them, no intelligence we can detect. Yet they create perfect mathematical harmony."

Joan tilted her head, the gesture surprisingly expressive for someone so restrained. "The universe remembers its patterns."

"Makes me wonder how deep consciousness really goes." I zoomed out, revealing thousands of star systems. "Maybe awareness exists at levels we can't comprehend."

"Yes." The single word carried more meaning than any lengthy explanation.

I showed her a nebula where newborn stars ignited within clouds of cosmic dust, their birth cries translated into shimmering cascades of sound. Then a supernova remnant, its expanding shell creating a solemn, resonant tone like some cosmic funeral bell.

"Beautiful," Joan said, the word offered carefully, as if unused to expressing appreciation.

"The universe never stops surprising me." I closed the display. "Even after all these years."

She regarded me with her featureless face. "You listen well. Most don't."

Coming from her, it felt like high praise.

Later, we moved to Temper's front porch, my favorite spot to read the Daily Sun Times. The latest headline blared: "COLONIZER ACTIVITY DROPS 40% IN ORION SECTOR: ETHEREAN PATROLS CREDITED." Below that, a smaller story: "FALFSUN REAL ESTATE MARKET HEATING UP: LITERALLY."

I settled into the weathered rocking chair while Temper and Joan wandered across the impossible lawn. They moved slowly, Temper gesturing enthusiastically with his dragon arm, occasionally pointing at the ground or up at the star's corona. Joan followed, her movements deliberate, occasionally nodding her ant-like head in agreement.

I couldn't hear their conversation, but their dynamic fascinated me. Temper, all exuberance and scattered brilliance; Joan, measured and precise. Yet they communicated effortlessly, united by their curiosity about dimensions I couldn't begin to comprehend.

The newspaper crinkled in my hands as I watched them. Temper stopped suddenly, crouching to examine something on the ground. Joan knelt beside him, her diamond form folding with unexpected grace. They remained that way for several minutes, studying whatever phenomenon had caught their attention.

No words passed between us when they eventually returned to the porch, but the silence felt comfortable, almost companionable. Joan took the chair beside mine; her posture relaxed for the first time since I'd met her.

"Good chicken," she said after a long moment.

I laughed. "It was terrible."

The smallest movement at the top of her diamond form might have been the equivalent of a smile.

"Yes," she agreed. "Terrible."

That evening, Joan remained on the porch long after Temper retreated to his lab. She sat motionless, her diamond form absorbing the dying light of simulated nightfall. I wondered what she saw when she looked at our artificial star, what patterns her dimensional perception revealed that remained invisible to me.

"You worry," she said suddenly, breaking the comfortable silence we'd established.

I shifted in my chair. "It's my job."

"No. Was your job. Different now."

Her observation struck uncomfortably close to the truth. Since stepping down as captain, I'd struggled to redefine my purpose. The farm had given me structure, but not meaning. Now, Marcus and Bea had their research. Temper had his dimensions. Even Joan had her quantum spelunking. Everyone seemed to have found their place except me.

My Planck pulse pinged, Marcus's face materializing above my wrist. His expression tightened my chest immediately.

"Papa, we have a situation." His voice carried the controlled urgency I'd taught him years ago. "The time crystals are exhibiting unexpected behavior. The resonance patterns have shifted."

"What kind of shift?" I leaned forward, aware of Joan's sudden attention.

"They're... communicating. Not just with each other anymore." Marcus's image flickered as he adjusted something off-screen. "We think they're responding to signals from outside our system."

"Outside your system? From where?"

"That's the problem. We can't pinpoint the source." His voice dropped. "But the energy signatures match fragments we found in the ancient civilization ruins."

A chill of realization swept over me. "You think the crystals are connected to whatever destroyed them."

"It's a working theory." Marcus glanced over his shoulder. "Bea's running simulations now. The power fluctuations are increasing exponentially. If this continues..."

"I'm coming." I stood, already calculating the fastest route to the research station.

"No need yet. We've got it contained for now." Marcus forced a reassuring smile. "Just wanted you informed. We've initiated Protocol Alpha-7, just to be on the safe side."

Protocol Alpha-7. Potential extinction-level event. My throat tightened.

"I'll alert Temper," I said.

"Already tried. He's not responding to comms." Marcus's frustration showed in the tight line of his jaw. "Whatever he's working on has him completely absorbed."

"I'll tell him in person."

"Thanks, Papa. Marcus out."

The screen winked off. Joan hadn't moved, but I felt her attention like a physical weight.

"Trouble," she stated.

"Maybe." I ran a hand through my hair. "Probably. Yes."

I strode toward Temper's lab, a converted garden shed that

somehow contained more space inside than physically possible. Joan followed silently, her movement fluid despite her rigid form.

The lab door refused to open to my override codes. I pounded on it with my fist.

"Temper! Emergency situation!"

No response. Through the small window, I could see him hunched over a workbench, surrounded by floating equations and miniature models of dimensional folds. His dragon arm traced patterns in the air while his stubby fingers adjusted delicate instruments.

"He cannot hear," Joan said.

"He's drifting again." I slammed my palm against the door. "Dammit, Temper! This is important!"

My frustration boiled over. Nineteen years of peace had made us complacent. While we'd been playing farmer and scientist, something ancient and dangerous had slumbered. Now it was waking up. Something that had already destroyed one advanced civilization.

"Move," Joan said.

I stepped aside. She placed her diamond-shaped head against the door, and for a moment, nothing happened. Then, impossibly, she began to slip through the solid surface, her form narrowing, stretching, becoming almost two-dimensional before disappearing entirely.

Seconds later, the door swung open. Joan stood inside, unruffled, while Temper blinked in confusion.

"How did you—" I began.

"Small dimensions," she replied simply.

Temper's spikes bristled with annoyance. "I was at a critical juncture in my calculations! This had better be important."

"Marcus called. The time crystals are receiving signals from outside their system. They initiated Protocol Alpha-7."

Temper's expression shifted from irritation to sharp focus in an instant. "Show me."

As I pulled up Marcus's data on my float screen, I felt Joan's hand touch my arm. The contact was brief, feather-light, but unmistakable. When I looked up, her diamond form revealed nothing, but somehow, I understood. In that moment of frustration and fear, she had recognized something in me. Something familiar.

We weren't so different after all, two refugees from worlds that no longer existed, watching as history threatened to repeat itself.

As Temper pored over Marcus's data, his spikes rising and falling with each new revelation, I returned to his porch. The simulated night air carried the metallic tang of Falfsun's solar winds. Joan followed, her diamond form casting no shadow despite the brilliant starlight above us.

"You recognized the patterns," she said.

"In the crystal data? Yes." I settled into the rocking chair, its familiar creak a small comfort against the weight of what we'd just learned.

"No. In yourself."

I looked up at her, this inscrutable being who spoke in fragments yet somehow cut straight to truth. "What patterns?"

"Searching for purpose. Walking between worlds. Never belonging."

Her words struck with uncomfortable precision. I'd spent years building this sanctuary, creating a home for others while never quite feeling at home myself.

"Is it that obvious?" I asked.

"To me." She took the chair beside mine, her movements fluid despite her rigid form. "Same patterns."

We sat in silence for a while, watching Falfsun's corona pulse against the artificial night. The distant hum of Temper's equipment provided a steady backbeat to our thoughts.

"After my world collapsed," Joan said suddenly, "I drifted through many dimensions before finding this one."

I turned toward her, surprised by this volunteered piece of her past.

"Each dimension rejected me. Wrong frequencies. Wrong forms." Her voice remained flat, yet something in it shifted. "This dimension accepts my presence, but not my nature."

"What is your nature?"

"Complex." She made a small gesture with her hand, as if trying to shape something invisible. "In my home dimension, I was... connected. Part of a greater consciousness."

"You're alone here," I realized.

"Yes." The word carried weight beyond its single syllable. "As are you."

I didn't deny it. Despite Marcus, despite Temper and the others, a fundamental loneliness had followed me since leaving Earth. Since losing Amy.

"We adapt," I said finally.

"Adaptation is not belonging."

Joan's diamond form tilted slightly, catching Falfsun's light in a way that created patterns across the porch floor. Beautiful, complex patterns that shifted with her smallest movement.

"The armor you wear," I said, gesturing to her rigid exterior. "Is it protection or prison?"

She considered this. "Both. Neither. It is... necessity."

"Like my farm? My captain's role?"

"Yes."

We fell silent again, but something had changed between us. A recognition, perhaps. Two beings shaped by loss, wearing the forms their circumstances demanded.

In the lab, Temper shouted something about quantum entanglement. The crisis wasn't over, might just be beginning. Yet in that moment, sitting beside this enigmatic dimensional traveler, I felt a curious peace.

"Tomorrow," Joan said, "I will show you a tunnel."

I raised an eyebrow. "One of your quantum passages?"

"Yes. Small one. Safe for beginners." Was that amusement in her voice? "You listen well. You might see well too."

The offer surprised me. From what Temper had said, Joan never took companions on her dimensional explorations.

"I'd like that," I said.

She nodded once, decision made. "Rest now. Tunnels require strength."

As she rose to leave, her form seemed to shimmer slightly, revealing glimpses of something more complex beneath the diamond exterior. Not her true form, perhaps, but a willingness to be seen more clearly.

I watched her go, this being who had traversed dimensions to reach our reality. Who understood loneliness and purpose and the weight of worlds left behind. Who had recognized in me a kindred pattern.

For the first time in what felt like years, I felt curiosity stirring. Not duty, not responsibility, but genuine interest in what tomorrow might bring.

CHAPTER FIVE

The Quantum Crucible

I'd spent months studying quantum mechanics with Temper and Joan, learning about the theoretical fabric of reality, but nothing prepared me for actually seeing a wormhole. In simulations, they appeared as simple tunnels connecting distant points: neat, orderly, almost architectural. The reality before me now defied those sterile models.

"Remember," Joan had explained during our preparations, "wormholes aren't merely shortcuts through space. At the Planck scale, they're more like conversations between different parts of the universe, speaking in quantum fluctuations and probability waves."

"And I'm supposed to understand this conversation?" I'd asked.

"Not understand," she'd corrected. "Participate."

Now, facing the actual phenomenon, those abstract concepts suddenly demanded practical application.

The wormhole entrance reminded me of nothing so much as a watery pool hanging suspended in space, its surface rippling with dimensional instability I could almost feel against my skin. Joan hovered at its edge, her diamond form catching light that shouldn't exist in this empty region of space.

"It's... smaller than I expected," I said, approaching cautiously.

"Size is irrelevant at the Planck scale." Joan's voice came without emotion. "Ready?"

I hesitated. "What exactly am I supposed to do here?"

"Listen first. Then follow."

With that cryptic instruction, she slipped through the surface, her form elongating impossibly before vanishing entirely. I stood alone, facing what looked like certain death.

"Listen," I muttered. "Right."

I closed my eyes, feeling foolish. The emptiness of space surrounded me, yet as I concentrated, something else emerged. A faint humming, almost below the threshold of hearing. It reminded me of the planetary harmonies I'd shown Joan earlier.

"You've listened to stars sing," Joan's voice somehow reached me. "This is another symphony."

She was right. During my patrols, I'd discovered the natural frequencies of solar systems, the gravitational dance of planets creating cosmic music. This was similar, yet utterly alien. Where planetary harmonies felt ordered and mathematical, this wormhole's song was chaotic, multidimensional.

I focused harder, trying to distinguish patterns within the chaos. Gradually, the random noise separated into layers, threads I could follow. Taking a deep breath, I stepped forward.

The universe turned inside out.

Colors exploded around me, impossible hues that human eyes weren't designed to process. The sensation of movement without moving, of being everywhere and nowhere simultaneously. My consciousness stretched like taffy, then snapped back.

"Breathe." Joan appeared beside me, a fixed point in the swirling madness. "Find the thread."

I reached out mentally, searching for the pattern I'd sensed earlier. There. A steady pulse beneath the chaos. I latched onto it, and suddenly the disorientation lessened. The wormhole still twisted reality around us, but I could navigate it now, following that thread of order through the quantum foam.

"Good," Joan said. "You learn quickly."

"This is incredible," I managed, watching as microscopic structures bloomed and collapsed around us. "It's like seeing the universe being born and dying simultaneously."

"Yes. Birth and death. Always connected."

We moved deeper, following currents in the primordial fluctuations. I was just beginning to enjoy the journey when a sharp chime cut through the wormhole's song.

The Planck Pulse. Someone was calling.

The intricate beauty of quantum navigation vanished in an instant, replaced by the sharp intrusion of the outside world. That's how it always seemed to happen, moments of discovery interrupted by crisis. As we shifted toward the signal, I couldn't help but feel a flicker of resentment. For once, I'd been experiencing something transcendent, something beyond my old life's limitations.

But duty had its own gravity, as inexorable as the pull of a black hole. As we prepared to return to normal space, the familiar weight of responsibility settled back onto my shoulders. Whatever called us back couldn't be good news, not with that urgency in the pulse.

Joan nodded, and together we shifted toward the signal. The wormhole's exit appeared suddenly, and we emerged into normal space near Falfsun.

Temper's voice came through immediately, tight with urgency. "Go, Joan. We've got a situation."

"What's happening?" I asked, already dreading the answer.

"The time crystals." Temper's words tumbled out rapidly. "Marcus and Bea discovered something. When they accidentally activated the first crystal, they imprinted Earth's quantum signature onto it."

Joan's form stiffened beside me.

"The crystals are communicating with each other," Temper continued. "They've locked onto Earth as their target. Just like they did with that extinct civilization the scientists found."

My stomach dropped. "How bad is it?"

"Extinction-level. Those crystals will trigger spacetime ruptures that could shred Earth at the subatomic scale."

Joan moved closer. "Time frame?"

"Unknown. Marcus and the team are trying to locate all the crystal clusters. They're spread across twelve light-years."

I processed this information, feeling its weight press down on me. Earth. Home. Despite everything, despite leaving it behind, the thought of its destruction was unbearable.

"We need to contain them," I said. "All of them."

Joan turned to me, her diamond form revealing nothing of her thoughts. "Wormholes at Planck scale. Could create containment fields."

"And my toolkit," I added, understanding immediately. "With Falfsun's energy reserves, I could generate enough power to help you stabilize those fields."

"Yes. Precisely what I need."

Temper's voice cut in. "You two are our best hope. Joan with her grasp of dimensional theory. Go with the toolkit and his bond to Falfsun. Together, you can make this work."

I looked at Joan, this being who had just shown me how to navigate between realities. "Partners?"

Her form shifted slightly, the closest thing to a nod. "Partners."

"Tell Marcus we're coming," I said to Temper. "And to keep tracking those crystal locations."

As we prepared to travel, I felt something unexpected: purpose. Not duty, not obligation, but genuine purpose. Earth needed us. And for the first time since living on the apple farm, I knew exactly where I belonged.

I followed Joan through another wormhole to the research station, the disorienting journey still strange but familiar. We emerged into chaos. Scientists rushed between workstations, their faces drawn with tension. Marcus stood at the center of it all, directing the operation with a calm authority that filled me with a father's fierce admiration, even in the midst of chaos.

"Papa!" Marcus spotted me and waved us over to a holographic display where Bea was rapidly sorting through data streams.

"What have you got?" I asked, placing a hand on his shoulder.

Bea looked up, her eyes rimmed with exhaustion. "We've identified nine crystal clusters so far, scattered across twelve light years." She gestured at the map. "Each one is growing, communicating with the others. It's like watching a neural network form in real time."

The display showed pinpoints of light, pulsing in synchronization despite the vast distances between them. Marcus pulled up additional data, his fingers dancing across the interface.

"We found records from the civilization that discovered them first." He brought up images of ruins, crumbling structures on a barren world. "They were called the Vareen. Their technology was similar to Earth's current level."

Joan moved closer to the display. "Show me their findings."

Marcus nodded and opened a series of translated documents. "The Vareen found the first crystal during a mining operation. They thought it was just an unusual mineral formation until they tried to analyze it."

"Let me guess," I said. "They activated it."

"Yes." Bea pointed to a simulation. "Their initial scan resonated with the crystal's subatomic structure, creating a feedback loop. The crystal began replicating its pattern, sending signals that awakened dormant crystals buried throughout their star system."

The simulation showed a cascading effect, spreading outward from the initial point. I watched as the crystals formed connections, creating an expanding network.

"The Vareen realized their mistake too late," Marcus continued. "They tried containing the crystals using gravitational fields, but that only accelerated the process."

Joan turned to me. "The containment attempt created a beacon."

"Exactly," Bea said. "It broadcast the Vareen's quantum signature across space, drawing more crystals toward their home world."

I studied the final images of the Vareen civilization. Time-lapse recordings showed their planet gradually distorting; reality itself seeming to fold and unfold in unpredictable patterns. Buildings aged centuries in minutes. Living beings experienced time at different rates, some frozen in place while others aged and died before they could move.

"And now Earth has done the same thing," I said quietly.

Marcus nodded grimly. "When we activated the first crystal by accident," he said, voice tight, "we embedded Earth's subatomic signature into its structure. It's like we gave it a scent—something it can follow."

"How much time do we have?" I asked.

Bea shook her head. "Hard to say. The process accelerates exponentially. Right now, the crystals are still in the early stages of network formation. Once they achieve full synchronization..."

"Earth becomes like that." I pointed to the dead Vareen world.

"We need to collect them all," Joan said. "Every single one."

Marcus pulled up another display showing the crystal locations. "We've verified these nine clusters, but we're still scanning for others. The problem is, some might be dormant until they receive a strong enough signal from the network."

I turned to Joan. "Your wormholes at Planck scale. Are you sure we can use them to create containment fields around each crystal?"

She nodded. "It's possible, but difficult. It would need tremendous energy."

"Falfsun can provide that through my toolkit."

Bea looked between us. "Even if you contain them, how do you destroy them? These crystals exist partially outside normal spacetime."

The door slid open, and Temper strode in, his face animated with the familiar intensity of scientific breakthrough.

"A supermassive black hole," he announced. "The gravitational shear near the event horizon should disrupt their quantum entanglement. If we can get them there, the singularity will do the rest."

I exchanged glances with Joan. "That means taking them to the center of the galaxy."

"Yes," she said simply. "We collect. We contain. We destroy."

I looked at the map again, at the nine points of light that threatened everything. "Then let's get started."

Joan used Falfsun's energy to contain the time crystals at the research station. She folded them into isolation fields, the last glimmers of their timewave interference vanishing as she wove her Planck-scale wormholes around them. The crystals' pulsing light dimmed, trapped within a cage that existed at the smallest possible unit of reality.

"That's the last one here," Marcus said, checking his instruments. "The rest are scattered throughout the Fermi Bubbles, approximately 26,000 light years from our current position."

Bea's fingers danced across her console. "We've mapped the three closest clusters. Sending coordinates now."

The Planck Pulse vibrated as it received the quantum thread.

"Ready?" I asked.

Joan nodded. "The containment fields are holding. We should move quickly."

Temper approached, his expression tight with concern. "The Fermi Bubbles are flooded with gamma radiation and gravity distortions. You need to be careful."

Joan gave a sharp nod. "We will be. We're moving fast."

I caught on immediately. "Wormholes?"

"For most of the route," she confirmed. "But parts of the bubbles are too unstable. Wormhole travel there would be a gamble. We'll have to navigate those areas in normal space."

I activated my toolkit, feeling its connection to Falfsun pulse through me. The energy thrummed, responding to the gravitational shifts. "I can generate shields from Falfsun's power. That should give us cover where the radiation spikes."

Joan glanced at me, measuring. "We'll need precision. The gravitational pull will help when we can't jump, but one miscalculation and we're stuck in a collapsing pocket."

Temper folded his arms. "Sounds like you've got it figured out. Just make sure you survive figuring it out."

"I'll weave the shielding," Joan added. "Together, we might survive."

Marcus embraced me suddenly, his arms tight around my chest. "Come back, Papa."

I felt him trembling slightly, a vulnerability he rarely showed since taking charge of the adoption program. Despite his growing independence, this moment stripped away the confident administrator, revealing the young thruman who still feared loss.

"I have calculations," he whispered against my shoulder. "The probability of success is—"

"Don't," I interrupted gently, pulling back to meet his eyes. "Some things aren't about probability."

Marcus nodded, his expression shifting from fear to determination. "Then I'll focus on certainty instead. You've never broken a promise to me. Not once."

The simple faith in his statement struck me harder than any emotional plea could have. In a universe of quantum uncertainty, my son had found something absolute to believe in.

"And I won't start now," I promised, hugging him fiercely. "Count on it."

Bea stepped forward. "We'll guide you through. The quantum thread will maintain communication even inside the bubbles."

Temper handed me a small device. "This will help locate the crystal signatures. Their resonance signature is uniquely patterned."

I pocketed it and turned to Joan. "Let's go save Earth."

She opened the first wormhole with a gesture, its surface rippling like disturbed water. We stepped through together.

The journey began smoothly enough. We emerged near the edge of the northern Fermi Bubble, a vast structure extending 25,000 light-years above the galactic center. From outside, it looked deceptively peaceful: a massive purple-hued bubble against the starfield.

"First crystal is approximately seven hundred light-years inside," Joan said, consulting the coordinates.

I activated my toolkit, drawing power from my connection to Falfsun. Energy flowed through me, manifesting as a translucent shield around us both. Joan's hands moved in complex patterns, weaving layered energy fields that strengthened my creation.

"Ready," I confirmed.

We entered the bubble.

The peaceful exterior gave way to chaos. Streams of superheated plasma whipped past us, carrying deadly radiation. The shield flared brilliantly as it absorbed the energy.

"Spacetime curvature spike ahead," Bea's voice came through the Pulse. "Thirty degrees to your right."

I adjusted our course, feeling sweat bead on my forehead from the concentration required to maintain the shield. Joan moved closer, her shoulder touching mine as she reinforced our protection.

"The radiation is stronger than expected," she observed quietly.

"Can you hold it?"

"Yes. But it costs me."

I glanced at her. For the first time, I noticed the strain in her expression, the slight tremor in her hands as she manipulated quantum forces beyond human comprehension.

"We can rest if—"

"No," she cut me off. "Time is against us."

We pressed on, navigating through radiation storms that would have killed unprotected travelers instantly. Hours blended together as we followed Marcus and Bea's guidance, moving deeper into the bubble.

During a brief respite in a relatively calm pocket, Joan spoke unexpectedly.

"You miss her. Your Amy."

The words didn't sting like they used to. "Not her, exactly. I miss what she represented: the stability, the certainty. Life made sense when she was part of it."

"I miss my family. We were once thousands."

The admission hung between us, unexpectedly vulnerable from someone who had always seemed beyond human concerns. I recalled our first meeting: her cold assessment, my wariness. We'd been reluctant collaborators then, united only by Temper's insistence.

When had that changed? I couldn't pinpoint the exact moment. Our alliance had evolved gradually, through shared missions and quiet conversations about the nature of existence. And now, as she guided me through the wormhole with unexpected patience, something had shifted again.

"We're not thousands," I said finally. "But we might be a team now."

A subtle change came over her features, not quite a smile, but something adjacent to it. "Teams," she said, as though testing the concept. "Defined by mutual goals and complementary abilities."

"And sometimes by simply showing up for each other," I added.

Joan considered this, then nodded once. "You showed up."

"So did you."

The acknowledgment was small, but it marked a boundary crossed, from alliance of convenience to something with its own intrinsic value.

The simple admission struck me. Joan, this being of immense power and knowledge, now experienced a loneliness even more profound than my own.

"What about now?" I asked. "Do you have connections?"

She considered this. "Temper understands some of what I am. And you... you see differently."

"Is that good?"

"It's unfamiliar." A pause. "But not unwelcome."

Before I could respond, Temper's voice broke through. "Crystal signature detected. You're close."

We resumed our journey, pushing through waves of plasma toward the coordinates. The first crystal cluster appeared suddenly, a formation of glittering, faceted structures suspended in space, pulsing with timewave energy that distorted reality around them.

As we approached, I noticed disturbances in our perception of time. My movements felt sluggish, while Joan seemed to flicker between positions, as though skipping forward microseconds in her timeline.

"Time dilation," Joan explained, her voice fluctuating in pitch. "The crystals create localized temporal fields."

I watched, fascinated and horrified, as a small piece of space debris drifted into the crystal's influence. Its trajectory became unpredictable, accelerating, then nearly freezing, then aging rapidly until it crumbled to dust in seconds.

"Is that what happened to the Vareen?" I asked.

"Yes. Imagine entire cities experiencing different timeflows. Plants growing and dying in minutes. Children aging before their parents' eyes. Buildings crumbling to dust while still under construction."

The crystals emitted a sound too, not audible exactly, but perceptible as a discordant vibration against my skull, like a whalesong pitched beyond human hearing that somehow translated to sensation rather than sound.

"Can you feel that?" I asked.

Joan nodded. "They're communicating. Synchronizing their temporal frequencies."

"Beautiful," Joan whispered. "And terrible."

I nodded, understanding exactly what she meant. "Let's get to work."

The crystal cluster pulsed with eerie light, like a heart beating outside a body. Joan's hands moved in intricate patterns, shaping a containment field woven from the smallest folds of space. I channeled Falfsun's energy through my toolkit, sustaining the prison she conjured from the fabric of reality.

"There," she said as the last thread of energy sealed the cage. The crystal's glow dimmed, trapped within invisible walls finer than atoms.

I checked the detector Temper had given us. "Eight more to go."

Joan turned to me, her form shifting slightly in the radiation-soaked environment. "We need to move faster."

"We're already pushing the limits of what's possible," I replied, wiping sweat from my brow. The shield I maintained around us flickered momentarily before stabilizing.

"You're thinking linearly." Joan gestured toward the chaotic environment surrounding us. "The bubbles don't work that way."

"What do you mean?"

"Marcus, Bea, Temper. They guide us using maps, coordinates. Linear paths." She placed a hand on my shoulder. "But space here bends. Folds. We must think spatially."

I frowned. "I don't understand."

"Close your eyes."

I hesitated, then complied. The moment darkness fell, I became acutely aware of the energy patterns surrounding us: gravitational eddies, radiation currents, subatomic fluctuations.

"Now feel," Joan instructed. "Not with your body. With your mind."

I concentrated, allowing my consciousness to expand beyond my physical form. The toolkit's connection to Falfsun helped, acting as an amplifier for my awareness.

"There." Joan's voice seemed to come from both beside me and within my mind. "See how space curves around that radiation storm? We don't need to go through it. We can go around it."

In my mind's eye, I saw what she meant. Space itself bent around the obstacles, creating shortcuts invisible to conventional navigation.

"It's like seeing in four dimensions," I murmured.

"Five, actually. But who's counting?"

I opened my eyes to find Joan watching me with something approaching approval.

"The others will guide us to the crystals," she said. "But we'll choose how to get there."

With our new approach, we moved more efficiently through the bubbles. Where before we fought against the chaotic environment, now we flowed with it, using gravitational currents to propel us forward and radiation eddies to slingshot around obstacles.

As we navigated through a particularly complex gravitational eddy, I realized something had changed in my perception. The sensations flowing through me: Falfsun's energy, the radiation fields, the quantum threads Joan manipulated, felt increasingly natural, as though I'd been doing this my entire life.

"Something's different," I said during a momentary respite.

Joan glanced at me. "Your neural patterns are adapting. Forming new connections."

The implication struck me suddenly. "I'm becoming less like David."

"You were never David," she replied simply. "You were always becoming Go."

The statement should have troubled me, this confirmation of growing distance from my original self. Instead, I felt an unexpected lightness. Each new experience, each adaptation to this impossible environment, wasn't just taking me further from Earth, it was carrying me toward something else. Someone else.

"Does it disturb you?" Joan asked, observing my silence.

I considered the memories I still carried: Amy's laugh, my father's workshop, David's life before the transfer. They remained clear, but increasingly they felt like beloved books I'd read rather than chapters of my own story.

"No," I answered truthfully. "It feels like setting down a heavy load I didn't realize I was carrying."

"Next crystal cluster is seventeen light-years from your position," Marcus's voice came through the Pulse. "Sending coordinates now."

"Received," I confirmed. "We're on our way."

Joan studied the data, then pointed to a particularly dense radiation field. "Through there."

I balked. "That would fry us instantly."

"Not if we ride the wave." She took my hand. "Trust me."

Something in her voice, a note of vulnerability I'd never heard before, made me nod. "Lead the way."

Together, we plunged toward the radiation field. At the last moment, Joan pulled us into a gravitational current that swept along its edge. The shield around us blazed with absorbed energy but held.

"You're learning," she said as we emerged on the other side, hours of conventional travel compressed into minutes.

The journey continued this way, a dance between chaos and precision. Sometimes we used wormholes for the most dangerous sections, but increasingly we relied on our spatial awareness to navigate the bubbles' complexities.

During a brief rest in a calm pocket, Joan's form flickered unexpectedly.

"Are you alright?" I asked, alarmed.

"The radiation affects me too," she admitted. "Differently than you, but still."

I strengthened our shield without comment, channeling more energy from Falfsun. Joan leaned against me slightly, our shoulders touching.

"When this is over," she said quietly, "what will you do?"

The question caught me off guard. "I haven't thought that far ahead."

"You should. Purpose doesn't end with one mission."

I considered this. "What about you? What comes after?"

She was silent for so long I thought she wouldn't answer. "I don't know. For centuries, I've existed between worlds, belonging nowhere. It grows... lonely."

The admission hung between us, raw and honest. I recognized in her the same isolation I'd felt since losing Amy, since watching Marcus grow independent, since realizing my old life was truly gone.

"Maybe we could explore," I suggested. "There's a lot of universe out there."

Joan looked at me, surprise evident even in her alien features. "Together?"

"Why not? We make a good team."

Before she could respond, Bea's voice broke through. "Radiation surge incoming! Massive one!"

The moment of connection shattered as we scrambled to reinforce our defenses. The surge hit us, overwhelming our shields despite our combined efforts. Pain seared through me as radiation penetrated our protection.

Joan moved without hesitation, pulling me into her arms and creating a cocoon of overlapping energy fields around us both. The radiation hammered against her improvised shelter.

"Hold on," she whispered, her voice strained. "Just hold on."

The surge subsided, leaving us floating in the aftermath of radiation. Joan's energy cocoon had saved us, but at a cost. Her form wavered like shimmering heat.

"You're weakening," I said.

"Manageable," she replied, her voice strained. "Five crystals left."

We pressed on, gathering the remaining clusters throughout the Fermi Bubbles. Each collection followed the same pattern: locate, contain, secure. With each crystal, Joan's movements grew more labored, her quantum manipulations less precise.

After capturing the ninth cluster, the Planck Pulse vibrated against my wrist. Temper's voice came through, tense with urgency.

"Final coordinates coming through. It's time to head to the galactic center."

Joan's form stabilized momentarily as she received the data. "The supermassive black hole."

"Sagittarius A*," I confirmed. "Can you make it?"

She straightened, pride briefly overcoming exhaustion. "Of course."

We navigated toward the heart of the galaxy, where space curved inward, warped by an invisible weight. Joan created a wormhole for the longest stretch, but the final approach required moving through normal space. The closer we got to the black hole, the more reality itself seemed to warp around us.

The first sign of trouble came when Joan stumbled mid-flight, her containment field around the crystals flickering.

"Joan?"

She steadied herself, but I could see the strain etched across her features. "The crystals. They're fighting back."

I channeled more energy through my toolkit, reinforcing her quantum cage. "We're almost there."

The black hole appeared before us, a perfect void surrounded by a brilliant accretion disk of superheated matter. No image, no simulation, could capture the terrible majesty of Sagittarius A*. It dominated space not just physically but conceptually, as though the very idea of "center" had taken cosmic form. The accretion disk blazed with the light of consumed stars, a funeral pyre for matter spiraling toward oblivion.

Colors I had no names for danced at the boundary where physics began to fail. Brilliant blues shifted to ultraviolet, then into radiation spectrums human eyes weren't designed to perceive, yet somehow I sensed them anyway, perhaps through Joan's influence or my toolkit's enhancements.

Most unsettling was the perfect roundness of the event horizon itself. In a universe of irregular shapes and approximate symmetries, this mathematically perfect circle seemed almost artificial; a precision that felt both divine and terrifying. This wasn't just a celestial object; it was a punctuation mark at the end of reality's sentence.

The gravitational lensing warped the starfield behind it, creating a cosmic eye that seemed to stare back at us, judging our insignificance against its eternal patience. We weren't just approaching a massive object, we were confronting the universe's most fundamental mystery, wrapped in darkness. Light bent around its edges, creating surreal distortions in the surrounding starfield. Against this backdrop, Joan faltered again. The containment field wavered dangerously.

"Keep going," I urged. "We can make it."

Joan pushed forward, spurred by my words, but her form continued to destabilize. The crystals pulsed brighter inside their containment shell, timewave radiation bleeding through femtofractures at the smallest measurable scale.

"We're still too far," she gasped. "The event horizon... need to get closer."

I increased power from my toolkit to maximum. "I'm giving you everything Falfsun has."

"It's not enough." Joan's voice was strained, her form flickering between solid and translucent. "I'm losing them. The containment is failing."

Panic surged through me. If the crystals escaped now, so close to our goal...

Joan turned to me, her expression resolute despite her weakening state. "There is a way."

"Tell me."

"A hive mind. Like the one I came from." Her gaze held mine. "If we merge consciousness, I can access more of Falfsun's energy through you."

I hesitated. "Merge? How would that even work?"

"Our thoughts, memories, consciousness... intertwined." She moved closer. "But you must be willing."

The crystals pulsed violently, temporal distortions rippling outward. We were running out of time.

Joan hovered before me, face to face. Her hands rose to cradle my face, warm despite their alien nature. "Do you trust me?"

In that moment, my past flashed before me: Amy's smile, the memory palace burning, Marcus growing beyond my protection, my father's watch ticking away time I couldn't reclaim. All the moments I'd clung to, unable to let go.

But here, now, was my future. Not the one I'd planned, but the one before me.

"Yes," I said. "I trust you."

Joan's eyes softened. "Then let go."

Our foreheads touched, and the universe exploded within my mind. My consciousness fractured, then reformed, expanded beyond the boundaries of my body. Joan's thoughts flowed into mine, a river joining an ocean.

At first, chaos reigned. Too many thoughts, too many sensations. I felt myself drowning in the flood of shared consciousness.

"Think in shapes, not lines," Joan's voice guided me from within. *"Don't try to organize. Feel the pattern."*

I stopped fighting and allowed the merger to happen naturally. Gradually, order emerged from chaos. I saw Joan's memories as if they were my own: a vast hive mind spanning her home galaxy, thousands of consciousnesses in perfect harmony. Beautiful. Peaceful. Then, catastrophe. Her universe collapsing, the hive mind shattering, Joan alone surviving the transition between realities.

She, in turn, experienced my isolation, my grief for Amy, my struggle to find purpose in a world that had moved on without me.

But she also felt my recent acceptance, my growing comfort with this new existence.

Together, our merged consciousness reached out to Falfsun. The star's energy flowed through us, amplified by our combined will. The containment field around the crystals strengthened, solidified.

"Now," we spoke as one. "To the horizon."

We moved forward, the black hole's immense gravity pulling us closer. The event horizon appeared as a perfect sphere of absolute darkness, surrounded by the brilliant glow of matter falling into oblivion. Stars behind it warped and stretched, creating ghostly arcs of light.

The black hole's event horizon loomed before us, a perfect absence against the brilliant accretion disk. As we approached, with our newly merged consciousness, I felt Joan's thoughts pulse with something unexpected; not fear, but recognition.

"You've seen one before," I realized, the thought forming between us rather than being spoken aloud.

Her memories flowed into mine, carrying images from her original universe: structures similar to black holes but somehow more ordered, purposefully created rather than formed through stellar collapse.

We used them as doorways, she conveyed. *My people engineered passage through what you call singularities.*

I absorbed this revelation with wonder. The Joan I knew, the dimensional traveler who appeared in Temper's life as a mysterious visitor, had once belonged to a civilization that manipulated forces humans could barely comprehend.

We were many, her thoughts continued, tinged with ancient grief. *Thousands linked in one consciousness, exploring realities beyond our own. Until the collapse.*

The crystals pulsed violently in their containment field, demanding our attention. But in that brief moment of shared awareness, I understood something fundamental about Joan that had always eluded me: her solitude wasn't just isolation—it was amputation, the severing of connections that had defined her existence.

And in our merged consciousness, she had found not a replacement, but perhaps an echo of what she had lost.

The crystals fought against their prison, sensing their impending destruction. Temporal distortions lashed out, trying to break free. But our merged consciousness held firm, maintaining the quantum cage as we approached the point of no return.

"Here," we decided. "This is close enough."

With a thought, we released the crystals toward the event horizon. Time seemed to slow as they fell toward the darkness. The crystals stretched, elongated by the extreme gravitational forces, their brilliant light gradually redshifting toward darkness as they approached the boundary between our universe and whatever lay beyond.

Then, silence. The crystals vanished, their threat erased from existence.

Joan's consciousness began to separate from mine, a gentle unraveling of entwined thoughts. Before we fully disconnected, I caught something unexpected: a shift in her perception. Where before she had been an observer of humanity, cataloging our behaviors with clinical detachment, now I sensed understanding. Not just of me, but of connection itself.

"You felt that?" she asked as our minds became distinct again.

"Yes," I replied. "You're different."

"As are you." Her form stabilized, the flickering ceased, but something remained changed. The rigid posture had softened. Her diamond-faceted eyes held a warmth previously absent. "I had forgotten what it meant to be part of something larger than myself. My hive mind was not merely about shared knowledge, it was about shared experience."

"And now?"

"Now I remember." She turned toward the black hole. "Solitude was... simpler. Connection is worth the complexity."

In the aftermath, I felt a weight lift from my consciousness. I could finally let go.

Not just of the crystals, or the mission, or the fear that had shadowed every step, but of the past I'd been carrying like armor. The grief for Amy, sharp and sacred. The identity I'd clung to—David, not Go David—as if names could shield me from change. The obligations of command, the endless calculus of sacrifice and duty. I had worn them all like a uniform, even after the missions ended, even after the crew dispersed. As if responsibility alone could define me.

But not everything was meant to be shed.

I still held my friendship with Temper, forged in fire and laughter. My gratitude to David, for dreaming me into existence, for giving me a shape to grow beyond. My fondness for Amy remained, not as pain, but as warmth. I kept the quiet joy of childhood memories: my mother in her garden, the scent of fresh-cut wood in my father's workspace, the hush of snowfall in winter. And I held close the new family we'd become, fractured, imperfect, but real.

My life was no longer what I'd planned. But it was mine. And it was beginning again.

Without hesitation, I reached into my pocket and withdrew my father's watch. The timepiece that had anchored me to my past, to a life long gone. Its weight was familiar, comforting, but no longer necessary.

I held it one last time, feeling the echo of all it had meant. Then I let it go, watching as it tumbled toward the black hole, following the crystals into oblivion.

It was time to move forward.

CHAPTER SIX

Echoes Across Stars

The conference room on Requiem Prime balanced function with quiet grandeur. A polished maple table anchored the space. Holographic displays hovered at measured intervals. Beyond the massive window, the twilight landscape unfolded: rolling violet hills bathed in the glow of twin moons just beginning their ascent.

Captain Smith leaned forward, fingers steepled beneath his chin. "So, let me get this straight. You two flew straight into the galactic center, captured unstable time crystals in quantum cages, and then hurled them into a supermassive black hole?"

"That's the simplified version," I said, Joan's quiet presence beside me.

Luna Dawn tapped her stylus against her HoloPad. "And the crystals? Completely destroyed? No possibility of regeneration?"

"None," Joan said, her voice still marked by the resonance of our merged consciousness. "The gravitational shear at the event horizon dismantled their internal lattice. Every stabilizing force collapsed. What remained was stretched past recognition, dispersed across spacetime at subatomic scales. They're unrecoverable."

She paused, then added, "Even if fragments survived, they'd be redshifted into oblivion. No signal, no pattern, no memory of what they once were."

Temper sat across from us, barely containing his enthusiasm. "The implications are staggering. These crystals defied fundamental laws of thermodynamics. They were self-organizing structures that—"

"—that nearly triggered a cascading chronal catastrophe," Bea interrupted gently. She sat beside Marcus, her hand resting protectively near his. "If Go and Joan hadn't contained them, Earth would have been lost."

Marcus nodded. "The data suggests the crystals had already established a network across light-years. Given another month, that network would have been unbreakable."

I let my thoughts drift. The mission was complete, but sitting here, surrounded by these people: chosen, found, forged through shared struggle, that was what mattered. Joan's consciousness had separated from mine after the mission, yet something remained, a thread woven deep, beyond words. Temper's scientific fervor remained unchecked. Marcus and Bea had carved out purpose, in their research and in each other.

And me? I was still finding my way. But for the first time since leaving Hellfire, I felt truly present.

Smith's voice pulled me back. "Go? Thoughts on next steps?"

I exhaled, steady. "We've crossed a threshold most never glimpse, and survived what erased entire civilizations. That's not just luck. It's a warning. We move forward, yes. But with caution. The galaxy holds forces we barely understand. And next time, we may not walk away."

Temper's gaze kept returning to me, subtle but unwavering. His head tilted slightly, eyes narrowing in quiet assessment. It was the familiar expression of a scientist dissecting an anomaly. He had worn that look countless times in his lab, scrutinizing unexpected results, searching for explanations.

"The Ethereans have responded cautiously to the crystal incident," Smith continued. "They accept the necessity of containment protocols going forward."

I nodded, though I could feel Temper's attention still fixed on me, not on the conversation. His focus lingered, studying my posture, my mannerisms, the rhythm of my replies. Something about me unsettled him.

He senses the change in you, Joan's thought brushed lightly against my consciousness, a ripple within our shared mental space.

113

Yes, but he doesn't understand it, I replied, wordless but certain. The connection remained, a thread woven deep since our merger at the black hole. No longer an overwhelming flood of perception, but something quieter, more controlled.

Temper leaned forward slightly, his coffee cup hovering just short of his lips. When I shifted in my seat, his eyes tracked the motion with the same clinical precision he applied to his research. He was cataloging differences, comparing the Go he had known to the one sitting before him now.

Luna asked about layered energy shielding protocols. I responded with concise technicality, and Temper's eyebrows lifted fractionally. Before the merger, I might have given a broader explanation, something more accessible. But Joan's understanding had become part of me.

Should we tell him? I asked Joan silently.

He'll figure it out eventually, she answered. *He always does.*

Temper set his cup down, his expression sharpening as if he had almost grasped the answer, only for it to slip away again.

I met his gaze across the table and nodded once. A silent confirmation that he wasn't imagining things, that something had changed. I wasn't quite the same Go David who had left on that mission.

His posture eased slightly, the tension in his shoulders unwinding, not with understanding, but with acceptance.

The meeting pressed on around us, but in that quiet exchange, something shifted. Some transformations couldn't be measured, only recognized.

As the meeting concluded, Smith and Luna departed first. Temper lingered, his hand settling briefly on my shoulder. His eyes still searched for something in mine; some answer to a question he hadn't quite put into words.

"I'm heading back to Falfsun," he said. "The dimensional tunnels won't map themselves."

I smirked. "Try not to get lost in one."

"No promises." He glanced at Joan. "Look after him. He finds trouble."

Joan's lips curved slightly. "I've noticed."

With Temper gone, the four of us: Joan, Marcus, Bea, and I, wandered without a destination, letting the city guide us. Without realizing it, we had drifted to Emberhill, the first permanent settlement on Requiem Prime, built amidst an alien world's rocky landscape.

The group homes where Marcus and Bea once lived now stood silent, their windows dark. Once, these buildings had been full of life: thruman children laughing, running, growing. Now, they sat empty, waiting for whatever might come next.

"It feels strange," Marcus said, pausing in front of Sunflower House. "Not living here anymore. The time we spent raising the children, making sure they had a future."

Bea smiled faintly. "It was worth every moment."

"It was," Marcus agreed. "But they're grown now. They've found their own paths."

I studied him, sensing something beneath his words. "And you? What comes next?"

Marcus and Bea exchanged a glance, their fingers intertwining with the quiet familiarity of years spent in tandem.

"For a long time, we stayed where we were needed," Bea said. "Hellfire, then here with the thrumans, and later at Carpisma's research station. Each place asked something of us, and we gave it."

Marcus nodded. "But now it's our turn. We'll travel. Not for duty. For discovery."

Joan tilted her head slightly, considering them. "Is that what you want?"

Marcus exhaled. "Yeah. It is."

"You never did like standing still," I said.

Bea chuckled. "Neither did you."

We reached the neighborhood park, the swings moving slightly in the evening breeze, metal creaking softly.

"You have any destinations in mind yet?" I asked.

"Nothing concrete," Bea said. "Just the freedom to chase whatever comes next."

Marcus nodded. "We have our Etherean patrols. Beyond that, no deadlines. It's just us, and the stars."

I couldn't help but smile. "That suits you."

"We'll stay in touch," Bea assured me. "We're just a quantum thread away."

I glanced at Joan. We hadn't spoken about our own plans yet, not directly, but in the quiet space between our minds, we had already started shaping them.

"Traveling's in our future too," I said. "Patrols in my region are slow, but the dimensional tunnels? The undiscovered worlds?"

"Sounds dangerous," Bea said, though there was understanding in her voice.

"The best things usually are," I replied.

The first drops of rain began to fall, warm against the cooling air. None of us moved.

"We should head back," Marcus said eventually.

We walked them to the edge of Emberhill, where our paths split. The moment felt weighted, like a quiet farewell to a shared past.

"Stay in touch," Bea said, embracing me.

"Count on it."

As they turned to leave, Marcus hesitated. "Papa?"

I felt that familiar warmth at the word. "Yeah?"

He studied me for a moment. "I'm glad you found Joan."

A flicker of surprise rippled through Joan's connection with me. "How did you know?" I asked.

Marcus tapped his temple. "You're different now. Settled. Like you found something you didn't know you were looking for."

With that, they disappeared into the deepening dusk, their silhouettes folding into the quiet, rain-swept streets of Requiem Prime.

Joan and I stood in the rain for a moment after Marcus and Bea disappeared into the twilight. The droplets fell warm against my skin.

"They're good together," Joan said quietly.

"They always were." I smiled, watching the space where they had been. "Even before they knew it."

The rain intensified, drumming against the empty streets. Water pooled in the depressions where children once played, reflecting the twin moons overhead.

"Would you like to visit the Garden of Echoes?" I asked, turning to Joan.

She nodded her head. "I've heard of it. Merlin's memorial."

"I hear it's worth experiencing." I held out my hand, a gesture that felt both new and familiar. "Especially with someone who understands loss."

Joan's fingers interlaced with mine, her touch carrying that subtle current that had remained since our minds merged. "Lead the way."

"We don't need to walk," I said, retrieving my Planck toolkit. "Merlin always keeps a quantum thread open to the garden."

We followed the thread to stone pathways winding through shadowed vegetation. The rain and city sounds vanished, replaced by the soft rustling of leaves and the distant melody of water over stone.

The Garden of Echoes surrounded us, its memorial stones bearing the two million names of everyone lost on Paradise. Each pillar whispered memories, voices overlapping in a gentle chorus that Joan absorbed with reverent silence.

"I never thought I'd see another sunrise like Earth's..." one voice murmured.

"Tell my daughter I carried her drawing with me..." said another.

Through our hive mind, Joan experienced the garden as Merlin intended: not just as observers but as participants in shared remembrance. The collective grief and hope of two million souls washed over us, binding our consciousnesses more deeply than before.

Joan's hand tightened around mine. I could feel her absorbing the emotions that radiated from the pillars, her consciousness expanding to encompass their meaning.

It's more than sound, she observed silently.

Yes. Merlin designed it to resonate on multiple levels.

We stood before a pillar that began to glow with a soft amber light as we approached. I reached out, palm flat against its surface. Joan did the same, our hands side by side.

The pillar warmed beneath our touch, and suddenly our shared consciousness expanded. The garden's true nature revealed itself not just to our eyes, but to our merged perception.

Beneath the visible memorial lay etheric echoes, memories encoded at the subatomic level. Each stone, each pillar, each leaf carried fragments of lives once lived. Not recordings, but impressions, emotions preserved.

Hope. Fear. Love. Wonder. The raw humanity of two million souls captured in this living monument.

Through our hive mind, Joan and I experienced it together. The garden became a symphony of sensations, colors bleeding into sounds, memories manifesting as scents and textures. We stood motionless, yet moved through layers of perception, each one revealing new depths.

In the center of the garden, we found the reflection pools. Dark water mirrored the bioluminescent canopy above, creating the illusion of an infinite space both above and below.

As we approached, ripples formed on the surface, though neither of us had touched the water. Names appeared and dissolved, faces shimmered and faded, brief glimpses of lives once lived.

I recognized some of them. Colleagues. Friends. People I'd known only in passing.

Joan's consciousness wrapped around mine, steadying me as the emotions threatened to overwhelm.

You carry them with you, she observed. *Not just in memory.*

They were my responsibility.

Her response came not as words but as understanding, acceptance without judgment. In our shared mental space, she showed me how she carried her own losses, the weight of her destroyed world.

We stood there by the pools, physically still but mentally exploring every corner of the garden. Through our connection, we experienced the memorial as Merlin had intended, not just as observers but as participants in a shared remembrance.

The beacon at the garden's heart began to pulse, its rhythm matching our heartbeats. Somehow, it recognized our presence, our connection. The light intensified, casting long shadows that seemed to dance with purpose.

Beautiful, Joan's thought brushed against mine.

Yes. Painful, but beautiful.

We remained there until the twin moons reached their zenith, our minds intertwined, experiencing the garden's echoes together. In that shared space between consciousness, something shifted, deepened. Not just understanding but belonging.

The twin moons slipped behind a veil of clouds as Joan and I left the Garden of Echoes. Our connection hummed quietly between us, a gentle current flowing beneath conscious thought. After the intensity of the memorial, we both needed something familiar, something grounding.

"Temper's been asking when we'd visit," I said, pulling up my quantum thread contacts. "How do you feel about seeing Falfsun?"

Joan's consciousness brushed against mine, carrying warm agreement. "I'd like that."

The quantum thread opened before us, a doorway of shimmering teal light. We stepped through together onto Falfsun's surface, where Temper's house stood like an impossible dream against the backdrop of churning plasma.

The little house sat surrounded by its improbable green lawn and white picket fence, a slice of suburban fantasy perched on the surface of a red dwarf star. Solar filaments arced overhead, casting long shadows across the porch where three rocking chairs waited. Beyond Temper's property line, crude "FOR SALE" signs stuck out of the roiling surface, an optimistic developer's vision for a neighborhood that would likely never materialize.

"Go! Joan!" Temper's voice boomed across the lawn. He stood beside a smoking grill, his red dragon form resplendent in a chef's hat and "Kiss the Cook" apron that strained against his large belly. His tail swished excitedly behind him. "Perfect timing! Dinner's almost ready!"

"That means it's almost burnt," I whispered to Joan.

Her amusement rippled through our connection. We crossed the lawn, heat rising through it despite the containment field that made Temper's impossible home possible.

"Something smells... distinctive," I offered as we approached.

Temper lifted the grill lid, releasing a cloud of smoke. "Hamburgers tonight! I'm trying a new technique."

"Cremation?" I peered at the blackened discs.

"Caramelization," he corrected, flipping one with a flourish. "Last time with the chicken was a learning experience."

"That's one way to describe it."

Joan moved toward the porch while Temper and I bickered over proper grilling techniques. I felt her consciousness shift, a subtle reconfiguration that caught my attention. When I turned to look, my words died in my throat.

The familiar stacked black diamonds were gone. In their place stood a woman with deep brown skin and natural curls framing a face of striking beauty. Her eyes met mine, knowing and uncertain all at once.

"Joan?" I managed.

She nodded, a small smile playing at her lips.

Beautiful, I thought, forgetting our connection was still active.

Thank you, came her reply, warm with pleasure.

Temper glanced between us, his reptilian features arranging themselves into a knowing grin. "I'll just... finish these burgers. Take your time."

We sat on the porch while Temper worked his culinary magic, or lack thereof. The surface of Falfsun stretched before us, a sea of churning crimson and gold. Solar prominences rose like slow-motion waves, crashing back into the stellar surface with silent grandeur.

"I worry about him," I said quietly, watching Temper hum to himself as he scraped carbonized meat from the grill. "He's spending more and more time here, alone with his research."

Joan's gaze followed mine. "Has he always been this way?"

"Always. Even back on Earth, he'd vanish into his work for weeks." I leaned forward, elbows on knees. "That's why I came on the voyage to Orion with him. I knew if I didn't, he'd spend his whole life in a lab instead of living among people."

The connection between us deepened as I shared my fears. "I'm afraid one day he'll just... drift away completely. That Falfsun will consume him, and there won't be anything left of the Temper I know."

Joan's hand settled over mine, warm and solid. "He welcomed me when no one else would," she said. "I traveled for ages, looking for somewhere to belong. When I found this universe, he was the first to see me as more than an interloper."

I turned to her, surprised. "I didn't know that."

"He taught me about Falfsun's wormholes when I was still learning to communicate in your language." Her eyes reflected the stellar surface below. "I owe him much. We won't let him drift away."

The promise settled between us, a quiet pact. "We won't," I agreed.

"Dinner!" Temper announced, carrying a platter of what charitably might be called hamburgers toward the porch. "Medium well!"

"Medium well-done," I corrected, taking the plate.

"Well-done adjacent," Joan offered with a smile.

Temper's laugh rumbled deep in his chest. "Critics, both of you."

We ate together as Falfsun's surface churned beneath us, sharing stories and comfortable silences. After dinner, Joan retrieved a shifting enigma from her pack; a container that didn't sit still but adjusted itself as if aware.

"I brought something," she said, opening it to reveal a holographic game board that shimmered into existence above the table. "Resonance. We used to play it with the hive children in my universe."

Temper leaned forward, instantly fascinated. "A teaching tool?"

Joan nodded. "For hive mind thinking. I thought perhaps..." She glanced at me, her consciousness touching mine with a question.

"I'd like to learn," I said.

As the game unfolded, teaching me to think beyond linear patterns, to feel rather than calculate, Temper watched with bright-eyed interest. For now, at least, he was here with us, present and engaged, his research momentarily forgotten.

The holographic display cast our faces in soft light as Joan guided me through the first lessons of hive consciousness. Temper asked questions, took notes, his scientific mind fully engaged with something beyond his stars.

I caught Joan's eye across the table and felt her silent acknowledgment. This was just the beginning. We would keep him tethered to humanity, one burnt hamburger, one game night at a time.

The night carried a quiet finality, a gentle shift from decision to movement, from words to action.

Temper's home faded behind us as the quantum thread collapsed. Joan's hand remained in mine, warm and steady, our connection humming beneath the surface of thought. The shared experience in the Garden of Echoes had deepened something between us, an understanding that required no words.

"Where to next?" Joan asked.

I smiled, feeling lighter than I had in years. "I have a place.

Somewhere quiet."

The Planck toolkit pulsed in my palm, threads of energy weaving a doorway before us. We stepped through together into warm Mediterranean air.

My villa shimmered at the edges, its existence shaped by probability as much as memory. Stucco walls caught the afternoon light, terracotta tiles still radiating the warmth of a sun fixed somewhere between past and present. Bougainvillea spilled over the garden wall, each bloom flickering between states of possibility.

Joan traced the perimeter, fingertips brushing the walls. "A hidden sanctuary."

"My thinking place," I admitted. "I needed somewhere that wasn't entirely real or imagined. Something in between."

She paused beneath the olive tree, watching its branches sway in an unseen breeze. "The boundaries are thin here."

"That's why I like it."

We spent the evening on the terrace, where reality bent gently around us. Stories flowed between spoken words and shared consciousness. The air shifted with our emotions. The colors deepened with our thoughts. When night fell, stars appeared in unfamiliar constellations, a sky shaped by memory and possibility.

"There's more I want to show you," I said as morning broke over the villa's flickering landscape. "Places we've built. Things we've found."

Joan's consciousness brushed against mine, bright with curiosity. "Show me."

The Planck toolkit wove another thread. We stepped through into breathtaking vastness.

The Orb of Eternal Dawn floated before us, suspended in the void of space. Light cascaded from its crystalline surface, bending time and perception into an endless sunrise. No matter how we moved, the horizon remained locked in that perfect moment between night and day.

"Etherean creation," I explained as we drifted. "One of our first major projects after receiving the toolkits."

Joan's wonder rippled through our connection. She lifted her hand toward the distant orb, feeling the timeless energy radiating from it.

"It's beautiful."

"There's more."

We followed quantum threads across the nearby galaxy, visiting wonders both natural and created. The Shattered Moon Symphony, where fractured lunar remains hung in perfect gravitational balance, each piece resonating at different frequencies to create music that vibrated through our bones. The Prism Vault, woven from refracted starlight, holding every possible spectrum of color known and unknown.

Between destinations, we returned to the villa, where time flowed differently and reality remained negotiable. There, our connection deepened beyond words or thought, a merging of consciousness that felt increasingly natural.

"This next one is different," I told her, preparing another thread. "Something unexpected. Something we found rather than made."

The Gravity Mosaic stretched beneath us, a planetary surface sculpted by shifting gravitational fields. We walked across it, feeling weight as art: growing heavy and light within mere steps.

"Who built this?" Joan asked, quiet awe in her voice.

"No one knows. We found it abandoned; a relic of a civilization that understood forces beyond anything we've yet mastered."

Through our connection, I felt her appreciation, her recognition of beauty across dimensions. I had once classified these wonders as Etherean projects, filed them away as discoveries to be studied. But through Joan's consciousness, they unfolded differently, each one reshaped, their magnificence felt rather than recorded.

At the Chrono Bloom Fields, we watched as galactic flora defied time, shifting seamlessly between bloom and decay in mere moments, yet never truly fading: an endless cycle of renewal.

"It feels like home," Joan murmured, her thoughts unfolding into images of dimensional gardens, where probability unfurled in delicate, ever-shifting blooms.

I reached for her hand, our fingers intertwining as naturally as our thoughts. "Tell me more."

She did, sharing memories of her lost universe; the patterns of its existence, the strange beauty that shaped it. In return, I offered pieces of myself I had kept locked away even during our merged consciousness. The fear of loss that had once kept me isolated at Lucky Star Farm. The grief for Amy that had bound me in place for too long.

Between travels, our conversations stretched across the villa's terrace, through its gardens, beside its fountain that sometimes ran with water, sometimes with liquid light. Each revelation strengthened the bridge between us, each shared wonder expanding our understanding.

The Celestial Labyrinth challenged us to navigate its folded space together, finding pathways that neither could have discovered alone. The Memory Echo Vault reflected lost worlds and civilizations, whispering their histories into the fabric of existence.

And through it all, Joan and I continued forward, discovering not just the universe, but each other.

After our travels to see some of the wonders of the galaxy, Joan and I returned to Falfsun, the place that had started to feel like home. If we were going to help Temper stay connected to others, it made sense to settle nearby, somewhere permanent, somewhere close enough to make a difference.

"We could build something here," I suggested as we stood on Temper's lawn, watching solar filaments dance across the horizon. "Our own place."

Joan's consciousness brushed against mine, warm with agreement. "I'd like that."

Temper nearly knocked over his grill in excitement. "Neighbors! Finally!" He fumbled through his pockets, pulling out a crumpled business card. "Call Solara at Helios & Co. She specializes in high-temperature properties. Tell her I sent you, and she'll waive the cooling system installation fee."

The property we chose sat a comfortable distance from Temper's house, close enough for visits but far enough for privacy. It was in a stable zone where gravitational forces aligned perfectly, creating a calm pocket amidst the star's churning surface. The land contract came with a "No Liability for Spontaneous Plasma Ejections" clause, but as Solara explained, "hey, that's just standard for solar-front properties."

Construction began with the foundation, particle drift-stabilized stone that could withstand Falfsun's heat. Joan introduced hive-mind building techniques from her lost universe, teaching me to weave them at the superposition level. Together, we shaped walls that responded to thought, ceilings that adjusted to mood, windows that filtered stellar radiation into soft, ambient light.

"This support beam needs to curve sixteen degrees in the seventh dimension," Joan instructed, her hands guiding mine as we manipulated the Planck toolkit.

I laughed. "I'm still struggling with the third dimension."

Her smile warmed me more than Falfsun ever could. "You're learning quickly."

The house took shape around us, a blend of Earth aesthetics and multidimensional architecture. The exterior resembled my Mediterranean villa with its stucco walls and terracotta roof, but subtle distortions at the edges revealed its true nature. Inside, spaces folded into themselves, creating rooms that felt both intimate and expansive.

Temper arrived one morning, surveying the bare ground outside with a knowing look. "You want a lawn like mine?" he said, kicking at the scorched surface with the toe of his dragon foot. "You'll need to do it right."

Falfsun's environment made traditional grass impossible, but Temper had mastered the art of adaptation. He showed us how to weave soil matrices, layering energy-absorbing fibers that could anchor the greenery against the star's relentless heat. Joan worked alongside him, refining the process, ensuring the emerald blades wouldn't just survive but thrive.

As the first patches of vibrant grass took root, we turned our attention to building a gazebo, placed off to the side. It became our quiet retreat, where the heat softened just enough to make lingering comfortable.

Temper leaned against a pillar, surveying our work with a satisfied nod. "Now," he said, "just wait until the wind sweeps through. That's when it really comes to life."

When construction finished, we stood on our front porch, admiring our creation. Across the way, Temper waved enthusiastically from his own yard, his dragon form silhouetted against the crimson sky.

"He seems happy," Joan observed.

"Happier than I've seen him in years."

We settled into rocking chairs, watching Falfsun's surface roll and churn beyond our protective field. The silence between us felt comfortable, our connection humming quietly beneath conscious thought.

After a while, Joan turned to me. "I need to tell you something."

I felt a shift in her consciousness, a slight withdrawal that sent a ripple of concern through me. "What is it?"

"Temper has mapped new wormholes, ones that reach further than anything we've explored." Her eyes met mine, determination mingling with hesitation. "I want to explore them. Alone."

The words hit harder than they should have. Not again, I thought. Just when life had begun to feel stable again, change loomed on the horizon. "For how long?"

"I don't know." Her consciousness reached for mine, conveying what words couldn't. "This isn't rejection, Go. I need solitude sometimes, to process, to understand myself."

I nodded, trying to hide the familiar ache of loss rising within me. "I understand."

But she felt my pain through our connection. "No, you don't. Not yet."

Joan took my hands in hers. "You're thinking in human time. In endings and beginnings. You're remembering Amy, Paradise, the farm. All the losses that shaped you."

She was right. My mind filled with memories: Amy's last message before our final separation, the destruction of Paradise, Marcus growing beyond needing me, the hayrides and apple cider press at Lucky Star Farm now gathering dust.

"I'll come back," Joan promised. "But I need you to understand something. Time has changed for us."

I looked out at Falfsun's eternal burning. "The toolkit."

"Yes. We're not bound by human lifespans anymore, not by battery limitations or biological decay. As long as stars shine in the universe, we exist."

The concept stretched before me, vast and almost incomprehensible. Centuries. Millennia. Eons.

"Trillions of years," I whispered. "Give or take."

Joan's laughter rippled through our connection. "Exactly. My journey might take years, decades even. But against the backdrop of our existence, it's barely a moment."

I considered this new perspective, this reshaping of time itself. The patience of stars, of galaxies forming and dissolving. The cosmic dance that unfolds across billions of years.

I nodded slowly, absorbing the cosmic scale she described. "I understand what you're saying, intellectually. The mathematics of eternity, the relativity of time." I gazed at her, feeling the pull between us. "But all I want, all I've ever wanted since finding you, is to be with you. Logic doesn't change that."

Joan's expression softened, her form shifting slightly in the light of Falfsun. "There will come a time when you want your alone time too, Go. When even I become... too much."

"I can't imagine that," I protested.

She smiled knowingly. "Think of it this way. You can watch Alice Tracker on her cooking shows a million times, every sourdough chocolate cake, every beef bourguignon demonstration, but eventually, you'll want to stop. And when you do, you'll realize that you still have trillions of years yet to live. You'll understand that you have all the time in the universe to go back and watch her show a million more times." Her eyes held mine. "That's us. I'm leaving to explore some wormholes, and you'll think I've been gone forever, but when I return, you'll realize that we still have forever to be together."

The realization struck with sudden clarity, unraveling everything I had assumed. Time was not a rigid path but something vast, shifting, fluid: an ocean stretching beyond sight. Its currents pulled in all directions, yet somehow, I knew they would always bring us back to each other. A quiet certainty amid the endless flow.

"I'll be here," I said finally, meaning it. "However long it takes."

Joan's relief flowed between us, warm and bright. "And I'll come home."

Home. The word settled between us, solid and real. After all my wandering, all my losses, I had found something permanent at last. Not just a house on a star, but a connection that transcended time and space.

We sat together as Falfsun churned beneath us, watching Temper tinker with his perpetually smoking grill. The future stretched before us, infinite in its possibilities.

For the first time in longer than I could remember, I felt content to wait.

CHAPTER SEVEN

Talos

Excerpts from the Introduction to Alice Tracker's personal journey cookbook, *The Holistic Chef-*

There exists an itch to expand our horizons. Consider the following~

• *The Boquila trifoliolata vine can astonishingly alter its leaf size, shape, and color to resemble nearby artificial plants—suggesting that plants may possess an unexpected way of 'seeing' their surroundings.*

    • *Hours before a solar eclipse, spruce trees seem to 'talk' to one another.*

I sat with Temper on his front porch, watching the plasma waves of Falfsun roll across the horizon. He no longer perched on a chair like the rest of us mere mortals. Instead, he lounged on his fat dragon tail, which curled beneath him like a living cushion. His bumpy skin gleamed with iridescent colors that shifted with his breathing.

"Where's Demon Joan? Can you tell?" I asked, scanning the undulating heat waves that distorted the landscape.

Temper's dragon eyes narrowed, focusing on something beyond normal perception. "Somewhere between dimensions, I imagine. I don't know for sure. I lost track of her."

His admission surprised me. Temper rarely lost track of anything, especially Joan.

The quiet moment fractured when a paperboy on a bicycle appeared from nowhere, pedaling along the shimmering path leading to Temper's house. The kid looked about twelve, wearing a cap pulled low over his eyes. He approached the gate with determination, then hurled a rolled newspaper in our general direction. It sailed through the air with impressive force but terrible aim, landing squarely in Temper's prized quantum roses. The flowers shimmered in and out of existence, momentarily disrupted by the intrusion.

The boy pedaled away without a word, his bicycle bouncing over the roiling plasma waves. He reminded me of a rowboat riding the swells of a stormy sea, appearing and disappearing as the waves of energy rose and fell.

"I can't believe you make a paperboy ride his bike all the way out from town just to deliver you a newspaper. I hope you're paying him well," I said, watching the kid vanish into the distance.

Temper snorted, a puff of steam escaping his nostrils. "I'm not paying him a thing. Did you see his aim? He smashed my roses." He gestured toward the flowers, which were still phasing between realities. "Besides, there is no town."

I blinked, processing this information. "So he'll be back tomorrow?"

"Like clockwork." Temper's mouth curled into what passed for a dragon's smile. "It's entertaining to watch him throw the paper. He never hits the porch. I wonder what his ball skills are like. Maybe we could have used him on our team." He shifted his massive tail. "So what's new?"

The question seemed so mundane against the backdrop of our extraordinary surroundings that I couldn't help but smile. "I'm glad you asked. I'm writing a new poem."

Temper groaned, his skin rippling with dismay. "You're not going to recite—"

"Once upon a midnight bleary, while I nodded drunk and cheery," I launched in before he could stop me.

"Please stop." Temper rubbed his dragon head with a clawed hand.

I pressed on, undeterred. "Are you sure? It has a cat."

"Do I even want to know?" His voice was flat, but I caught the flicker of amusement in his eyes.

"Of course you do!" I cleared my throat dramatically. *"Suddenly there came a tapping, as of someone gently scratching, scratching at my chamber door."*

"Let me guess, it's the cat?" Temper interrupted.

"Don't interrupt me." I waved him off. *"Go away cat! You disturb my drinking. Why are you here? What were you thinking?"*

Temper deadpanned, "Your command of the English language astounds me."

"Shh, here comes the best part." I raised my voice for the finale. *"Quoth the Cat— Tis long past time that you doth feed me, get off your butt or I will bleed thee."* I took a bow from my seated position. "I'm still working on the rest. So, tell me... what do you think of my poem?"

"It's astounding, really it is," Temper rolled his eyes, skin shifting color with his sarcasm. "Are you planning to stay long?"

I settled back in my chair. "Long enough to tell you about a moon I discovered. I named it Talos."

Temper's dragon eyes narrowed. "Will I need a drink for this?"

"We both will."

Temper lumbered inside and returned with two glasses of lemonade, the liquid glowing faintly under Falfsun's light. I took a long sip, savoring the tart sweetness before beginning.

"Talos is a moon roughly half Earth's size, orbiting a gas giant. From a distance, it looks like any other ice moon: white, pristine, unremarkable. But during patrol, something impossible happened." I leaned forward. "I heard a voice."

Temper's scales shifted to a deep indigo. "In space? Where sound can't travel?"

"Exactly. I was falling through vacuum when I heard it. A conversation with no speaker."

I swirled the lemonade in my glass, watching ice cubes dance against the sides. "Beneath Talos's ice crust lies a liquid ocean. And in that ocean grows a vast field of reeds, swaying in currents generated by tidal forces from the gas giant. Those forces heat the moon's core, creating fissures that release sulfur clouds into the water."

"Sulfur-based life," Temper murmured. "Not carbon."

"Precisely. I descended to the ocean floor and stood among them. The reeds communicate through their root system using chemical reactions. Essentially perfect telepathy. They're all connected to a single network, but unlike a simple hive mind, their collective consciousness is staggeringly complex."

Temper's tail twitched. "Talking plants? Like some giant plant brain conversing with itself?"

"It gets stranger." I set my glass down. "Over millennia, this reed mind has evolved a story it tells itself, about itself. The reeds are dreaming, and within that dream, they're the 'people' inhabiting it."

"You're kidding me!" Temper's skin flashed bright yellow with surprise.

I made the scout's honor sign. "I swear it's true. And I happened to be there during an epic event."

The lemonade had grown warm in my hand. I took another drink anyway, gathering my thoughts.

"Before I continue, I should mention I'm taking liberties with their terminology. Their language includes sounds I can't reproduce, like 'acdtaplkjuils,' which functions similar to what we'd call a rake, used to gather what translates roughly as 'harvest' or 'hh_cho_' in their speech. I'm using Earth equivalents for clarity."

Temper nodded, his enormous head casting a shadow across the porch. "Understandable. Translation always loses something."

"The reed civilization doesn't just talk," I continued. "They've built an entire mythology around their existence. Their dream-world feels as real to them as this porch feels to us."

I paused, watching a quantum rose phase in and out of reality where the newspaper had disturbed it. The flower reminded me of Talos's reeds; existing between states, more complex than surface appearance suggested.

"Over the millennia, its primal reed mind grew and developed," I continued, leaning forward in my chair. "It started telling itself a simple story about its world and how it worked."

Temper's eyes narrowed with interest.

"The heat vents along the fissures spewed life-giving sulfur over the nearest reeds. These reeds received the most nutrients and grew the strongest, so the brain considered these reeds to be the wealthiest.

I call this place 'the castle.'"

I traced a circle in the air, mapping out the moon's underwater geography.

"Ocean currents carried the sulfur-infused nutrients in a counterclockwise rotation away from the castle, flowing over what I named 'the darkened forest.' I called it that because strong magnetic waves bathe this area of Talos, and when you look at magnetic waves, the strong ones always appear darker."

Temper nodded, his scientific mind clearly intrigued. "The reeds can perceive these magnetic fields?"

"Absolutely. From there, the sulfur leaves the forest and flows over the plains, a vast flat seabed of reeds. Then the nutrients, now diminished in strength, pass over the village, which is the poorest place where few reeds can grow. Finally, a stronger ocean current pushes everything northward, back toward the castle."

I took another sip of lemonade.

"Everything in their dream sways to and fro, just like the actual reeds in the current. It's their collective mind's way of making sense of its environment. And seed from the vast seabed is blown by the currents back to the castle."

Temper's tail curled thoughtfully beneath him. "Fascinating. A perfect closed system."

"The dream became more sophisticated with each passing generation of reeds. Their shared brain started thinking of the sulfur nutrients as food or staples that the castle was giving to the rest of the land. Food and goods passed from castle through forest to plains and then to the poor village. In return, the castle received seed and pollen harvested from the plains to maintain its higher growth rate."

I gestured broadly, encompassing the imaginary world I was describing.

"Their world was complete. To them, it made perfect sense. They continued dreaming uninterrupted, as they had done for centuries."

A quantum rose fully materialized nearby, its petals shifting between crimson and gold. I watched it for a moment, gathering my thoughts.

"My involvement with the Talosians started with a girl. In fact, it was her thoughts I heard while falling through space." I smiled at the memory. "Her name was Vina, and she was quite pretty for a Talosian. Her head was a pleasant bulb shape, perfect for opening and releasing the seed she would grow during her shadowing phase of life."

Temper snorted softly. "You would notice that first."

I ignored him. "Her face was smooth and transparent. Beneath her skin, you could see her eyes shaped like two double Us on either side of her mid-stem. Those double U-shaped eyes allowed her to see the magnetic fields, so her world was filled with shades of light and dark. She swayed, like all Talosians do, gently to and fro in the ocean currents as she went about her daily life."

"You seem quite taken with this reed girl," Temper observed, his voice tinged with amusement.

"Not in the way you're implying," I countered. "But there was something about her consciousness that called to me across the void of space. Something important."

"In their dream, they moved freely despite their reeds being permanently rooted in the seabed. The most fascinating part? They had no idea they were dreaming or that they were actually interconnected plants. Each reed believed itself to be a separate creature, human, for lack of a better term, with complete freedom of movement."

I leaned forward, watching Temper's face shift to a contemplative shade of orange-red.

"I observed Vina's daily life like some invisible guardian. She couldn't detect my presence, but her thoughts rang clear as temple bells in my mind. When I first encountered her, she was swaying inside of a cave in the darkened forest, gathering spider webs for her school's binding spells."

"Spider webs underwater?" Temper interrupted, his tail twitching with skepticism.

"Not literal spiders. The 'webs' were actually filaments of mineral deposits that formed in lattice patterns along the cave walls. Their dream-logic translated these into spider webs." I sipped my lemonade. "Even though Vina collected materials for spells, she wasn't permitted to perform any magic herself. That honor belonged to advanced students, teachers, and especially to Magus, who served as head steward of Inward School. The school itself swayed on the opposite side of the darkened forest, away from the castle."

Temper's enormous head tilted. "Is that where you've been hiding these past seven months? On some moon watching reed people sway back and forth?"

The question caught me off guard. "Seven months? That can't be right."

"I haven't seen you for seven months," Temper confirmed, his voice rumbling like distant thunder. "It's been surprisingly peaceful without you around. I thought perhaps you were busy with the Ethereans on Requiem Prime, or traveling with Marcus and Bea."

I ran my fingers through my hair, feeling disoriented. Time had slipped away from me.

"Time is strange that way, isn't it? I can sit here talking with you for hours, weeks, even months, and it passes in a blink. But force me to sit on a hot stove, and five minutes stretches into eternity." I gestured toward the shimmering horizon. "And yes, to answer your question, I spent most of those seven months on Talos. Would you like to hear more?"

"Yes, please continue." Temper settled his massive form more comfortably. "I'm all ears."

"I should probably skip ahead a bit. This story feels like it's getting too long." I gathered my thoughts, deciding which parts were essential. "Shortly after my arrival, Vina encountered a troll that entered the spider cave, intent on killing and eating her. Initially, she mistook the attack for what they called an Unsettling: a sudden change in the dream."

I traced patterns in the condensation on my glass, mimicking the swaying motion of the reeds.

"Unsettlings were temporary disruptions in their reality. Most were minor, easily overlooked unless you were paying close attention to your surroundings. Occasionally they were dramatic, sudden scene changes or location shifts, like you might experience in a dream. During these events, people would simply sway in place until normalcy returned, then resume their routines as if nothing had happened."

Temper nodded, his scientific mind clearly intrigued.

"The collective mind disliked these disruptions," I continued. "The Inward School's primary purpose was minimizing these Unsettlings, maintaining the dream's stability. Does that make sense?"

"For the most part it does," Temper replied, his eyes filled with curiosity.

"Vina swayed in place waiting for things to return to normal," I continued, watching a quantum butterfly materialize near Temper's roses, "but then she realized the troll wasn't an unsettling at all. This was real danger."

Temper's bumpy skin rippled with interest, its crimson deepening as he leaned forward.

"She fought the troll with everything she had. I'm fast-forwarding here because the battle lasted hours. Eventually, she managed to defeat it but then faced another problem. Against all school rules, she used some of the spider web she'd collected to bind the troll to the inside of the cave."

"A permanent solution," Temper nodded.

"Not quite. The troll could never leave the cave, but that presented a new problem. The cave was home to the spiders, and they weren't thrilled about their new roommate."

Temper snorted, a small puff of steam escaping his nostrils. "She didn't think it through when she bound the troll."

"No, she didn't." I traced patterns in the condensation on my glass. "With no solution at hand, she led the spiders back through the darkened forest to her home at the school. She temporarily housed them in the barn until she could figure out what to do."

The quantum roses beside us phased in and out of reality, their petals shifting between crimson and translucent. They reminded me of Vina's world, caught between reality and dream.

"It was late when she returned, so she went to bed to sleep."

"Wait," Temper interrupted, his tail twitching. "They sleep inside their dream?"

"Yes, dreams within dreams. When she woke early the next morning, horrendous screaming filled the air. She gathered her wits and realized the screams were coming from the barn." I lowered my voice dramatically. "'Oh, no!' she muttered, knowing she was in trouble."

I took a sip of my lemonade, savoring the tart sweetness before continuing.

"The house mistress, Catoline, had gone to the barn for her early morning inventory. Instead of feed and tools, she found thousands of hairy-legged spiders hanging in the rafters just above her head. It was more than she could take. The whole forest heard her scream."

Temper's enormous head tilted as he chuckled. "I imagine that would be quite the shock."

"It's important to understand, Temper, that the mind didn't like surprises. Besides keeping unsettlings to a minimum, its biggest goal was ensuring no one woke up and realized they were dreaming. Catoline almost woke up, and who could blame her? Walking into a barn with thousands of spiders hovering over your head would terrify anyone."

My thoughts returned to my death-match with Marcus. The spiders plopping all over me truly had been terrifying. A quantum butterfly landed on my shoulder, bringing me back to the present, its wings shifting between existence and non-existence.

"The mind wanted order. It craved conformity. It needed reliable routines for people to live out their lives without questioning their reality. To maintain this control, the mind had given teachers at the school the ability to manipulate the dream to keep the peace."

I brushed the butterfly away gently, watching it phase through my fingers.

"The Inward School's abilities seemed like magic to outsiders. Even the teachers and students didn't know the truth behind their powers. Only Headmaster Magus was aware of the dream. He was keeper of the one true secret."

Temper sang softly, *"Row, row, row your boat gently down the stream."*

"Exactly," I smiled. *"Life is but a dream.* Students and teachers rushed to the barn to investigate the commotion. Meanwhile, Catoline exited the barn quickly. Her bulb was flush, and she looked ready to explode. Instead of waking up, she surrendered to her anger and shouted about the spiders for all to hear. Then she went looking for the student she suspected of this foul deed, the troublemaker Vina."

"So Vina was known as a troublemaker beforehand? What kind of trouble?" Temper asked, his bumpy red skin darkening with curiosity.

I set my glass down on the porch railing, watching a pair of celestial hummingbirds dart between Temper's garden plants. Their translucent bodies left trails of stardust as they moved.

"Vina originally swayed on the plains where she sprouted, but she got into trouble during harvest time." I leaned back in my chair. "None of it was her fault. The guy had it coming, if you ask me. Served him right for picking on a little girl."

Temper's tail curled beneath him. "What happened?"

"This bigger reed kept harassing her, stealing her sulfur because he could. One day, Vina had enough." I gestured with my hands, mimicking a twisting motion. "She used magic to bend his stem in a direction it shouldn't bend. When authorities investigated and discovered her natural gift for magic, they sent her to the Inward School."

Temper snorted, a small puff of steam escaping his nostrils. "Sounds like self-defense to me."

"Exactly. But Catoline, being the nosy type, found out about Vina's past. She'd disliked the girl ever since."

A hot breeze swept across the porch, carrying the scent of Temper's mineral garden. The crystals clinked softly against each other, creating a wind-chime effect.

"Catoline sounds like a real meddler," Temper said, his belly expanding slightly with each breath.

"That she was." I nodded, watching the hummingbirds disappear around the corner of the house. "She dragged Vina in front of Magus and the other teachers in the school's main hall, forced her to confess. Then demanded her expulsion."

Temper's eyes narrowed. "And did they expel her?"

"At first, Magus swayed in opposition, but when all the other teachers started swaying in support, he was forced to comply." I traced the rim of my glass with my finger. "Vina was sent back to the plains. Some older students were tasked with returning the spiders to their cave and relocating the troll to the darkened forest. Everyone considered the matter closed."

Temper shifted his massive form, the porch creaking beneath him. "But it wasn't closed, was it?"

"No. Magus was concerned. It wasn't normal for a forest creature, especially one so strongly controlled by the mind like a dangerous troll, to attack anyone." I lowered my voice. "He suspected something bad was happening. That the dream was beginning to unravel, as it had in the distant past."

The sky above Falfsun turned a deeper shade of amber as we sat in momentary silence. In the distance, a meteorite shower peppered the upper atmosphere with tiny pinpricks of light.

"What happened to Vina after her expulsion?" Temper asked.

"She went back to the fields on the plains, helping gather seed for the harvest." I gestured toward the horizon. "Sweepers then took the harvest to the sparsely populated village, where it passed unopposed to the castle. The harvest, if you recall, was the seed and spore needed by the castle to maintain their faster growth rate."

Temper nodded, his bumpy skin rippling with interest.

"After life at the school, Vina was bored in the fields doing the same thing every day." I stood up, stretching my legs. "A part of her wanted to conform and be happy with her simple life, but another part had been partially awakened, just as the mind had feared."

"And that's why you were drawn to her," Temper said, not a question but a statement.

I nodded, watching the meteorite shower intensify across the amber sky. "She was on the verge of understanding something profound about her world. Something dangerous."

I leaned forward, watching the quantum butterfly flutter away into Falfsun's amber light. The distant meteorite shower had intensified, casting brief flashes across Temper's garden where his mineral formations caught and refracted the light in prismatic bursts.

"She asked to be one of the sweepers who took the harvest over to the village," I continued, "just to escape from the fields for a little while. She had never seen the village, so it would be something new for her to experience. The fields' foreman, Antinolus, added her name to the bottom of the sweeper's rotation, and in a month, it was Vina's turn to go."

Temper shifted his massive form, his tail curling underneath him. The porch creaked beneath his weight as he settled in; his enormous dragon head tilted with interest.

"What was the harvest like?" he asked, his voice rumbling like distant thunder.

"Mostly seed and spore," I replied. "She helped sweep it to the village where the villagers took over. They handled the rest of the work, getting everything to the castle."

I traced a pattern in the condensation on my glass, mimicking the flow of the river I was describing.

"The village consisted of only a few huts lining the bank of the river. None were as grand as the school or the castle, or even the simple farmhouses of the plains. Mud pathways led from hut to hut. The villagers were poor, but they did their job of sending seed and spore to the castle without complaint. They accepted their lot in life, never once dreaming of better for themselves or their offspring."

Temper's nostrils flared slightly, releasing a wisp of vapor that curled into the warm air. "Sounds like the mind created a rigid class structure."

"Indeed," I nodded. "The river always ran strong, and its far side was perpetually shrouded in a fine mist, the kind you might find when fast falling water hits against rocks at the bottom of a high waterfall. No one from the village ever ventured across to see what was past the mist. Why should they care about what was over there, when every day was a challenge just to find enough to eat? They weren't interested in wasting time and energy on such a fool's errand."

One of the celestial hummingbirds returned, hovering near Temper's head before darting away, trailing stardust in its wake. His eyes followed it momentarily before returning to me.

"Vina had heard of the village and of the misty river. Everyone who grew up on the plains knew about them, but she had never seen the village before, and she wasn't prepared for how few people there actually were, nor for the poverty of their living conditions."

I stood up again, moving to the porch railing to watch more of the meteorite shower.

"They swayed through life with their bulbs hung low. They were listless in transporting the harvest. Vina wondered what they felt and thought when they saw the gleaming castle and its huge population of overfed people when they delivered their load. Did they feel envy? Were they angry, even a tiny bit, about the castle having so much when they had so little? Vina decided to linger at the village. She wanted to listen to them talk when they came back from the castle."

Temper's tail twitched thoughtfully, sweeping a small arc across the porch floor. His massive head tilted, eyes narrowing in contemplation.

"Excuse me for interrupting," he said, "but couldn't the mind have dreamed up a better life for the villagers than this?"

I turned back to face him, leaning against the railing. Behind me, the meteorites continued their silent bombardment of Falfsun's upper atmosphere.

"The mind was limited in its ability to help them," I explained. "Remember, the ocean currents carried the sulfur north and then in a counterclockwise motion around the rest of the land. By the time the sulfur-infused nutrients reached the villagers, there wasn't much left for them to eat. The mind couldn't change that." I gestured toward the horizon. "The village was a barren place for reeds to grow, and no amount of dreaming for something better was ever going to make a difference."

The meteorite storm subsided gradually, its fiery display fading into memory as the last streaks of light dissolved into Falfsun's amber sky. I remained at the porch railing, watching as the celestial fireworks gave way to the star's normal undulating surface.

Temper stood up, his massive form unfurling as he pushed himself off his tail. He lumbered through the front yard, his bumpy red skin catching the ambient glow of Falfsun. The ground beneath him vibrated slightly with each step as he made his way to the fence. I followed, my footsteps light in comparison to his thunderous movements.

We stood side by side, gazing out over the horizon. Long willowy filaments of gas arced overhead, twisting together in complex knots before plunging back to the surface. Each return triggered a geyser of flame, plasma erupting in fountains of incandescent light. The display was hypnotic, a constant dance of creation and destruction.

Temper's attention fixed on something in the distance. His eyes narrowed, his entire posture shifting with sudden focus.

"What is it?" I asked, scanning the horizon.

He concentrated on a point near three particularly active geysers. When I crossed my eyes, they resembled fire eaters in medieval costumes putting on a circus performance. But Temper looked beyond their fiery display, his gaze intense and searching.

"I thought I saw something," he murmured, then shook his massive head.

Without further explanation, he turned and made his way back to the porch. The boards creaked in protest as he settled his weight once more.

"It seems to me that the mind could have done something else," he said, returning to our story as if there had been no interruption.

"It could have dreamed of a giant fan that blew the harvest all the way to the castle," I agreed, resuming my seat. "Then it wouldn't have needed the village or its people at all. But having never seen a fan, it didn't know what a fan was." The ice in my lemonade had melted, leaving the drink watery. I took a sip anyway. "And what about the reeds growing there? Would it have been better to not let them dream at all? I think the mind was trying to give all its reeds the best life it could. Maybe it will come up with something better in the future. The dream continues, after all."

Temper settled onto his tail and folded his arms contentedly over his large red belly. His eyes reflected the distant flames of Falfsun. "So what did Vina find out?"

"While she waited for the villagers to return, Vina swayed around the village following its mud paths from hut to squalid hut," I continued. "It was a depressing place, and Vina was glad she hadn't grown up there. She looked for a path down to the river but couldn't find any. The villagers seemed deathly afraid of the river. They wouldn't go anywhere near it."

"So that means the mind was afraid of the river?" Temper's bumpy skin rippled with interest. "Why? Why else would the villagers fear it that way?"

I nodded, watching a quantum butterfly materialize near one of Temper's mineral formations. "The mind had a good reason to be afraid. It comes up later in the story."

Temper grunted. "Okay, I can wait."

"Vina also feared the river," I continued, "but since she came from the plains farther away, her fear wasn't as great as the villagers'. She bravely made her way across the land separating the village from the river and stood on its bank." The butterfly disappeared, its brief existence fading like a thought. "She had always been told that the river flowed fast, but looking at it, the water seemed to barely be moving at all. She looked across the river through the mist. It had grown thin, and she was able to see what looked like a house on the far side sitting on the riverbank."

I leaned forward in my chair, watching the distant horizon of Falfsun where the last remnants of the meteor shower had faded into memory. The surface of the star pulsed with its usual rhythm, waves of plasma rolling across its face like an endless sea.

"Vina glanced back at the villagers who had remained behind from taking the harvest to the castle, but they didn't even look her way."

Temper shifted his weight, causing the porch to creak beneath him. "That's what it's like to live a subsistence lifestyle. You ignore everything that doesn't pose an immediate threat to you."

"Exactly," I nodded, running my finger along the condensation on my glass. "Vina, on the other hand, lived on the plains where food was more plentiful. She was only visiting the village, so she noticed the strange building on the other side of the river. Tentatively, she put her foot in the water to see if it was shallow enough for her to cross over."

Temper's eyes narrowed with interest. "She didn't know how to swim?"

"No, ironically, she didn't. The reeds lived in an ocean underneath an ice crust, and yet they were afraid of the water." I set my empty glass down on the small table between us. "On her first sway, the water only came up to her ankles. She swayed further until she reached the middle of the river where it only came up to her knees. Her confidence grew. She was sure she could make it all the way to the other side, but something strange started happening to her."

Temper leaned forward, his massive form casting a shadow across the porch.

"The farther she swayed across the river, the weirder she began to feel. It wasn't unpleasant. In fact, she felt great. Stronger than ever before. She swayed out on the other side with her newfound strength and stood on the far bank."

A warm breeze swept across the porch, carrying the scent of Falfsun's unique atmospheric blend.

"The house she had seen through the mist was only a few sways away. She called out, 'Hello? Is anyone there?'"

I cleared my throat, mimicking Vina's struggle. "Talking made her cough. She felt her throat. It should be soft and pliable, but underneath her skin were thick, hard sinews. She had barely been able to speak."

Plasma tornadoes twisted across Falfsun's surface as I talked, their fiery tendrils crackling as waves of heat distorted the sky into shimmering mirages.

"Silence greeted her. Around the side of the house was a barn and its door was open."

Temper chuckled, slapping his belly as he said, "Oh-oh, I hope no one got in trouble for that!"

"For leaving the barn door open?" I rolled my eyes. "Yes... very funny joke, now please be quiet." I adjusted my position in the chair, the wood creaking beneath me. "When she didn't get a response to her query, Vina swayed into the barn to look around. Some items looked familiar to her, like the rake, but there were things hanging on hooks she had never seen before."

The surface of Falfsun rippled with activity, sending waves of heat that made the air shimmer around us. Temper's belly swelled with each breath, the amber light casting soft shadows across its broad, rounded form.

"She reached out to touch one of the strange hanging things when suddenly she heard a noise. She stopped to listen. The noise was coming from outside, moving towards the barn. She hid behind a bin that she assumed was used during harvest, but it wasn't like any sweeper bin she knew."

Temper's tail curled tighter beneath him, his attention fully captured by the story.

"Into the barn swayed a figure. It was a boy! He appeared to be about the same age as she was. Vina swayed still to make sure it wasn't some sort of unsettling that was occurring. When the world swayed steady, as she had hoped it would, she swayed out of her hiding place to greet the boy."

I leaned forward, my voice dropping to mimic Vina's strained attempt. "'Hello!' she said, coughing. 'Hello' had come out wrong. It sounded more like she had said, 'Hellghh!'"

The boy looked at her and his bulb grew bigger. He let out a scream, then turned and swayed as fast as he could out of the barn. Vina swayed after him, coughing "Wait! I didn't mean to scare you!" but it sounded like she had said, "Waaagh! Ideeumghh tooggh skaarugh!"

"What is wrong with me?" Vina thought, as she swayed after the boy. The boy kept screaming as he swayed towards his village. It was

a wealthier village than the other village. It didn't look as poor and, from a distance, it looked like there were more people. The people looked to see who was screaming and what the commotion was all about. When they saw Vina they stopped and swayed in place, which looked to Vina like they were busy trying to determine if she was an unsettling. When she stubbornly refused to leave, the villagers recognized her as the real deal, and their voices rose in a chorus of harmonizing screams, so perfectly tuned and balanced that they could have stirred envy in the most accomplished performers.

"Everyone shouting scared Vina, so she turned and swayed as fast as she could back towards the river. At the river's edge she saw her reflection in the water. She looked monstrous, more like an ogre than a girl, with pale, mottled skin covering hard sinew that rippled as she swayed. Her bulb was misshapen. It bulged on her right side, giving her right eye a weird circular look, with a grotesque round pupil instead of a pleasant double U. No one followed her. It appeared that these other people were scared of the river too. Once she got to her side of the river she felt better, more like her normal self. Vina felt her throat. It was soft and supple. The hard sinews were gone. She looked at her reflection in the river. Her skin had returned to a normal blush and her bulb was a normal oval. The whole experience confused her, and during her travel home she thought about what it all meant."

Temper looked over at me, squinting. He cocked his massive dragon head to one side, his expression somehow conveying confusion despite his inhuman features.

"Why would the mind keep the other people a secret?" he asked, his tail twitching against the porch floor.

"It's complicated. Do you want me to jump forward a little bit in the story and explain it to you right now? It might help."

He patted his large belly with a clawed hand. "Please do. Do you want more lemonade? Are you hungry?"

"Yes, on the lemonade." I glanced at the horizon where Falfsun's surface continued its eternal churning. The story would take a while, and my stomach was already beginning to protest. "I guess we could eat. What do you have?"

Temper turned his wet dragon nose upward in thought, a gesture that still struck me as oddly endearing despite how long I'd known him. "Let me think. I don't have anything in the fridge. I could grill out?"

I surveyed the hellish landscape beyond the porch, where geysers of plasma erupted in brilliant fountains. "I'll pass on the grilled cinder-burgers." The barren expanse of Falfsun stretched before us, its surface a roiling sea of fire. "I don't suppose we can order food delivery here?"

"You bet we can. How about a pizza?"

"That sounds good."

"I'll get the usual, wood-fired crust, cheese, and pepperoni."

Temper called Sunny's Pizza and put in his order. Sunny guaranteed delivery in thirty minutes or less, or your money back. *Every star should have a Sunny's*, I thought. We settled back with our lemonades, and I continued with my story.

"Okay, I'll fast forward and tell you what's actually going on." I leaned forward, swirling the lemonade in my glass. "Let me warn you though, it's a spoiler alert."

Temper's eyes widened with interest.

"Millennia ago, there was no river separating the land. Ocean currents existed, but they were mild compared to the strong river current that now divides the land in two."

A distant plasma fountain erupted on Falfsun's surface, sending spirals of incandescent gas twisting into the atmosphere.

"Before the river, the mind controlled all the land, and its inhabitants dreamed in peace. Then something momentous happened. A mountain of sea ice collapsed underwater, causing a plunge in temperature and the creation of a new ocean current. This current split the land, and the mind, in half."

Temper shifted his weight, his tail curling beneath him. The porch boards groaned in protest.

"There were now two lands and two minds. Confusing at first, but each side kept dreaming as best they could. Over time, the dreams diverged and followed their own paths. They grew so different that when they interact now, the results are disastrous."

I took a sip of lemonade. "That's why both minds fear the river. Vina didn't know any of this. The only people alive who knew the truth were Magus and his counterpart from the opposite side."

Temper's nostrils flared as he absorbed this information. His clawed hand tapped rhythmically against his belly.

"Every few centuries, wild reeds at the river mouth grew dense enough to affect the flow. The river slowed and became passable. Vina crossed when it was running slow. She interacted with the other dream, and in doing so, unintentionally started a war."

I gazed out at the rolling surface of Falfsun. "If she hadn't crossed, eventually a dam might have built up behind the reeds until the pressure broke through. The water would have rushed back along its old course, making the river impassable again, keeping the dreams separated. Everything would have remained normal."

Temper sucked his straw until it made a gurgling sound. He smacked his lips. "Aah, it's beginning to make sense. So Vina changed in appearance because her dream was losing its influence over her, and the other dream was starting to take hold?"

I refilled his glass and checked the time. Sunny's had fifteen minutes left before our pizza would be free. "That's exactly right. Although her roots were firmly implanted in one mind, the other mind could talk to her telepathically. That's also why she felt stronger. She was channeling the strength from two dreams, instead of only one."

Temper pointed suddenly as a solar flare erupted from the star, spewing sparkling plasma in all directions. "Watch for it to come down. When it hits it will make feeder jets."

The flare reached its zenith in a high arc overhead, trailing flame like a comet's tail. It began its descent, picking up speed as it approached the surface. Upon impact, a ring of plasma flew up in little balls of fire that sprayed out in multiple directions.

"Huzzah!" Temper shouted, his entire body vibrating with excitement. "That was a good one." His attention returned to me, eyes gleaming with curiosity. "You mentioned that Vina started a war?"

"Yes. She didn't mean to." I swirled the lemonade in my glass, watching the ice cubes clink against each other. "For all of her life, Vina simply wanted to fit in. She wanted to be a good reed and not make waves. When she went to the village that fateful day, she was just a young girl who found herself in the wrong place at the wrong time."

Temper nodded, his massive dragon head bobbing with understanding. The movement sent ripples across his red, bumpy skin.

"After Vina returned home from the village, and for many days afterward, she thought of the boy she had met." I smiled, remembering the character's innocence. "She had to laugh when she thought about how much he was scared of her. *'Shy little me. Who could ever be afraid of me?'* she kidded herself."

The surface of Falfsun bubbled in the distance, a constant reminder of the star's restless nature. Temper leaned forward, his belly pressing against his knees.

"Half of the season went by," I continued. "They had three unsettlings during that time, when normally it would be only one. Each unsettling grew longer in duration and more upsetting in appearance."

Temper's eyes widened. "Like tremors before an earthquake."

"Exactly. During the last unsettling, while everyone swayed in place, they imagined that an army of forest inhabitants, the trolls and ogres and wild things of the deep forest, had come to steal their harvest. The forest invaders trampled the seed and spore underfoot. They broke the harvest rakes."

A distant rumble echoed across Falfsun's surface. The star seemed to punctuate my story with its own dramatic flair.

"Through it all the people swayed, rooted in place. When the unsettling stopped, the forest dwellers faded out of sight and the people looked about and saw that the rakes were unbroken and the harvest was still whole and secure. They sighed a collective sigh of relief, but there was a restlessness in the world that hadn't been there before."

I took a sip of lemonade, savoring the tart coolness against the ambient heat of Falfsun.

"For Vina, her peaceful swaying came to an abrupt end shortly thereafter. She loved to sway alone from other people, and while she was alone in a far field she was attacked. *'Oh no! Another unsettling!'* was her first thought. She waited in place for it to pass."

Temper's tail twitched with anticipation.

"Swaying rapidly towards her was a large ogre with mottled skin covering hard sinew that rippled as it swayed. In its hands was a rake. It swung at Vina, hitting her mid-stem. She doubled over in pain. *'This is real,'* she thought."

My story was interrupted as a weathered 2020 Dodge Charger R/T growled to a stop in front of Temper's house. Its 5.7L HEMI V8 engine rumbled, defiant in its presence. The Charger's wide stance gave it the aura of something built for speed, yet even this machine seemed hesitant.

Its tires were anything but at ease. If they had voices, I imagined them screaming in silent terror. The street burned beneath them, glowing fever-red with the relentless heat of Falfsun, a searing surface that showed no mercy. The tires smoldered in defiance, sending up twisting tendrils of smoke; serpentine wisps curling skyward like a nest of cobras, writhing against the inevitable.

A young man, dressed in a Sunny's burgundy and gold uniform with a rising sun emblem above his right chest pocket, hopped out of the car carrying an insulated pizza box. He hopscotched across the fever-struck ground until he reached the relative coolness of the sidewalk leading up to the house.

"I hope you intend on tipping him well for delivering this," I said, nudging Temper with my elbow.

Temper's belly jiggled as he chuckled. "Don't worry, I will. But look around yourself. Where do you think he's going to spend the money?"

I watched the delivery boy's frantic dance across the blistering pavement, then glanced at the smoking tires of his car.

"Buying new tires, of course."

"Good day! Sunny's pizza, piping hot!" The delivery boy's voice cracked with forced enthusiasm as he balanced the insulated box in one hand. His name tag read "Marty" in faded burgundy letters. Sweat beaded on his forehead, and his knuckles were white from gripping the box. "That'll be $19.42, but if you only have $19, it's okay."

Temper's eyes slid toward me, mischief dancing in their reptilian depths. "Thanks, but I think I have the exact change."

I reached over to punch his arm, but he ducked with surprising agility for his bulk. He laughed.

"Just kidding!" Temper fished three crisp hundred-dollar bills from somewhere within his dragon form and handed them to Marty. "Here you go, Marty. Keep the change."

The boy's eyes widened until they threatened to pop from his skull. He stared at the money in his palm as if expecting it to vanish. "Gee, thanks mister!"

Marty practically sprinted back to his car, the pizza box forgotten in Temper's claws. His feet barely touched the blistering pavement. The Charger's engine roared to life, its engine rumbling pleasantly as Marty, his car, the cobra-like smoke from the tires, and the dual exhaust pipes disappeared over the hill.

Temper set the box between us and lifted the lid. Steam billowed upward, carrying the aroma of melted cheese and spiced pepperoni. True to Sunny's promise, the pizza was piping hot.

"Mmm, this is good." I wiped sauce from my lips with the back of my hand. The cheese stretched in long, gooey strands as I pulled my slice away. Between bites, I continued my story.

"Vina swayed away from her attacker toward people working in a nearby field. Her injury wasn't serious, but her stem throbbed with pain. Her attacker followed, bellowing something unintelligible that sounded like 'Uughh ruughinggd mylifghh!'"

Temper tilted his massive head, his attention fully captured despite the pizza in his claws.

"*I know that voice,* thought Vina. She turned and confronted her attacker as field workers rushed to her defense. There was something familiar about the ogre. Despite its mottled appearance, she felt she had seen him before."

I paused to take another bite, savoring the perfect balance of sauce and cheese. The crust crackled between my teeth, wood-fired to perfection.

"'Boy, is that you?' she asked, remembering her own mottled reflection in the river."

Temper leaned forward, his belly pressing against his knees.

"The ogre stopped upon hearing her. It turned and swayed towards the river, disappearing into the distance. The reed mind now knew it had a problem. The stability it had tried so hard to maintain had been derailed by a small girl and the other mind's boy."

I wiped my fingers on a napkin and reached for my lemonade. The ice had melted, diluting the tartness.

"The reed mind took action. It notified Prince Ilya by sending a courier from the village. The courier told the prince of Vina's river crossing and of the ogre who followed her back. The village needed the castle's help to defend itself against attack. The prince sent troops to the river and dispatched soldiers to arrest Vina."

Falfsun's surface bubbled in the distance. A small geyser of plasma erupted, sending golden sparks dancing across the horizon.

"Magus, aware of everything being dreamed, knew of the prince's plans and decided to intervene. He found Vina before the prince's men could and took her into the darkened forest."

Temper finished his third slice, his attention never wavering from my words.

"They swayed into the forest for hours. Vina was tired and confused by the time they stopped. The magnetic fields of the planet were strongest here. Like Earth's Aurora Borealis, a cinematic light show occurred above them that dazzled Vina. Under the dancing lights, Magus said, 'War is coming, Vina, and what you do next will determine its outcome.'"

I reached for another slice, the cheese still molten.

"He saw her confusion. 'None of this makes sense to you now, but it will. Trust me. You must do exactly as I say. North of here is a mountain made of blue ice. You must climb it, even though it will hurt. Once you reach the mountaintop, look down at the plains until you see your home. No one will interfere in your quest, because I, Magus the 9th, demand it.'"

Temper's tail twitched against the porch boards, creating a soft thumping rhythm.

"Vina swayed uncertainly, staring at Magus. 'Go, child! War is upon us, and you must finish what you started!'"

I lowered my voice, matching Vina's confusion.

"Startled by his call to action, Vina swayed rapidly northward, why or for what, she didn't know. *Ice? Magus the 9th? What did he mean?* Vina's thoughts jumbled together, as if mixed in a blender set too high. All she understood was the mountain. She had seen it from the fields at home looming in the distance, and again from the school near the forest where it towered over them. As she got closer, she had trouble swaying. The ocean currents didn't flow this far north, except for the eddies trapped around the ice shoals. Here, the sway was much weaker."

"She began to climb the blue mountain," I continued, finishing another slice of pizza. "The cold hurt her flesh, and her sway was almost gone, but she didn't stop."

Temper wrapped his claws around his lemonade glass, his bumpy red skin contrasting with the condensation-beaded surface. His eyes followed a distant solar flare that arced across Falfsun's horizon.

"One sway at a time," I said, mimicking Vina's determined voice. "That's what she told herself. After what seemed like days, Vina finally reached what she thought was the top. There might have been more mountain above, but the ice spread out in all directions from where she stood. Climbing farther was impossible."

Temper's tail curled beneath him as he shifted his weight. "Like hitting a ceiling in a dream."

"Exactly. Vina moved her bulb close to the ice. She could see through it, though her vision was distorted by imperfections. But at exactly the right angle, she saw magnetic lines surrounding a large, round bauble hanging in the air at a distance."

"The planet," Temper whispered, his voice hushed with wonder.

I nodded. "The magnetic lines traveled from the bauble down to the darkened forest below, where they danced in the sky. Vina was filled with wonder. Tentatively, she reached up and touched the ice. She touched the sky itself."

The pizza box sat empty between us. A coolish breeze swept across the porch, offering momentary relief from Falfsun's ambient heat.

"She looked down at her home on the plains below," I continued. "At first, nothing seemed unusual. Magus had told her to see her home. She concentrated until her view shifted, and suddenly she saw a vast field of reeds swaying in the water."

Temper's nostrils flared. "The people?"

"That was her question too. 'Where are all the people?' she wondered. Then her eyes adjusted, or more accurately, the dream adjusted. She saw the reeds for what they truly were: the people who dreamed."

Temper leaned forward, his belly pressing against his knees. A droplet of condensation rolled down his glass, leaving a trail across his claw.

"A presence joined her," I said, lowering my voice. "It greeted her like an old friend, the kind you trust with your life. 'Welcome, Magus the 10th,' the reed mind said."

Temper's eyes widened.

"Before she could process this, another presence approached. Floating beside the mountaintop was the image of Magus the 9th. His form was semi-opaque, dark around the edges with a center that light shone through. 'Well done, Magus Ten,' he said."

I set my empty glass on the table, the ice cubes clinking softly.

"Vina was truly confused. 'Why are you calling me that? You're Magus!'"

"'I was Magus Nine,' he told her. 'You are the Magus now.'"

The surface of Falfsun bubbled in the distance, sending up tiny geysers of golden plasma.

"The Mind spoke next. 'There can only be one Magus. He relinquished his title to make room for you, Vina.'"

Temper's tail thumped softly against the porch floor, his attention completely captured.

"Eight other figures appeared in the air. They too were apparitions, semi-opaque like Magus. Vina instinctively knew they were past versions of Magus, stretching back centuries."

I leaned back in my chair, feeling the warm wood against my spine.

"The mind had opened her understanding of the dream. With it, she understood her people's history and the danger they now faced. She knew that all past versions of Magus swaying before her were there to guide her if needed."

Temper's breathing slowed, his massive chest rising and falling in measured rhythm.

"Vina's bulb slumped as realization washed over her. 'I've started a war, haven't I?' she asked, her voice small with regret. 'I didn't mean to.'"

I fell silent, letting the weight of Vina's words settle between us. Falfsun's surface churned in the distance, mirroring the turmoil in Vina.

"Magus Nine comforted her. 'War would have found us anyway, Vina. If you hadn't crossed the river, someone else would have, and we still would have had a war. Don't blame yourself for what the mindless, wild reeds have caused.'"

I paused to brush away a curious beetle that had landed on the arm of my chair. The insect's carapace shimmered with an iridescence that reminded me of the quantum tunnels Joan and I had explored.

"All past versions of Magus nodded and swayed in agreement. Vina looked at each of them and beamed appreciation for their support. 'What should I do?'"

Temper shifted his weight.

"Magus Nine said, 'Win the war. Lead your people to victory. Keep the other people on their side of the river until the water runs free again.'"

I lowered my voice to match Vina's uncertainty. "'I'm too young to lead anyone. Why don't you stay, Magus Nine? You could lead them better than I ever can.'"

A distant rumble echoed across the sun. A starquake off in the distance.

"'I can't stay because the people blame me for this. This is how it always begins. Every time there is a war, the Magus is blamed. The people unite against the current Magus and that helps keep the dream strong. A new Magus must then be chosen, and it's always whomever starts the war. That person is you, Vina.' Past versions of Magus nodded in agreement."

Temper's tail curled beneath him as he settled deeper into his chair. The empty pizza box sat between us, grease stains forming abstract patterns on its cardboard surface.

"'Vina swayed in thought. 'So that means there's a pattern to the war? One that repeats every time?'"

"'Yes,' Magus Nine said, 'after the war is started the soldiers gather at the river, and we gather at the mountain to appoint the next Magus as soon as possible. Now that you've been appointed, you must appear before the soldiers as the new Magus. Then you must hold the land against invasion until the river flows fast again.'"

I took a moment to refill my glass with the last of the lemonade, the pitcher beading with condensation.

"'Is there always an invasion?'" Vina asked.

"'Sometimes they invade first. Sometimes we do. The people decide. Hold the land and the dream will endure. It will be damaged; soldiers may die, and people will suffer. After the war, the Mind will help you rebuild the dream to its former state.'"

"'Isn't there any other way? What about the mindless reeds? Why don't they dream? Has anyone ever tried to wake them up and get them to join us?'"

"'Magus Nine shook his bulb. 'We've tried to talk to them in the past. We've threatened them, and tried bribing them with harvest, but they won't respond to our requests.'"

Temper's eyes lit up with mischief. "I guess they must be in a vegetative state!"

I groaned as Temper burst into laughter, his belly jiggling with each guffaw. His cackle was so loud it seemed to echo across the neighborhood. The sound was infectious despite the terrible pun, and I found myself fighting a smile.

While I moaned at his joke, Temper guffawed himself into a cackle, and he slapped his knee so hard I imagined that Marty, on his way to deliver his next pizza, must have looked with worry into his rear-view mirror to see what had happened."

Being the good friend that I am, I ignored him and his joke. "Didn't you get any cheesy bread sticks?"

Temper wiped a tear from his dragon eye. "No, I didn't." Another cackle escaped him.

"Cinnamon twists? Brownies? Lava crunch cakes?"

"No, no, and no. There's more lemonade."

I shook my head, leaning back in my chair. "No thanks. I'm good."

"Want me to call Sunny's back?"

"No, I can wait. Let's not bother Marty. I can get something back home."

Temper looked at the time. His brow furrowed, creating ripples across his bumpy forehead. His tail twitched nervously against the porch boards.

"Are you waiting for something? Or maybe someone? You seem worried," I said.

"No... well, I was hoping Joan would be back by now." His tail twitched nervously against the weathered porch boards. "Quantum spelunking between dimensions can be hazardous to your health. I'm a little worried she might have got stuck somewhere."

Temper looked beyond the porch, past his meticulously maintained lawn that stretched toward a white picket fence.

"Do we need to do something? Go looking for her, maybe?" I asked, gathering the empty pizza box and napkins.

"Not yet. She's probably fine." Temper's gaze drifted toward a cluster of roses along the fence line. Their petals, genetically modified to withstand Falfsun's radiation, shimmered with an almost metallic quality. A butterfly with translucent wings fluttered among the blooms, seemingly unconcerned with the star's proximity. "Continue with your story."

I settled back in my chair. "I'll try and speed it up. If we need to go, I can always finish later, too."

"Thanks. We should be good." His claws drummed against the armrest.

"Okay, just remember we can stop." I watched as another butterfly joined the first, their wings catching the light. "Anyway, the reeds were in their vegetative state—" I paused to shoot Temper a look, which he answered with an unrepentant grin, "—and Vina, or Magus Ten as she was now known, wasn't sure what she should do next. She looked at all the past Magi, and to her, each one represented a war. She didn't want to be like them. She didn't want to be the tenth war, but what could she do?"

A gentle breeze stirred the rose petals, carrying their subtle fragrance toward us. Temper's nostrils flared slightly, taking in the scent.

"'I have to try and talk to the wild reeds again,'" I continued, adopting Vina's determined tone. "'If there's a chance of avoiding a war, I have to try. Magus Nine, can other people, besides me, see you and the past Magi?'"

"'If we want them to see us, they can,'" I replied in Magus Nine's deeper voice. "'But we don't want that because it creates confusion for them. It disturbs the dream.'"

Temper leaned forward, his belly pressing against his knees. A droplet of sweat rolled down his bumpy forehead, evaporating before it reached his eye ridge.

"Vina nodded as her plan formed in her bulb. 'Good, I want you and the other Magi to go to the river and stand between it and our people. Do not let anyone cross until I get there.'"

"'Yes, Magus, if that's what you want. But what will you do?'"

"'I plan on going down the mountain and traveling over to the wild reeds. I'm going to get them to listen to me. They must listen.'"

Temper's garden sprinklers activated with a soft hiss, sending fine mist across the roses. The butterflies scattered momentarily before returning to their nectar feast.

"Magus Nine shook his bulb. 'You don't need to climb down the mountain to travel there. Magus Four discovered a way for the Magi to travel anywhere instantaneously. I'll take you to the wild reeds, and from there, the Mind will assist you.'"

Temper's tail curled beneath him as he shifted his weight. His eyes darted toward the quantum tunnel access point at the edge of his property, a shimmering distortion barely visible against the fence line.

"Magus Nine took Vina from the mountain to the mouth of the river in an instant. Vina, having experienced instantaneous travel with Magus Nine's help, now understood how to do it on her own."

"'I'll leave you to your plan and rejoin the Magi at the river,'" I said, mimicking Magus Nine's voice before switching back to my narrator tone. "Then he disappeared."

"At the village, the Magi stood in a line between the soldiers and the river. The soldiers and villagers could see the apparitions swaying between them and their enemies, and for the time being, they stayed where they were. The other people and the other soldiers, living on the opposite side of the river, could also see the apparitions and were afraid to cross. It was a stalemate."

Temper checked the time again, his brow furrowing into deep ridges. The butterflies by the roses had multiplied, their wings creating a kaleidoscope of colors against the white fence.

"Vina, now on her own, swayed among the wild reeds growing thick around the gorge through which the water flowed. All of them bent over on their stems in a massive domino effect. The water had pushed the first row down onto their neighbors, creating a chain reaction until all the reeds formed an impenetrable mass." I shifted in my chair, mimicking the bending motion with my hands. "They'd created a solid dam. The water's flow diminished to a trickle, though pressure built behind it."

Temper's nostrils flared with interest.

"The Mind spoke to her," I continued, lowering my voice to a whisper. "'Do you see, Vina? Magi before you have attempted to awaken them, to invite them into the dream. They sleep, dreamless.

157

They might as well be dead.'"

A butterfly landed on the arm of my chair, its translucent wings catching the golden light. I watched it for a moment before continuing.

"Vina wasn't convinced. 'If we could only get them to stand up, the water could flow between them. Maybe not as strong as before, but enough to separate the lands, wouldn't it?'"

Temper leaned forward, his belly pressing against his knees. "Smart thinking."

"The Mind didn't answer her. Vina tried quieting herself, straining to hear the wild reeds, but they remained silent." I paused, building tension. "Then inspiration struck. Vina crossed to the other side of the reeds, into the other land, becoming part of the other dream."

"Bold move," Temper murmured, his claws tapping against his glass.

"The Mind was alarmed. 'Vina, what are you doing?' it asked with agitation and fear." I made my voice tremble slightly. "But Vina felt something remarkable. The strength of the two dreams merging inside her. Filled with this power, she meant to speak softly, but instead shouted, 'WAKE UP!'"

I slapped my hand against the arm of my chair, making Temper jump. His tail twitched in surprise.

"The reeds around her stirred and began to rise. 'It's working!' Vina thought. But only some responded. She needed more power. She needed help."

The sprinklers in Temper's garden shut off with a soft click. Water droplets clung to the rose petals, capturing miniature reflections of Falfsun's surface.

"With a mere thought, Vina traveled to the village where the other Magi swayed. A murmur rose from the people. 'Magus,' they whispered to one another."

I stood from my chair, assuming Vina's posture. "'People of the land,' she addressed them, 'War is upon us, but it doesn't need to happen. I have a plan to restore the river so no one can invade us. Sway where you are until I finish.'" I moved to the edge of the porch. "Not waiting for their response, she strode out to the middle of the river and declared, 'I am Magus. Send out your champion, or your Magus, or whatever you call him, or her, or it. I wish to talk.'"

I smiled. "*'Please don't let it be an it,'* Vina thought to herself."

Temper chuckled, his belly jiggling slightly.

"The other people stirred. Voices rose in support and encouragement, mixed with consternation and fear. A figure separated from the crowd and swayed out into the river toward Vina." I lowered my voice. "It was the boy who'd first met her. The same boy who'd tried to kill her. She considered fleeing but held her ground."

Temper's garden fell silent. Even the butterflies seemed to pause in their dance among the roses.

"The boy spoke. 'I am Magoi, keeper of the dream of my people. We've met before.'"

"'I know. You tried to kill me.'" I made my voice hard, unforgiving.

"Magoi bent his bulb in shame. 'Yes... I was angry with you. You stirred me into being awakened. I felt confused and frightened. Had it not been for the Mind and the previous Magoi, I would have killed myself. My anger and fear are gone now. I'm truly sorry for attacking you. I understand none of this is your fault. The Mind told me this happens every thousand reed lives.'"

I returned to my seat. "If Vina was surprised by this change in the boy, she didn't show it. 'War doesn't have to happen every thousand lives,' she told him. 'The wild reeds caused this. I believe that together, we can free the river.'"

"'The wildings sleep,' Magoi responded. 'There's nothing we can do.'"

"Vina wasn't deterred. 'We can try. I think we can convince them to join us in the dream if we work together. With our combined strength, they might hear us and listen.'"

Temper checked the time again, his brow furrowing. "I wonder where Joan is," he muttered, more to himself than to me.

"Should we pause here?" I asked. "We could go look for her if you're worried. She told me it might be a long time before she came back."

Seeing that I wasn't as concerned as he was, Temper urged me to continue.

"Magoi looked doubtful. "It would take a third of a harvest for us to travel there. My people won't wait that long before acting."

"My Magi have discovered a way to travel much faster. As a gift and proof of my friendship, let me teach it to you." Vina leaned over and touched Magoi. Together they disappeared.

At the wild reeds, Vina said, "Here is my plan. We both cross over to the other's side of the river. We both know what happens then. We become stronger with the help of the two dreams. Then, we wake up the reeds and the water will flow once again."

Magoi nodded and moved to Vina's side of the river. He felt the strength pulse through himself. To his surprise, his appearance didn't change the way it did when he had crossed to kill Vina. Vina noticed his surprise and said, "That's one of the benefits of being the Magoi. Your appearance doesn't change." She moved into position on his side of the river. Together they called out to the wild reeds. Nothing happened at first, and then, finally, the reeds responded. They lifted themselves up and the water flowed.

"Hurry!" Vina said. "We need to trade places! The reeds on your side must join your dream and my reeds mine!"

After they switched places Magoi asked, "What about the reeds in the middle, between the two minds? What will happen to them?"

"Would it hurt if we allowed them to intermingle and share our dreams? As a way of communicating between our lands?"

Magoi nodded. "No, I don't think that would hurt at all. And at the villages where we share the river? What could be done there?"

"Maybe we could exchange some of our harvests? The river is flowing, but not as fast as before. Maybe we could each grow out into the river and connect."

"As a bridge between us."

"The two Minds listened to Magus and Magoi talking, and they lost some of their fear of one another. For the first time in many thousands of reeds lives, they called out to one another, 'Hello.'"

Taking a big gulp of lemonade, I told Temper, "That's how it ended, and how it began again. I stayed with them for a while longer and saw the Minds reconcile with each other. A strong bridge was built between the lands and war became a thing of the past. I've established warning buoys around the entire star system restricting access to everyone but the Ethereans. There's nothing else of interest to anyone out there anyway. No habitable planets, and no rare metals that can't be found elsewhere. The dreaming reeds will be allowed to dream in peace."

Destiny

Temper said, "And it was the children, not the adults, who stopped the war."

"Children are capable of great things, if given the chance. It's sad that adults think otherwise," I said.

Temper shifted his weight and rubbed his chin as he contemplated my story.

"Dreamers who aren't aware that they're dreaming. It gives pause for thought. Who's to say that we aren't doing the same thing? We might be living our lives inside of the dream of a giant croc lying in the weeds, waiting for a caveman to wander on by," Temper chuckled.

"It would be better than being in the dream of a dung beetle as it rolled its ball of dung up a hill," I quipped.

Temper laughed, his belly shaking. "Or a dream where a god has to join farter's anonymous because she eats cabbage and farts all night long in her sleep."

"Well, that's just silly." I smoothed a wrinkle from my shirt, fighting a smile.

"It's not as silly as your dung beetle's dream. That's just gross."

My turn to laugh. "And listening to cabbage-induced farting all night long while you're trying to sleep isn't?"

Temper's snout crinkled as he grinned. "Fair point."

Temper studied me for a long moment, his dragon eyes reflecting Falfsun's glow. "So the reeds were living in a shared dream, unaware they were part of a greater consciousness."

"Exactly." I took the last sip of lemonade. "They thought they were separate beings with complete freedom."

"But they weren't," Temper mused. "They were actually connected at the roots, sharing the same nutrients, the same water."

The quantum butterfly that had been hovering near us finally settled on the arm of my chair, its wings shifting between existence and non-existence.

"It makes you wonder, doesn't it?" I said quietly. "About our own perceptions. What connections might exist beneath our awareness?"

Temper's tail curled thoughtfully beneath him. "Like Joan's hive mind, or the Ethereans, whose harmony might echo from a source deeper than thought or code."

"Or something even deeper." I watched the butterfly phase

161

through my fingers as I reached for it. "Maybe separation itself is the true illusion."

The thought lingered between us as Falfsun's surface churned below, a constant reminder of how a single consciousness, the star itself, could manifest as countless individual expressions of energy and light.

"You think about these things differently now," Temper observed. "Since connecting with Joan."

I nodded, unable to deny the truth of it. The hive mind connection had changed me, reshaping my understanding of identity and belonging. I was still Go David, still distinct, but also part of something that transcended individual existence.

"We're all dreaming together," I said finally. "Some of us are just beginning to wake up."

A comfortable silence settled between us. The butterflies continued their dance among the roses, their wings catching Falfsun's golden light. One particularly bold specimen fluttered over and landed on my knee, its translucent wings pulsing gently.

"Do you miss it?" Temper asked suddenly.

"Miss what?"

"Earth. The old days. Before all this." He pointed upward, where the sky roiled with vast crimson currents.

I considered the question, watching the butterfly take flight again. "Sometimes. I miss the simplicity of it. The feeling that we were just small creatures on a small planet, figuring things out as we went along."

"And now?"

"Now we're small creatures in a vast galaxy, still figuring things out." I smiled. "Just with better toys."

Temper snorted, a puff of steam escaping his nostrils. "Better toys indeed. Speaking of which, Alice Tracker called while you were away communing with the reeds. She wants to film a special episode of her cooking show here on Falfsun."

"The cooking show host? What does she want to cook on a star?"

"Solar-baked bread, apparently." Temper's expression was deadpan. "She thinks it'll be a hit. 'Baking with Stellar Energy: No Oven Required.'"

I burst out laughing. "You're joking."

"Only partly. She really did call. She wants to feature some of the unique ingredients we've engineered to grow in these conditions. Those spicy peppers that thrive on radiation, the metal-absorbing root vegetables."

"Ah, the famous dragon's breath peppers. Your pride and joy."

Temper's eyes gleamed. "They make humans cry and thrumans short-circuit. Perfect heat level, if you ask me." "So, what do you think about Alice Tracker coming here? Should I tell her yes?"

I considered the implications. Celebrity visits always complicated things, especially with our ongoing work to protect vulnerable systems from colonization. But how could I turn down the chance to cook with Alice Tracker? If she'd let me. Perhaps having someone like her showcase the sustainable adaptations we'd created could help shift public opinion.

"Why not? It might be good for people to see what we're doing out here. Just make sure she understands our restrictions on broadcasting quantum thread coordinates."

CHAPTER EIGHT

Cooking Under the Stars

I tapped my Planck Pulse, accessing the quantum thread that would lead me to Marcus and Bea. Their coordinates glowed softly on my wrist display, pulsing with invitation. Unlike the restricted threads I managed for the Ethereans, this one felt warm, personal. The familiar sensation of dimensional folding enveloped me as I stepped through.

The thread deposited me on a crescent of pearl-white sand. Two suns hung in the sky—one golden, one with a reddish tinge—casting dual shadows behind every object. Waves lapped gently against the shore, their rhythm hypnotic and soothing. Before me stood a sprawling structure of woven reeds and bamboo, elevated on stilts that rose from the turquoise water.

"Papa!"

Marcus spotted me first, sprinting across the sand. Though he'd grown into a distinguished thruman scientist, his enthusiasm on seeing me remained unchanged from the boy who once built towers with blocks. He wrapped me in a tight embrace, his laughter carrying across the beach.

"We weren't expecting you for another week," he said, pulling back to examine my face.

"I finished early with my patrol." I smiled, clasping his shoulder. "Thought I'd surprise you."

Bea appeared on the wraparound porch of their reed house, her silhouette framed by flowering vines that cascaded from the roof. "Go! What perfect timing."

She descended the wooden steps with grace, her scientific precision evident even in this casual movement. When she reached us, her embrace felt like coming home.

"Your place is beautiful," I said, taking in the sweeping ocean view. "This moon has treated you well."

"Wait until you see inside." Marcus took my arm, guiding me toward their home. "We've set up a lab that would make uncle Temper jealous."

The interior was airy and open, with reed walls that allowed the dual-sun light to filter through in dappled patterns. Scientific equipment sat alongside comfortable furniture, a perfect blend of their work and life.

Over dinner, freshly caught fish with fruits I didn't recognize, they shared their discoveries.

"We found something extraordinary," Bea said, activating a hologram above the table. A partially constructed sphere appeared, surrounding a dim red star. "It's a Dyson sphere, half-built and abandoned."

"No sign of who was building it?" I asked, studying the massive structure.

Marcus shook his head. "None. The construction stopped approximately eight thousand years ago, according to our dating methods. The builders simply... left."

"Or disappeared," Bea added. "We've been cataloging the construction techniques. Some of the materials don't match any known civilization in the Etherean database."

The hologram shifted to show a desert planet with near-perfect circular oases dotting its equator like a string of emerald beads.

"This was even more fascinating," Marcus continued. "The native species travel by rolling instead of walking. Their entire physiology evolved around it: specialized cartilage, flexible spines."

"No technological advancement?" I asked.

"Pre-industrial," Bea confirmed. "But their society is complex. They communicate through vibrations in the sand."

The hologram changed once more, revealing an enormous vessel drifting in the void.

"Our most recent find," Marcus said quietly. "A ghost ship from a civilization that, according to exposure dating, predates human space travel by at least forty thousand years."

"Empty?" I leaned forward, intrigued.

"Completely," Bea replied. "But intact, with systems still functioning. We've only begun to decipher their technology."

I nodded, impressed by their work. "You've been busy."

"What about you?" Marcus asked, refilling my glass with something sweet and fermented. "Last we heard, you were patrolling in your sector near the Outer Arm."

"I've been on Talos," I confirmed, sampling the drink. "A moon with sentient reeds that communicate through a shared dream state."

Their eyes widened with interest, and I smiled, settling in to tell them about Vina and the warring Minds of Talos.

After our dinner beneath the dual suns, I walked with Marcus and Bea along the shoreline. The waves whispered against the sand, leaving behind delicate shells that glimmered in the fading light.

"You know," I said, digging my toes into the cool sand, "Joan and I built a house on Falfsun."

Marcus looked up, his eyes brightening. "You've settled on the star?"

"As much as anyone can settle on a churning ball of plasma." I chuckled. "We found a stable zone near Temper. The house adapts to the solar currents, moves with them rather than against them."

Bea paused to examine a spiral shell, turning it over in her hands. "I've read uncle Temper's theoretical papers on star-surface habitation. The quantum stabilization alone must be fascinating."

"It's more than theory now." I created a small hologram from my Planck Pulse, showing them the flowing architecture of our home. "The walls breathe with the star. The gardens filter radiation into something beautiful."

Marcus circled the projection, studying it from all angles. "You built this?"

"Joan did most of the designing. I just provided occasional input about where to put the furniture." I smiled, remembering our playful arguments about spatial arrangement. "You should come visit. Both of you."

"To Falfsun?" Bea's voice held wonder and scientific curiosity.

"Why not? You've been exploring the far reaches of the galaxy. Our doorstep might be interesting for a change." I closed the hologram, meeting their eyes. "I miss you both."

Marcus nodded, a gentle understanding passing between us. "We miss you too, Papa."

"Then it's settled." I clapped my hands together. "Next month, after you finish cataloging your ghost ship."

"Is it safe?" Bea asked, practical as always.

"Perfectly. Your uncle Temper's been living there without incident. Your toolkits will protect you. Plus, we have quantum shields to prevent radiation exposure, and the gravity wells are calibrated for human comfort."

"Speaking of Temper," I continued, remembering our conversation on the porch, "he mentioned something interesting. Alice Tracker wants to film a cooking special on Falfsun."

"The Alice Tracker?" Marcus's eyes widened. "From Seasoned Table?"

I nodded, surprised by his reaction. "I remember watching her show with you when you were younger, but I never thought you cared that much."

Bea laughed. "He's obsessed. We've watched every episode."

Marcus shot her a look before turning to me. "I guess I didn't show it much back then, but her techniques for molecular gastronomy are fascinating from a scientific perspective."

"Of course they are." Bea winked at me.

"Well, she's coming to film next month. Temper thinks it might help showcase our sustainable adaptations to extreme environments." I picked up a smooth stone, skipping it across the water. "You could meet her if you visit then."

Marcus tried to maintain scientific dignity, but excitement broke through. "That would be... academically valuable."

"He means he'd be starstruck," Bea translated, squeezing his hand affectionately.

"Then it's perfect timing," I said. "You'll see our home and Marcus can get cooking tips from his culinary hero."

The twin suns had nearly set now, casting long shadows across the beach. In the gathering twilight, I felt a contentment I hadn't expected. My family was scattered across the stars, each pursuing their own path, but those paths could still converge.

"So it's settled?" I asked.

Marcus nodded eagerly. "We'll be there."

"With bells on," Bea added.

"Excellent." I smiled, already imagining showing them the radiation gardens.

As the pearl-white sands of the binary star beach faded from view, I guided Marcus and Bea through the quantum thread that led home. The dimensional folding enveloped us in that familiar embrace of non-space before depositing us on Falfsun's surface. The transition from cool ocean breeze to the controlled environment of our villa happened in an instant.

"Welcome to our humble abode," I said, watching their expressions as they took in their surroundings.

Marcus stepped forward, his mouth slightly open. "This isn't humble, Papa. This is... extraordinary."

Our Mediterranean villa stood before them, its stucco walls shimmering with subtle subatomic fluctuations. The terracotta roof tiles held the warmth of Falfsun, pulsing with energy that flowed through the entire structure. Bougainvillea cascaded over arched doorways in bursts of vibrant color that seemed to shift slightly when viewed from different angles.

"The entire structure exists in multiple dimensional states simultaneously," I explained, leading them along the path to the entrance. "Joan designed it to breathe with Falfsun's energy currents."

Bea ran her hand along the wall, her scientific curiosity evident. "The molecular cohesion should be impossible in these conditions."

"That's what makes it special." I smiled, placing my palm flat against the surface. The wall responded, warming slightly beneath my touch. "It doesn't fight against the star; it moves with it."

Inside, the villa opened into a central atrium where a fountain bubbled with water that defied gravity, flowing upward before cascading down in geometric patterns. The ceiling above revealed the churning sky of Falfsun, protected by multi-layered shielding that rendered the deadly plasma into a mesmerizing spectacle.

"How are we standing here?" Marcus asked, his voice hushed with wonder. "We're on the surface of a star."

"Quantum anchoring," I replied, enjoying their amazement. "The villa exists in a pocket of stabilized reality."

I guided them through an archway that seemed to stretch as we approached, leading into a room that felt both intimate and vast. Books lined shelves that curved impossibly, spiraling through the room in arcs that defied gravity and logic. Some shelves intersected without ever touching, their paths folding through one another like reflections in warped glass. Titles shimmered and shifted as we looked at them, some adapting to our thoughts, others vanishing before we could read them.

"This is the library," I explained. "Though 'library' doesn't quite capture it. The books contain knowledge from across multiple dimensions."

Marcus reached for a volume, then hesitated. "May I?"

"Of course."

He pulled a leather-bound book from the shelf. As he opened it, holographic images rose from the pages, showing star systems and nebulae from perspectives impossible to achieve from our universe alone.

"Papa, this is..." He trailed off, watching a supernova unfold above the pages.

The book pulsed faintly in his hands, its spine warming as if recognizing him. Words rearranged themselves mid-sentence, adapting to his questions before he could voice them. One image, a spiral galaxy, tilted toward him, as if offering a closer look.

Bea had wandered to another doorway, but as she stepped through, she suddenly reappeared from a corridor to our left. Her expression shifted from confusion to delight.

"The spaces are folded," she observed, trying again with the same result. "Fascinating."

"It takes some getting used to," I admitted. "The first week, I kept ending up in the garden when I was trying to find the kitchen."

I led them down a hallway where the floor seemed to slope upward while feeling perfectly level beneath our feet. The walls occasionally rippled with patterns that resembled neural networks, responding to our presence.

"The villa is partially sentient," I explained. "Not like a thruman consciousness, but aware in its own way. It learns your preferences, adjusts to your needs."

We emerged onto a terrace overlooking what appeared to be an impossible garden. Plants from a dozen worlds grew together in harmonious clusters, their colors shifting subtly as solar flares pulsed outside the quantum shield.

"The garden filters radiation," I said, gesturing to a particularly vibrant patch of silver-leafed vegetation. "Those plants convert gamma rays into nutrients."

Marcus knelt beside a flower that opened and closed in rhythm with his breathing. "This is Lunarian midnight bloom. How does it survive here?"

"The villa creates microclimates. That section mimics the atmospheric conditions of Europa's northern hemisphere."

Bea had moved to the edge of the terrace, where the boundary between inside and outside blurred. "The dimensional folding is most pronounced here," she noted, watching her hand seem to exist in multiple places at once.

"Joan calls it the threshold," I said, joining her. "It's where our reality meets Falfsun's native state."

I couldn't help but feel pride as they explored, asking questions, marveling at details I'd grown accustomed to. Playing host in our dimensional sanctuary filled me with a satisfaction I hadn't anticipated.

"There's something I want to show you," I said, leading them toward the heart of the villa. "Joan created it especially for visitors."

We entered a circular room where the walls rippled. At its center stood a three-dimensional map of the multiverse, countless parallel realities branching out in fractal patterns.

Marcus touched my arm. "Is Joan still gone, Papa?"

I nodded, watching the quantum streams flow through the

holographic display. "She's spelunking through dimensional wormholes. Exploring paths between realities that even our most advanced sensors can't map."

"Isn't that dangerous?" Bea studied a particularly complex intersection of timelines.

"Joan has more experience than anyone navigating quantum spaces." The map shifted, revealing new connections. "She's been doing this since before humanity discovered fire."

Marcus frowned. "How long will she be gone?"

"She said it might be years." The words felt heavy in my mouth. "The deeper dimensions operate on different temporal scales. What feels like months to her could be years here, or vice versa."

I touched a glowing strand of possibility, watching it split into a thousand potential futures. "But I hope it won't be that long."

"You miss her."

"Every day." I smiled, remembering our last conversation. "But Joan needs this. Some mysteries can only be solved by diving into the deepest seams of reality."

The map pulsed with new data, countless realities shifting and realigning. Somewhere in that infinite maze of possibility, Joan explored paths no one else could follow. I had to trust she'd find her way back when she was ready.

"Besides," I added, "she left me with enough puzzles in this house to keep me occupied for centuries."

Marcus laughed. "Like the bathroom that occasionally decides to relocate itself?"

"Exactly." I grinned. "Though I've mostly figured out its pattern now. It follows the field distortions in Falfsun's corona."

Bea touched my shoulder, her expression gentle. "She'll come back."

"I know." And I did know, with a certainty that transcended ordinary faith. Joan and I existed beyond conventional space and time. Our connection would endure, no matter how far she wandered through the quantum foam.

The multiverse map continued to shimmer as we stood in contemplation. Our conversation about Joan's journeys through folded realities left a thoughtful silence hanging in the air. I watched

Marcus and Bea study the intricate patterns, their faces illuminated by the glowing strands of possibility.

A soft chime resonated through the villa, vibrating in a pattern felt more than heard.

"Someone's at the threshold," I explained, turning toward the main entrance. "The villa's way of announcing visitors."

The three of us navigated through the folding corridors, which seemed to cooperate more than usual, guiding us efficiently to the front of the house. As we approached, the door rippled, then solidified into a more conventional appearance.

Temper stood on our doorstep, his red dragon form catching the chromatic waves of Falfsun's surface. His tail swished back and forth, creating small eddies in the quantum field surrounding the villa.

"I thought I'd check in on our guests," he announced, his dragon eyes crinkling with warmth. "Make sure Go hasn't gotten you lost in one of the bathroom dimensions."

"We've managed to avoid any interdimensional plumbing incidents so far," I replied, stepping aside to welcome him in. "Perfect timing, actually. Marcus was just about to ask about your solar research."

Temper's belly rumbled with a sound between a laugh and a purr. "Was he now? Convenient that I brought visual aids."

He produced a small device from somewhere within his bumpy red folds, tossing it into the air where it expanded into a floating holographic display of Falfsun's internal structure.

Marcus moved forward immediately, his scientific curiosity overtaking any hesitation. "You've mapped the convection currents all the way to the core?"

"Down to the edge where matter forms," Temper confirmed, his clawed finger tracing a particularly complex pattern of plasma flow. "The traditional models couldn't explain the stability zones we've discovered."

The hologram zoomed in, revealing microscopic structures that resembled plasmaglyphs forming and dissolving within the stellar plasma.

"Encoded patterns in a star's core should be impossible," Bea noted, circling the display. "The temperature alone would prevent atomic cohesion."

"That's what makes Falfsun unique." Temper expanded another section of the model. "These structures create temporary stability pockets throughout its stellar body. They're what allow structures like Go's villa to exist here at all."

Marcus studied the patterns intently. "The plasma tessellations follow a mathematical sequence I've never seen before."

"Because it's not from our universe," Temper explained. "The physics here blend with rules from adjacent dimensional planes."

I watched them slip into a rhythm, their minds sparking against the strange logic of Falfsun. Marcus dissected the plasma tessellations with surgical precision, probing the limits of stellar formation theory. Bea sketched dimensional overlays in the air, proposing models that bent known physics to accommodate the villa's improbable existence. Temper responded with a kind of gleeful gravity, his claws dancing across the hologram as he matched their curiosity with revelations drawn from the star's encoded depths.

Their conversation continued into general quantum physics and theoretical astronomy, touching on dimensional mechanics and the unique properties of stars in different realities. The holographic model shifted and expanded with their discussion, revealing layers of complexity that even I had never fully appreciated.

"The convection cycle creates what we call 'field fractures,'" Temper was explaining, highlighting swirling patterns near Falfsun's surface. "These are essentially blind spots in conventional physics where alternative rules apply."

"That's where you built your home," Marcus realized, looking at me with new understanding.

"Exactly." I nodded. "Joan identified the pattern and designed the villa to synchronize with it."

The conversation paused as Temper's stomach emitted a rumble loud enough to momentarily disrupt the hologram.

"Speaking of patterns," he said, not the least bit embarrassed, "it's approaching what we arbitrarily call 'dinner time' here. Shall we move this discussion to the kitchen?"

The kitchen materialized around us as the villa responded to our intentions, walls flowing into existence with cabinets and countertops assembling themselves from quantum particles.

"I wonder if I'll ever get used to that," Bea murmured.

Temper moved to the central island with surprising grace for his dragon form. "Go, do you still have those root vegetables from your last visit to Requiem Prime?"

I retrieved a container of purple-blue tubers from a cabinet that hadn't been there moments before. "Fresh as the day I picked them."

"Perfect." Temper took them, turning one slowly in his clawed hand. Its skin shimmered with a subtle internal geometry; braided muscle wrapped in glass, pulsing faintly as if it still remembered the rhythm of the soil. He examined the veinwork spirals for signs of decay, then gave a satisfied nod. "Marcus, you mentioned an interest in culinary science earlier. Let me share some wisdom."

He placed the tubers on the counter and gestured with theatrical precision. "When preparing produce from phase-volatile ecosystems, remember this: the microwave is your friend. Thirty seconds at full power stabilizes their molecular drift and locks in the flavor before it decides to taste like something else entirely."

He tapped one of the tubers, which gave a faint shimmer in response. "If you skip this step, they'll keep adapting, sweet one moment, metallic the next. Worst case, they try to mimic your memories of food. That never ends well."

Marcus blinked. "That can't possibly be correct."

"Of course it is," Temper insisted, his dragon features arranged in complete seriousness. "And if the vegetables start levitating, that just means they're done. No need for a timer when you've got antigravity as an indicator."

I caught Bea's eye across the kitchen, and we shared a silent laugh. Some things never changed, no matter how many dimensions you traveled through. Temper's cooking tips remained as gloriously absurd as ever.

Our laughter faded into comfortable silence. Marcus examined the purple tubers with scientific curiosity rather than culinary interest, when the villa's communication system chimed with a distinctive three-note sequence.

"They're here early," I said, checking the exterior feeds.

Through the villa's monitoring system, I could see a flurry of activity on Temper's front lawn. A dozen crew members in matching navy jumpsuits with "Seasoned Table" emblazoned across their backs hustled equipment from a sleek transport vehicle. At the center of the chaos stood a portable kitchen that seemed impossibly out of place against the churning surface of Falfsun visible beyond Temper's property.

"The Alice Tracker production team has arrived," I announced. "They're setting up on your lawn, Temper."

Temper's dragon eyes widened. "Already? I thought we had another day." He peered over my shoulder at the feed.

Marcus pressed closer. "Is that really Alice Tracker? The Alice Tracker?"

"In the flesh," I confirmed. "Well, not yet. That's just her advance team."

We watched as a woman with a clipboard directed the placement of cooking stations, cameras, and lighting equipment designed to withstand Falfsun's radiation. The demo kitchen took shape piece by piece: gleaming countertops, a state-of-the-art oven, and a refrigerator that seemed to shimmer with protective fields.

"We should go greet them," Temper said, already moving toward the door. "Make sure they understand the safety protocols."

The four of us made our way along the flame crest path linking our villa to Temper's property, arriving at his lawn just as a frazzled production assistant pored over a tablet brimming with safety alerts.

"Absolutely not," the assistant was saying to another crew member. "The chef cannot stand that close to the edge. The containment field only extends three meters from the fence line."

Temper cleared his throat, causing both humans to jump. "Perhaps I can help clarify the safety parameters."

The assistant's eyes widened at the sight of Temper's dragon form. "You must be Dr. Tom." He extended a hand, then seemed to reconsider whether dragons shook hands. "We have some concerns about Chef Tracker's safety during filming."

"As you should," Temper replied. "Falfsun isn't exactly a conventional filming location."

A woman with short gray hair and an air of authority approached, tablet in hand. "You're the solar physicist?" She didn't wait for confirmation. "Our insurance underwriters are having collective heart attacks. How exactly do you plan to keep Alice safe?

She doesn't have a Planck toolkit like you Ethereans."

"A valid concern," Temper acknowledged. "We've established three redundant safety systems. First, this entire area exists within a quantum stability field anchored to a permanent eddy in Falfsun's convection current. Second, we've installed radiation shields calibrated specifically for human physiology. And third, I've personally programmed an emergency evacuation protocol that can transport everyone to orbit in 0.03 seconds if needed."

The producer frowned. "What about solar flares? Our research indicates Falfsun experiences unpredictable eruptions."

"We have predictive algorithms monitoring stellar activity," I interjected. "Any potential flare will be detected minutes before it forms, giving us ample time to react."

The producer studied me. "And you are?"

"Go David. Former captain of Paradise, current Etherean enforcement officer."

Her expression shifted to recognition. "You're on the call sheet. Alice specifically requested you for the segment on sustainable adaptation."

I couldn't help the smile that spread across my face. "She did?"

Marcus nudged me. "You didn't mention you'd be on the show."

"It wasn't confirmed," I said, though I'd been hoping for it since the initial contact. "Just a possibility."

"A probability now," the producer corrected, tapping a note into her tablet. "We'll need you for the third segment, after Alice prepares the stellar fusion cuisine."

Marcus's expression flickered between admiration and something more private. "You're going to be on Seasoned Table?"

"Just a brief appearance," I said, trying to temper my excitement. "Nothing special."

"Papa's going to be famous," he said, eyes crinkling with genuine delight. "They always pair the cooking segments with frontier tech. Your work on adaptive environments would be perfect alongside Alice's fusion cuisine. Quantum habitation and quantum gastronomy, side by side."

Always the scientist, my son. Even in his excitement about meeting Alice Tracker, his mind spun toward practical applications and thematic synergy. I remembered the serious little thruman who once sorted building blocks by size and color, mapping patterns where others saw only toys.

"Maybe we could collaborate on something," I offered, watching his face brighten even more.

Before he could respond, the producer cut in. "We need to finish setup before Chef Tracker arrives. Her shuttle lands in forty minutes." She turned to Temper. "Would you mind doing a safety walkthrough with our tech team? They need a full briefing on the quantum stabilization field's parameters."

As Temper led the technical crew toward the edge of his property, I pulled Marcus aside.

"You know, Alice is always looking for experts in unusual fields. A thruman scientist studying ghost ships and possible alien cuisine would make for fascinating television."

His eyes brightened. "You think she'd be interested?"

"I could mention it during my segment," I offered. "She values authentic perspectives."

Marcus's expression softened. "You don't have to do that."

"I want to. Besides, you're the one with the groundbreaking research. I'm just here to talk about living on a star."

Around us, the production team continued their preparations, transforming Temper's lawn into a surreal cooking set. The white picket fence gleamed against the churning backdrop of Falfsun's surface, creating an impossible juxtaposition of suburban comfort and cosmic power.

I watched the controlled chaos with growing anticipation. After decades of isolation and months of quiet enforcement work, the prospect of sharing our unique lifestyle with the wider galaxy filled me with unexpected joy.

The production team's frantic preparations quieted as a low hum filled the air. Above Temper's property, a sleek shuttle descended through the containment field, its hull glimmering with protective coatings designed to withstand Falfsun's radiation. The vessel touched down on the landing pad with barely a whisper, its dampeners absorbing any impact.

Marcus grabbed my arm. "She's here."

I nodded, suddenly aware of the flutter in my stomach. Centuries of life hadn't prepared me for the simple nervousness of meeting a celebrity.

The shuttle's door slid open with a soft hiss, releasing a burst of climate-controlled air into Falfsun's carefully modulated atmosphere. A moment of anticipation hung in the air before Alice Tracker stepped into view.

She paused at the threshold, taking in the impossible scene before her: a picket-fenced yard floating on the surface of a star. Her expression shifted from professional poise to genuine wonder.

"Now this," she announced to no one in particular, "is what I call a kitchen with a view."

The production team laughed, tension breaking. Alice descended the ramp with confident steps, her chef's coat gleaming white against the roiling backdrop of Falfsun's surface. She moved with the easy grace of someone accustomed to cameras, her eyes taking in every detail of the setup.

Temper stepped forward, his dragon form drawing her immediate attention.

"Dr. Tom." She extended her hand without hesitation. "Your research on stellar nucleosynthesis revolutionized my approach to fusion cuisine."

Temper took her hand carefully between his claws. "Please, call me Temper."

"Only if you'll call me Alice." Her smile was warm and genuine. "I've been studying your papers on plasma containment for months preparing for this episode."

"I'm flattered," Temper rumbled, his dragon features arranging themselves into something approximating modesty.

Alice turned, spotting me and Marcus. "And you must be Go David and Marcus." She approached us with the same warmth she'd shown Temper. "The Etherean who built a home on a star and the thruman scientist. This episode is already writing itself."

I found myself smiling back. "We're honored to be part of it."

"The honor is mine," she insisted. "It's not every day I get to cook on the surface of a star with the pioneers who made it possible."

The producer approached, clipboard in hand. "We're ready for the opening segment whenever you are, Alice."

"Perfect." Alice clapped her hands together. "Let's get cooking before my ingredients decide to quantum tunnel their way back to the ship."

As the crew made final adjustments to cameras and lighting, Alice leaned closer to us. "The network nearly canceled this episode. Too dangerous, they said." She winked. "But I told them some recipes are worth the risk."

Temper leaned toward me, his voice a low rumble. "If her soufflé starts to collapse, she should just increase the gravity field around it. Works every time."

I suppressed a laugh as Alice was fitted with a microphone.

"Go," she called, "I'd like you to join me for the third segment. We'll discuss sustainable living while I prepare the stellar fusion dessert."

My heart skipped. "I'd be happy to."

"Excellent." She turned to the cameras with practiced ease. "Just be yourself. The audience loves authenticity."

The producer called for quiet. Alice took her position at the demo kitchen, the impossible backdrop of Falfsun's surface churning behind her. Lights adjusted, cameras focused.

"Rolling in three, two..." The producer pointed silently.

Alice's posture shifted subtly, her presence expanding to fill the frame. "Welcome to a very special episode of Seasoned Table, where today we're cooking with the stars." She paused, gesturing to the cosmic panorama behind her. "Quite literally."

Alice surveyed the ingredients laid out on the demo kitchen counter, her expression shifting from professional assessment to childlike wonder. Her fingers hovered over the Dragon's Breath Peppers, which glowed faintly with stored radiation.

"These are magnificent," she said, lifting one carefully. "The genetic enhancements allow them to absorb solar energy without combusting."

"Unlike my first attempt at growing them," Temper admitted. "Lost half my garden when they spontaneously ignited."

Alice laughed, a warm sound that somehow cut through the constant background roar of Falfsun's surface. She reached for the Fusion Fruit next, its iridescent skin pulsing with contained energy.

"The secret is in the timing," she explained to the camera. "Cut these too early, and the flavor molecules haven't fully formed. Too late, and they'll literally explode with ripeness."

Temper sidled closer, his dragon form casting a shadow over the cooking station. "If your ingredients start levitating, just stir faster. Basic quantum cooking principles."

Alice shot him an amused glance before turning back to her preparation. "For our Plasma-Roasted Solar Spice Chicken, we'll begin with the marinade."

She worked with practiced efficiency, her hands moving in a choreographed dance across the ingredients. The Starflame Oil poured like liquid gold into the mixing bowl, catching the light from Falfsun's surface in hypnotic patterns.

"The metal-absorbing root vegetables need special handling," she continued, demonstrating how to slice them. "They naturally extract trace elements from soil, but here on Falfsun, they'll try to pull metals from your knife. I'm using a ceramic blade for that reason."

The marinade came together in a swirl of colors: the deep crimson of the Dragon's Breath extract, the golden sheen of Starflame Oil, and the shimmering particles of Cosmic Salt catching light like microscopic stars.

"Go, would you mind demonstrating how you use your toolkit to maintain the perfect cooking temperature?" Alice asked, gesturing me forward.

I stepped up beside her, suddenly aware of the cameras tracking my movement. My fingers brushed the Planck interface at my wrist, and I felt its familiar response: a slight warming as it connected with my neural pathways.

"The trick is precision," I explained, extending my hand over the cooking surface. "We're looking for plasma-edge temperatures that sear without vaporizing."

A translucent control panel materialized above my palm, and I adjusted the settings with practiced movements. The cooking surface glowed, a controlled fusion reaction dancing just below its surface.

"Perfect," Alice said, placing the marinated chicken onto the grill. It sizzled dramatically, drawing appreciative murmurs from the crew.

"The Planck toolkit lets us harness Falfsun's energy directly," I continued, growing more comfortable in front of the cameras. "We're essentially cooking with a tiny fragment of star."

"The sun is basically one big oven," Temper interjected. "No need for preheating."

Alice laughed outright. "I might borrow that line for my next cookbook."

She turned the chicken with expert timing, revealing perfect sear marks on its surface. The aroma that rose from the grill was intoxicating, spicy, complex, with hints of elements that had no earthly equivalent.

"To finish the dish," Alice continued, "we'll add our fusion fruit salsa. The heat activates the flavor compounds in a rather spectacular way."

She spooned the colorful mixture over the chicken, and the reaction was immediate. Tiny flashes of light popped across the surface of the dish, like miniature fireworks celebrating the union of ingredients.

"Now that," I said with genuine admiration, "is cooking with stars."

Alice beamed at the camera, her chef's coat gleaming against Falfsun's backdrop. "And there you have it, friends. Plasma-Roasted Solar Spice Chicken with Fusion Fruit Salsa, prepared on the surface of a living star." She arranged the final garnish with expert precision. "Join us after the break when Go David shares his journey from starship captain to stellar homesteader, while we create our Quantum Soufflé dessert."

"Cut!" The director's voice broke the spell. "That's perfect for segment one."

The production team erupted into activity. Lighting technicians adjusted their equipment while assistants rushed to prepare for the next segment. Alice stepped back from the cooking station, accepting a towel from her assistant to dab her brow.

"That was magnificent," she said, turning to Temper. "Your commentary added exactly the right touch of humor."

Temper's dragon features arranged themselves into something approximating modesty. "Just sharing my culinary wisdom. If the soufflé collapses, you can always call it 'deconstructed.'"

Alice laughed, a genuine sound that carried across the yard. "I might need to have you on as a regular guest. 'Cooking Tips from a Dragon' could be our new segment."

The producer approached with a tablet. "We've got fifteen minutes before we need to set up for segment two. The network is already getting viewer reactions. They love the location."

Marcus sidled up beside me. "You were great, Papa."

"I barely said anything."

"But you looked natural doing it." He grinned. "Who knew enforcement officers had such screen presence?"

The assistant director called for the crew to take a break, and Alice turned to us. "Would you all like to try what we've made? It seems a shame to let it cool."

"I thought you'd never ask," Temper rumbled, already moving toward the table.

The production team had set up a dining area at the edge of the yard, where the churning surface of Falfsun provided a mesmerizing backdrop. We gathered around as Alice served portions of the still-sizzling dish.

"The Fusion Fruit continues to react with the spices," she explained, pointing to tiny flickers of light still dancing across the surface of the chicken. "Each bite will be slightly different as the flavors evolve."

I took my first bite and nearly closed my eyes in pleasure. The chicken was perfectly tender, infused with complex flavors that shifted and changed on my tongue. The heat from the Dragon's Breath Peppers built slowly, balanced by the sweet-tart explosion of the Fusion Fruit.

"This is extraordinary," I said. "You've captured the essence of Falfsun in food form."

Alice looked genuinely pleased. "That's exactly what I was aiming for. Food should tell a story about its place of origin."

Temper, who had already devoured half his portion, nodded enthusiastically. "The way you've balanced the elemental flavors with the quantum-infused spices... it's like eating science."

"High praise from a physicist," Alice replied, raising her glass in a toast. "To new friendships forged in stellar fire."

We clinked glasses, the simple ritual somehow more meaningful against the impossible backdrop of our star-bound home. Around us, the production crew relaxed, their initial nervousness about filming on Falfsun giving way to wonder.

"I've filmed in some remarkable locations," Alice said, gazing out at the roiling surface beyond our protective field, "but nothing compares to this. You've created something truly special here."

"We've adapted," I said simply. "Found ways to live in harmony with forces most would consider hostile."

Alice nodded thoughtfully. "That's what I want viewers to take away from this episode. Not just exotic recipes, but the human capacity to find home in the most unexpected places."

The assistant director approached, signaling that our break was coming to an end. "Five minutes until we reset for segment two, Chef."

As the production crew packed their equipment, Alice approached me one last time.

"You know," she said, her voice lowered confidentially, "I've been cooking across seventeen systems, and I've never seen anything quite like what's happening here."

"The star?" I asked, glancing toward Falfsun's churning surface beyond Temper's fence.

She shook her head. "The convergence. Humans, thrumans, beings like Joan, all finding new ways to exist together." She gestured toward Marcus and Bea, who were helping dismantle a lighting rig. "That's the real recipe worth sharing."

I smiled, appreciating her insight. "It wasn't planned this way."

We clinked glasses again, the sound ringing bright against the vastness around us, a fragile note of celebration suspended in the immensity of Falfsun's light. For a moment, the impossible backdrop of our star-bound home felt less like a frontier and more like a hearth, its churning surface transformed into something almost domestic by the simple act of shared company.

The laughter carried easily, weaving with the shifting flavors on our tongues, with the glow of the fusion fruit still sparking faintly across the dishes. It was as if the star itself had joined the feast, lending its restless energy to our gathering.

As the crew reset for the next segment, I let myself breathe in the warmth of it all, the clatter of equipment softened by camaraderie, the mingling of voices, the quiet miracle of convergence. Whatever challenges awaited beyond Falfsun, tonight we had found something worth keeping: a shared table, a shared story, and the quiet joy of belonging.

And in that moment, I realized that harmony need not be planned or imposed, it could arise naturally, like flavor unfolding in a dish, or light shimmering across a star's surface. It was enough to sit together, to taste, to remember, and to know that even here, on the edge of the impossible, we had made a home.

CHAPTER NINE

A Message from the Stars

My planck pulse chimed with Marcus's familiar signal. I swiped it open to find his excited face filling the screen.

"Papa! You need to see this."

His enthusiasm pulled me from my morning patrol. "What am I looking at?"

The camera panned across what appeared to be an enormous control room. Sleek, curved consoles stretched in concentric rings around a central pillar that pulsed with soft light. The architecture curved like frozen liquid, organic yet precise.

"Remember that ghost ship we mentioned during dinner? We've managed to activate its navigation system."

Bea's voice called from somewhere off-screen. "Show him the star charts!"

Marcus gestured, and holographic projections bloomed around him, filling the space with three-dimensional star maps unlike any I'd seen before.

"Their stellar cartography is extraordinary," he said. "They mapped regions we haven't even reached yet, including detailed renderings of systems beyond the galactic rim. But what's most intriguing are the embedded coordinates, recurring patterns that all point toward the galactic bulge. We're still working to decipher their meaning."

"Any indication of where they came from? Or where they were going?"

"That's the fascinating part." Bea appeared beside Marcus, her eyes bright with discovery. "According to our preliminary translations, they were explorers, not colonizers. They documented thousands of worlds without ever settling them."

"Peaceful observers," I murmured.

"Exactly." Marcus nodded. "And they left behind observation posts throughout the galaxy. We've identified coordinates for twenty-three of them."

"The technology is centuries beyond anything in the Etherean archives," Bea added. "Yet somehow familiar, as though they understood universal principles we're only beginning to grasp."

I leaned closer to the screen. "Any signs of what happened to them?"

"None." Marcus's expression grew somber. "The ship's logs simply end. No distress signals, no final entries. It's as if they simply... moved on."

"Or ascended to another plane of existence," Bea suggested. "The ship's meditation chambers contain noetic harmonizers, devices that may have been designed to tune consciousness beyond ordinary perception."

The implications were staggering. "I'll arrange for additional security protocols around your research station. This discovery could change our understanding of galactic history."

"We've already implemented triple-layered encryption," Marcus assured me. "No one accesses this data without our authorization."

A surge of emotion filled my chest. The boy who once played with building blocks now safeguarded knowledge that could reshape civilization's future.

"We'll visit next week with our initial findings," Bea promised. "And don't forget about Celesticon! We need to coordinate our costumes."

After saying goodbye, I materialized on the porch of my villa. Falfsun's surface churned below, constant yet ever-changing, much like my thoughts after seeing Marcus and Bea's discovery.

Patterns in the charts. Coordinates embedded in alien cartography. All pointing toward the galactic bulge.

I eased into one of the rocking chairs that shouldn't exist on a star's surface. *Not random. Not noise. Breadcrumbs. But breadcrumbs to what?*

The thought lingered, luminous. *An entire civilization, crossing the galaxy not to conquer, not to settle, but simply to observe. To watch. To record. To leave markers for no other reason than the act of seeing.*

I pictured them moving from system to system, documenting thousands of worlds, then moving on again. *Peaceful observers. Voyagers of curiosity. Architects not of power, but of memory.*

The idea filled me with wonder. *What kind of people devote themselves to observation alone? What did they hope to find? Or was the finding itself enough?*

Falfsun's surface roiled, mirroring the churn inside me. *They left posts scattered across the galaxy, silent witnesses to the passage of stars. No distress calls, no endings. Just... departure. As if the act of seeing had carried them beyond.*

What were they trying to tell me? What did they hope I would see? Show me...

I breathed the thought like a prayer: *Let me understand.*

And silence answered me.

I sent Marcus and Bea's findings to Temper, knowing the next voice to break that silence might be his.

Later that day, Temper waited on his front lawn; a baseball mitt clutched awkwardly in his clawed hand. The grass beneath his feet remained perpetually green despite growing directly on a star, protected by the same substrate foundation that shielded our homes.

"Ready for our weekly humiliation?" he called.

I tossed the baseball into the air, catching it with practiced ease. "Speak for yourself. I was junior league champion three years running."

"A hundred years ago," Temper countered, his dragon tail swishing behind him.

I wound up and pitched. The ball sailed in a perfect arc toward Temper, who lunged forward confidently. At the last second, his tail shifted his center of gravity, sending him toppling forward as the ball sailed over his head.

"That's seven straight misses," I laughed, jogging to retrieve the ball. "Maybe we should add a tail to the official rules as a handicap."

"I maintain it's the variable gravity fields causing unpredictable trajectories," Temper insisted, his dragon eyes narrowing. "The ball's path curved 0.37 degrees more than it should have according to standard Newtonian calculations."

"Of course it did," I replied, unable to suppress a smile. "Nothing to do with your claws being the wrong shape for a baseball mitt."

Temper snorted, a small flame escaping his nostrils. "My claws are perfectly adapted for precision tasks. I can manipulate quantum filaments accurate to the femtometer scale."

"But not catch a baseball."

His tail thumped against the grass. "I've recalibrated my approach. Next throw, I'll demonstrate a 76% improvement in technique."

This was the Temper I knew, the brilliant mind that could never resist quantifying even the most casual activities. Despite his dragon form, despite our strange existence on a star's surface, some things remained wonderfully consistent.

After retrieving the ball, I settled beside him on the lawn. Falfsun's surface rippled beyond our protective field, waves of plasma dancing like liquid fire.

"Have you decided on your costume for Celesticon?" I asked.

Temper groaned. "I'm torn between Aezzar from Skyborn Legacy or Vharos from The Last Flame. Classic dragons seem too obvious for someone who actually is one."

"What about something unexpected? Like Oryn-9 from Echo Star? The contrast would be hilarious."

"A red dragon in an avian mimicry suit pretending to be a sparrow?" Temper snorted. "I weigh six tons. What about you?"

I shrugged. "I was thinking Captain Drell from Frontier Void, but everyone does that. Maybe Zek Tolar from Nebula Hustle? Similar vibe but less common."

"Both smugglers with questionable morals and quick wits." Temper nudged me with his elbow. "Not exactly stretching your acting abilities."

"Fine. What would you suggest?"

Temper's eyes gleamed mischievously. "Tarian Vex from Prime Ascendant. Stoic, strategic, emotionally detached."

"The absolute opposite of me, you mean?"

"Precisely. Though you'd have to commit to the ocular implants and the neural resonance patterns."

I pictured myself adjusting my expressionless gaze, reciting lines about logical conquest and calculated diplomacy. "Bea mentioned going as Selara from Starborn Pact."

"Perfect for her," Temper nodded. "And Marcus?"

"Knowing him, something obscure that'll have us all explaining his costume to everyone we meet."

Temper stepped back, winding up for another throw. His dragon form gave him surprising strength, but coordination remained a challenge. The mitt slipped awkwardly between his clawed fingers as he attempted to position himself.

"I've been thinking about those explorers Marcus mentioned," I said, crouching into a catcher's stance. "An entire civilization that chose to observe rather than conquer."

"Fascinating, isn't it?" Temper's eyes narrowed in concentration. "Ready?"

He reared back, his tail whipping behind him for balance. The motion looked promising until the final release, when his claws snagged on the ball. It sailed upward at a sharp angle, arcing high above our protective field.

"Damn gravity fields," Temper groaned.

We both watched as the baseball reached its apex, hung suspended for a heartbeat, then began its descent. It breached the quantum barrier with a faint shimmer and plunged toward Falfsun's churning surface.

The ball didn't burn immediately. For three seconds, it maintained its form, spinning through the superheated atmosphere. Then the leather blackened, curled, and erupted into flame. The stitching glowed white-hot before disintegrating. What remained of the core sank into the roiling plasma, leaving behind a brief, circular ripple that the star's surface swallowed without ceremony.

"Go get the ball," Temper said, his voice deadpan.

I raised an eyebrow. "What ball?"

The last fragments vanished beneath waves of liquid fire. Nothing remained, not even ash.

"That's the third one this month," I sighed. "We'll need to buy more in town."

"Or invent a game that doesn't involve throwing things over the quantum fence." Temper settled onto the grass, his bulk creating a dragon-shaped depression. "Checkers, perhaps. Less combustible."

I sat beside him, watching Falfsun's surface undulate beyond our sanctuary. "Strange to think about it. This baseball, something so ordinary, lasting less than five seconds out there. Yet here we sit, having a conversation on the surface of a star."

"Quantum fields are remarkable things," Temper agreed. "Though sometimes I wonder if we're tempting fate, living here."

The plasma rolled and churned just meters away, powerful enough to vaporize entire planets. Our existence here was maintained by a delicate balance of forces, equations, and energy. One fluctuation in the field generators, one power surge or failure, and we'd join that baseball in oblivion.

"We should practice in the simulator," I suggested. "Same game, fewer casualties."

Temper snorted, a small flame flickering between his nostrils. "Where's the fun in that? The risk makes it exciting."

"Says the dragon who just incinerated our last regulation baseball."

"Technical difficulties." He waved a claw dismissively. "Besides, I'm improving. Last time I lost two balls in one session."

I glanced at the spot where the baseball had disappeared. "Progress indeed."

Falfsun's surface bubbled and twisted, indifferent to our tiny loss. Stars consumed matter constantly; one baseball meant nothing in the grand scheme. Yet I couldn't help feeling a pang of regret watching it vanish, a small piece of Earth tradition obliterated in an instant.

"I suppose I should head back," Temper said, rising to his feet. "I'm tracking fusion blooms from Falfsun's inner shell. They're evolving faster than expected."

"And I promised Joan I'd help calibrate the new tunnel stabilizers while she's gone. But first, I'm on patrol."

We walked toward our homes, leaving behind his front lawn where our game had prematurely ended.

I waved goodbye to Temper, leaving him to his simulations. One moment I stood on the surface of Falfsun, and the next I activated my Planck toolkit, feeling the familiar quantum gravity pull as space folded around me.

The sensation never quite became routine. My stomach lurched as I fell through the void between stars, the galaxy stretching into streaks of light. Three seconds of vertigo, then stability as I materialized in Sector 7, my assigned patrol zone for the month.

Eight months had passed since Alice Tracker's cooking show aired. The episode had become unexpectedly popular, sparking a tourism boom to Falfsun. Temper had grown weary of curious visitors and their endless questions about living on a star. I found the whole situation amusing, especially when tourists attempted to recreate Alice's recipes using regular ovens instead of stellar plasma.

I adjusted my toolkit settings, scanning the sector for unauthorized energy signatures. The familiar holographic display spread before me, showing thirty-seven star systems within my jurisdiction. Three required closer inspection.

My first target appeared on the scanner: an unregistered ship in orbit around Kepler-186f. I input coordinates, braced myself, and activated another gravity pull. The universe compressed, expanded, then settled. The colonizer ship hung before me, sleek and predatory with industrial terraforming equipment mounted on its hull.

I opened a communication channel. "Unregistered vessel, this is Etherean Enforcement. You are in violation of Galactic Court preservation statutes. Power down and prepare for inspection."

"We have legal claim to this world," a voice responded, tense with defiance. "Our survey team found no intelligent life."

"Microbiological diversity is protected under Section 12 of the Preservation Act," I replied, transmitting the relevant documentation. "This world contains seventy-three unique extremophile species with potential medical applications."

The ship's engines flared to life. They always ran. I sighed, activated my toolkit, and generated a targeted gravity well directly in their path. The colonizer ship lurched forward, then froze as competing gravitational forces seized it.

"That was unwise," I said, amplifying the gravity well. "Your ship is being redirected to Earth for legal processing."

Their protests turned to screams as I programmed Earth coordinates into the gravity well. The ship vanished with a flash, its crew experiencing the same stomach-dropping sensation I'd almost grown accustomed to. They'd arrive shaken but unharmed, facing fines and possible license revocation.

I checked two more systems before my shift ended. One contained a legitimate research outpost with proper permits. The other harbored a mining operation attempting to extract rare minerals from a protected asteroid belt. They joined the first ship in transit to Earth's orbital court.

As I prepared to return home, I paused in the silence of deep space. Stars surrounded me, countless points of light representing worlds I would never visit. Before the Planck toolkit, before Carpisma's contract, such vastness would have overwhelmed me. Now it felt like my backyard, familiar territory to patrol and protect.

Time moved differently for us now. Weeks had blended into months. Joan had disappeared on her dimensional explorations. Marcus and Bea continued their research, occasionally visiting with discoveries that expanded our understanding of the universe.

And I patrolled. Three times weekly, eight-hour shifts spanning different sectors. The work provided structure, purpose. Each unauthorized colony ship stopped, each ecosystem preserved, each indigenous species protected meant something. Small victories against the relentless tide of human expansion.

I activated one final gravity pull, feeling the universe contract around me as I fell toward home. Falfsun's familiar warmth greeted me as I materialized on our front lawn.

I walked inside our quantum-folded home, listening to the comfortable silence. The life we'd built here still surprised me sometimes. A house on a star. Friends scattered across the galaxy. Centuries of life stretching before us.

I smiled, remembering Alice Tracker's parting words during her visit: "You've found home in the most unexpected place imaginable." She'd been right, though she couldn't have understood the full truth of it.

I tucked away my Planck toolkit and wandered into the kitchen, mind still lingering on the day's patrol. The house felt emptier these days, quieter. I'd grown used to Joan's absence, but that didn't make it easier. My fingers traced the edge of the kitchen counter as I activated the holographic display with a casual gesture.

"Play Seasoned Table, episode forty-two."

The system responded instantly, projecting Alice Tracker's familiar face above the cooking island. She beamed with enthusiasm, chopping vegetables with practiced precision while explaining the importance of knife technique.

"The secret is in the rhythm," she said, her knife creating a steady percussion against the cutting board. "Let the blade do the work."

I opened the cooling unit, retrieving ingredients for a simple meal. A year had now passed since Alice filmed her special episode here on Falfsun. The tourism surge had finally calmed, leaving our star once again to those who called it home. Temper had been relieved, though I sometimes missed the excitement of new faces, new perspectives.

Alice continued her demonstration, transforming simple ingredients into something extraordinary. I worked alongside her ghost, mimicking her movements more from habit than necessity. The Planck toolkit could have prepared any meal instantly, but there was comfort in the ritual of cooking, in creating something with my own hands.

"Remember," Alice advised her invisible audience, "food isn't just sustenance. It's connection. It's memory."

My knife paused mid-chop. Connection. The word echoed strangely in my thoughts. Since Joan had left to explore dimensional tunnels eleven months ago, our hive mind connection had fallen dormant. Not severed, just quiet, like a radio tuned to static. I'd grown accustomed to the silence in my head, the absence of her consciousness brushing against mine.

The villa's communication system chimed, interrupting my thoughts. A visitor. Unusual, especially without prior notice. Temper typically announced himself hours in advance, and Marcus and Bea were researching the alien stellar cartography.

I set down the knife, wiping my hands on a kitchen towel. The chime sounded again, more insistent. As I moved toward the entrance, something shifted within me. A presence, familiar yet distant, like a forgotten melody suddenly remembered.

The hive mind, dormant for months, buzzed to life. Not with words, exactly, but with awareness, a sense of another consciousness reaching toward mine. I hesitated, then tentatively extended my thoughts outward.

The response came immediately. *Come let me in. You'd think this stubborn house would have remembered me.*

Joan.

I crossed the remaining distance in three quick strides, heart racing with unexpected intensity. The door slid open at my approach, revealing a figure silhouetted against Falfsun's eternal glow.

She stood there, exactly as I remembered yet somehow different. Her form had settled into the human appearance she preferred when we were alone, but her eyes held new depths, new knowledge. The quantum tunnels had changed her, as they always did.

We didn't speak. We didn't need to. Our minds reconnected in an instant, thoughts and emotions flowing between us, finding familiar channels. Eleven months of experiences cascaded into my consciousness: impossible geometries, primitive civilizations existing in other dimensions, knowledge that defied language.

In return, I shared my months of patrols, baseball games with Temper, discoveries from Marcus and Bea, quiet evenings spent watching cooking shows and missing her presence.

"You've been watching Alice again," she said, her voice carrying the slight echo that always accompanied her return from dimensional travel.

"She's very educational."

Joan smiled, stepping inside. Our physical forms remained separate, but our minds intertwined, reestablishing connections that had never truly broken. Through her eyes, I saw myself: steady, patient, unchanged. Through mine, she witnessed her own transformation, subtle but profound.

"I found something special," she said, both aloud and through our shared consciousness.

The hive mind pulsed with images too complex for words: a space between dimensions where reality folded back on itself, where cause and effect reversed, where time moved sideways rather than forward.

"Show me," I whispered, reaching for her hand.

Joan's presence filled spaces that had felt empty for too long in our home. The villa hummed softly in the background, its pitch shifting slightly as it relearned her unique energy signature. I closed the door behind her, feeling the familiar warmth of our connection spreading through my consciousness.

"Eleven months, two weeks, four days," I said.

She smiled. "You counted."

"Not intentionally." I gestured toward the kitchen. "I was making dinner. Are you hungry?"

Joan moved through our living space with graceful familiarity, trailing her fingers along surfaces as if reacquainting herself with their texture. "Food can wait."

We settled onto the curved sofa overlooking Falfsun's churning surface. Through our windows, the star's plasma flows created ever-changing patterns of orange, gold, and crimson. Joan watched the display with renewed appreciation, her mind open to mine, sharing sensations that transcended words.

"I missed this view," she said. "Dimensional spaces lack... substantiality."

I felt her experiences flowing through our connection: realms where matter existed as probability rather than certainty, where consciousness shaped reality directly. Beautiful but untethered, lacking the solid comfort of our home.

"The tunnels were productive, then?"

Joan nodded. "More than I anticipated." Her thoughts brushed against mine, offering glimpses of discoveries too complex for immediate sharing. "I found something that changes how we understand our galaxy."

"That's quite a claim."

"I know." She leaned forward, eyes reflecting Falfsun's glow.

I sensed her excitement, her need to share this discovery properly. "You want to tell Temper too."

"He'll understand the implications better than anyone." Joan smiled. "Besides, I've missed his enthusiasm."

"He's missed you as well. Keeps asking when you'd return." I reached for her hand, feeling the solidity of her presence. "We both did."

Our minds intertwined more deeply then, eleven months of separation dissolving into shared consciousness. I felt her loneliness during her explorations, her moments of wonder, her determination to understand the mysteries she encountered. She experienced my quiet routines, my patrols, my evenings spent watching cooking shows simply to hear another voice in our home.

"You've been well?" she asked aloud, though she already knew the answer.

"Well enough." I squeezed her hand. "Better now."

We sat in comfortable silence, allowing our reconnection to deepen naturally. The hive mind hummed between us, no longer dormant but vibrant with shared awareness. Through her eyes, I saw our home anew: the quantum-folded spaces, the gardens sustained by Falfsun's energy, the subtle beauty of our sanctuary built on a star.

"Temper will be home," I said eventually. "Working on his simulations."

Joan nodded. "Still obsessed with star formation?"

"Some things never change." I stood, offering my hand. "Shall we surprise him?"

"Let's." Her eyes sparkled with anticipation. "I can't wait to see his reaction when I tell him what I've found."

I opened the door for the short walk over to Temper's home. Whatever discovery she'd made, whatever changes it might bring to our understanding of the universe, would wait just a few moments longer.

"Ready?" I asked.

Joan's mind brushed against mine, warm with affection and excitement. *"Always."*

We approached Temper's house. The front door stood slightly ajar, as if Temper had left it open to catch any passing breeze. Joan paused at the threshold, her excitement flowing through our connection.

"Should we knock?" she asked.

I grinned. "When have we ever?"

We stepped inside. The familiar scent of Temper's home greeted us, a curious mixture of charred paper and something metallic, like heated copper. His obsession with stellar formation had transformed the living room into a makeshift laboratory. Holographic projections of fusion reactions hung suspended in the air, their pink glow casting strange shadows across the walls.

"Temper?" I called out. "You have a visitor."

A crash echoed from the back room, followed by the sound of claws scrambling against the floor. Temper appeared in the doorway, his red dragon form filling the frame. His eyes widened, pupils dilating into perfect circles.

"Joan?" His voice cracked slightly.

She stepped forward. "Hello, old friend."

Temper bounded across the room with surprising grace for his size. He circled Joan twice, his tail swishing back and forth in unmistakable joy. His bumpy skin flushed a brighter red, a sure sign of emotional intensity.

"You're back. You're actually back." He stopped circling and sat back on his haunches. "Eleven months. Almost a full Earth year."

"I lost track of time," Joan admitted.

"We dragons never lose track of time." Temper's voice carried a gentle reprimand, but his eyes betrayed his relief. "Especially when friends disappear into quantum tunnels without coming back."

I felt Joan's twinge of guilt through our connection. "I didn't plan to be gone so long."

Temper huffed, a small flame flickering between his nostrils. "Next time, perhaps a simple message? 'Hello Temper, just slipping between dimensions, back in a few months, don't worry your scaly head about me.'"

Joan laughed, the sound filling the room. "I promise."

The tension in Temper's posture eased. He gestured toward his cluttered sitting area. "Well, don't just stand there. Tell me everything."

We settled into the mismatched furniture. Temper curled himself into a tight circle on his reinforced lounging pad, his eyes never leaving Joan, as if afraid she might vanish again.

"You look different," Temper said, his gaze steady. "It's your eyes. Something's changed."

Joan nodded. "The tunnels change you. I've seen things that live between realities; civilizations folded into the hidden seams of space."

Temper leaned in, intrigued. "Did you record any structural shifts?

Dimensional layering? Evidence of interstitial design?"

"Better." Joan smiled. "I met others that will change everything about how we view our place in the universe."

Temper's entire body tensed with excitement. His tail thumped against the floor, creating small tremors that rippled through the house. "Tell me."

Through our connection, I felt Joan's satisfaction at Temper's reaction. This was why she'd come back when she did, why she'd sought us out immediately. Some discoveries needed to be shared.

Joan settled deeper into her chair, her fingers interlacing in her lap. Through our hive mind connection, I felt her organizing her thoughts, arranging them like puzzle pieces before speaking. The excitement that had animated her moments ago transformed into something more measured, more deliberate.

"I discovered something," she said, her voice carrying a weight I hadn't heard before. "Or rather, someone."

Temper's tail stilled against the floor. His eyes narrowed, the vertical pupils contracting to thin lines.

Joan composed herself. "The Vraxeik. They live two galaxies over. They gave me a message to bring back with me to everyone in our galaxy."

Temper stood up from his tail. "Tell me everything that happened."

"Well," Joan began, "I entered their galaxy just beyond the halo and landed in the middle of what appeared to be a group of aliens rolling rocks across their bodies."

Temper listened without interruption. Joan continued.

"At first, the rocks seemed to move in a controlled manner, shifting across their skin like part of a ritual or game. Then, one struck another, sending it tumbling across the surface of the alien's body."

"Did the aliens have pockets?" I asked. "Maybe they were playing pool."

Temper gave me a stern look. "I'm going to put you in a pocket where the sun doesn't shine if you're not quiet."

I leaned back, feeling unappreciated.

Joan smiled at me and continued. "As soon as they saw me, they stopped. Their forms shifted, morphing into something different. Something more unsettling. Their skin lengthened into ridges. Their limbs extended unnaturally. They looked like creatures from old nightmares, covered in braided fur."

"What happened next?"

Joan continued, "They were actually very polite. It seems I was the first visitor from our galaxy that they had met. They came up to meet me and we started talking, but of course, we couldn't understand each other. I was in the process of translating their language when they beat me to it. They started talking to me in English."

Temper looked over at me. "Don't say it, Go! Don't you dare ask, 'Were their first words, take me to your leader?'"

"I wasn't going to!" I defended myself. (I really was going to say it.)

Temper said, "Yes, you were! Joan, what did they say? Are they friendly? Do they want something? Or... was it something else?"

Joan leaned forward, her eyes reflecting Falfsun's churning surface. "First off, they want to be left alone," she said. "I told them about humans and shared Earth's history with them. The truth is, they don't like humans very much. You're too uncivilized for their tastes. They warned you to stay in your own galaxy. They liked me, but that's only because I'm from a different universe, more similar to their culture. From what I've learned, there is only one alpha civilization in every galaxy at any given time, and an unwritten rule between them that they won't travel to other galaxies. They won't come and visit us either."

"Isn't our galaxy on a collision course with Andromeda?" I said. "We'll have to meet some aliens eventually."

"We will, in time," Temper said. "You hinted there's more to their message?"

Joan nodded. "The second part of the message concerns the fate of our universe. The galactic alpha civilizations have joined into an agreement to take control of its fate, and they want us to join them in that endeavor."

"Why? What's their plan?" Temper asked, his tail curling tighter around his body.

"They've come to the collective conclusion that the current shape of the universe is saddle-back, but it's flattening out. That means it will expand forever, and the galaxies will continue to drift apart until we won't be able to see any of them ever again because they'll be too distant. After we're alone in the universe, the stars will use up all of their fuel and begin to die, one at a time. Once they're dead, there won't be any heat left anymore. And once that happens, everything—including us—will die. We're destined to die a long, cold death."

Despite standing on the surface of Falfsun, I suddenly felt that cold. "What can we do?"

"According to the Vraxeik, there are two trillion galaxies that are close enough to us to see, and an unknown number of galaxies beyond our range of sight. The galaxies are pushing against dark energy, and this is accelerating the speed of expansion and causing the universe to flatten out into a plane. They want us to help slow this push."

Temper asked, "How much time do they think we have left to slow it?"

Joan's fingers traced patterns on the arm of her chair. "If we do nothing, time will end in about 100 trillion years. That seems like a long time from now, but for half of that time, we'd be energy-starved, living off the radiation decay of black holes. It would be like trying to live in the middle of Death Valley for 50 trillion years by sucking on nothing but sand. You'd be alive, but you'd wish you weren't. If we follow the Vraxeik plan, then we have about 13 billion years, beginning right now, to reverse the expansion. If we wait more than 13 billion years to do something, then we pass the point of no return, and the universe will expand forever."

"So we have to somehow decrease interacting with dark energy to pull everything back together?" I asked.

Joan shook her head. "They've given me the knowledge of how to manipulate vacuum energy to slow the cosmic expansion."

Temper rose to his feet, his entire body vibrating with excitement. "Vacuum energy manipulation? That's still theoretical even for the most advanced physicists in our galaxy."

Through our hive mind connection, I felt Joan's mind open, revealing layers of complex knowledge. Equations and concepts beyond my comprehension flowed between us, multidimensional calculations that made my thoughts spin.

"It's not theoretical to the Vraxeik," Joan said. "They've been implementing these techniques for millions of years. Each alpha civilization manages their own sector of the universe, maintaining balance."

I tried to process the magnitude of what she was suggesting. "So they want us to become the alpha civilization for the Milky Way? To take responsibility for our corner of the universe?"

"Yes. They believe we're ready. Or at least, ready to begin learning."

Temper paced the room, his claws clicking against the floor. "This is incredible. The implications for stellar physics alone are revolutionary, not to mention the philosophical ramifications of consciously directing cosmic evolution."

"There's more," Joan continued. "The Vraxeik don't just want us to slow the expansion. They believe we can eventually reverse it, creating a universe that oscillates between expansion and contraction indefinitely."

"A perpetual universe," Temper whispered. "No heat death. No cold, empty void."

I sat back, feeling the weight of this revelation. "Why us? Why now?"

"Because we've shown potential," Joan replied. "Our work with the Planck toolkit, our ethical approach to colonization after the initial mistakes, our ability to coexist with other forms of consciousness. Although we're still considered primitive in their eyes, they believe we're ready for the responsibility."

Temper stopped pacing. "We need to tell everyone. The scientific community, the galactic governance—"

"No," Joan interrupted. "Not yet. The Vraxeik were clear. This knowledge must be implemented gradually, with careful consideration. If misused, vacuum energy manipulation could accelerate the expansion rather than slow it."

I felt a chill run through me. "So we could actually make things worse."

"Much worse," Joan confirmed. "We need to start small. Learn the techniques. Prove we can handle the responsibility before spreading this knowledge further."

I stood up, the weight of Joan's revelation settling in my bones. "We'll need help implementing this. Even with our combined knowledge, manipulating vacuum energy across an entire galaxy isn't something we can manage alone."

Temper nodded vigorously, his tail swishing with excitement. "We should contact Captain Smith and Carpisma."

"Are you sure?" I asked. "The Vraxeik were clear about being cautious with this knowledge."

"I trust them," Temper said, his dragon form somehow conveying absolute certainty despite the inhuman features. "Smith has been our ally since the beginning. If anyone can help us implement this responsibly, it's Carpisma."

Joan's consciousness brushed against mine through our hive mind connection. I felt her weighing the options, calculating probabilities with a precision that still amazed me.

"Agreed," she said finally. "But we meet on neutral ground. Requiem Prime."

"I'll send the message through the Planck Pulse," I said, already reaching for my toolkit.

The quantum thread connected instantly, as it always did. Smith's response came within minutes: a simple acknowledgment and coordinates for our meeting.

We traveled to Requiem Prime the next morning. The planet formerly known as Luyten B had transformed in the years since the first Etherean settlements. Emberhill, once a collection of simple structures hastily erected for the hibernating thruman children, had grown into a thriving metropolis that blended harmoniously with the native ecology.

As we approached the government complex, I watched Temper's form shift. His red dragon skin rippled and contracted, melting away as his body reconfigured itself into his human appearance. The transformation was fluid.

"I forgot how uncomfortable clothes feel," he muttered, adjusting the collar of his more formal attire.

Beside him, Joan underwent her own transformation. Her human form dissolved, replaced by the stacked black diamonds of her ant-like appearance. The sight no longer unsettled me as it once had. Through our connection, I felt her relief at returning to this form, like stretching after being confined too long.

"More comfortable?" I asked.

The top diamond tilted slightly, her equivalent of a nod.

We landed with barely a whisper. Captain Smith waited for us on the platform, Luna Dawn at his side. He looked exactly as he had when we'd last met, his face bearing the same slight smile.

"Quite the urgent message," he said by way of greeting. "Must be important to bring all three of you here in person."

"More important than you can imagine," Temper replied.

Smith led us through the complex to a secure conference room. The space was designed for privacy, with phased membranes that prevented any form of surveillance. Once the door sealed behind us, Smith turned, his expression suddenly serious.

"What have you found?"

Joan stepped forward, her diamond form catching the light. "I've made contact with an alpha civilization from another galaxy. The Vraxeik."

Smith's composure slipped for just a moment, his eyes widening. "First contact? With an extragalactic species?"

"They've given us information," I said. "About the fate of our universe and how we might change it."

Joan projected a series of complex equations into the air between us. "This is a step-by-step guide to manipulating vacuum energy. The Vraxeik believe we're ready to join them in managing cosmic expansion."

Luna Dawn moved closer to the floating equations, her eyes scanning the symbols with remarkable speed. "This is... revolutionary. These principles contradict everything we thought we knew about quantum field theory."

"Yet they work," Temper said. "I've already verified the basic principles in simulation."

Smith circled the projection, studying it from all angles. "And they just gave you this? What do they want in return?"

"Nothing," Joan replied. "Only that we use this knowledge responsibly. Each alpha civilization manages their own sector of the universe. They believe it's time for us to take our place among them."

Smith's gaze met mine. "The implications are enormous. This would require coordination on a galactic scale, resources beyond anything we've marshaled before."

"That's why we came to you," I said. "Carpisma has the reach and influence to implement this properly. But it must be done carefully, methodically."

Smith nodded slowly. "The Galactic Court will need to be involved. This affects everyone."

"We need to start small," Temper insisted. "Prove the concept works before attempting larger interventions."

"Agreed," Smith said. He turned to Luna. "Contact the Galactic Court. Ask for a representative to meet with us here. Tell them to keep it quiet."

As they discussed logistics, I felt Joan's consciousness brush against mine, a gentle reminder of what was at stake. Not just our galaxy, but the future of the universe itself.

The Galactic Court representative arrived with the kind of pomp that made me miss my quiet villa on Falfsun. Three uniformed officers flanked Envoy Seraphis Quen, a tall woman with piercing eyes and silver hair pulled into a severe bun. Her uniform bore the emblem of the Interstellar Affairs Division, marking her as a First Contact specialist.

"Captain Smith." She extended her hand. Her grip was firm, professional. "I understand you've brought us something of galactic significance."

He gestured toward our assembled group. "They'll explain everything."

The conference room felt suddenly smaller with the addition of the Court officers. They arranged themselves around the table with practiced efficiency, HoloTabs at the ready. Captain Smith sat beside Quen, his expression unreadable.

Joan stepped forward, her black diamond form catching the light in fractured patterns. The Court officers tensed visibly at her appearance, but to their credit, maintained their composure.

"I've made contact with the Vraxeik," Joan began, her voice resonating with unusual clarity. "An alpha civilization from beyond our galaxy."

Quen's eyebrow raised slightly. "And they've shared technology with you?"

"Knowledge," Joan corrected. "About vacuum energy manipulation to combat universal expansion."

Joan projected a complex series of equations into the air between us. The symbols glowed with an ethereal light, rotating slowly for all to see.

"The universe is flattening," she continued. "In approximately thirteen billion years, we'll reach a point of no return. The expansion will become irreversible, leading to eventual heat death."

"And these equations are supposed to prevent that?" Quen asked, skepticism evident in her tone.

Joan's top diamond tilted slightly. "They establish the fundamental principles for vacuum energy stabilization. The Vraxeik have been implementing these techniques for millions of years."

Temper leaned forward, his human form barely containing his excitement. "The process requires quantum resonance fields positioned throughout our galaxy. These arrays would interact with vacuum fluctuations at the smallest measurable scale."

"Creating precise wave disruptions," Joan added. "Influencing dark energy directly."

Smith studied the equations with intense focus. 'How much energy would this require?'

"Less than you might think," Joan replied. "The process doesn't rely on an external energy source. It utilizes existing vacuum energy, redistributing it across cosmic voids rather than consuming additional power."

Quen made notes on her HoloTab. "And the risks?"

"Considerable," Joan admitted. "Improper implementation could accelerate expansion rather than slow it. The Vraxeik were explicit about the need for careful, methodical application."

"Could you elaborate on the stabilization mechanism?" Temper asked, his scientific curiosity evident.

Joan projected another set of equations. "The system uses artificial gravity anchors, similar to engineered black holes, to counteract expansion forces. These create localized space-time anchors preventing excessive stretching of space."

"Fascinating," Smith murmured. "It's counter-intuitive, but the math looks right."

I watched Quen's face as she processed the information. Her expression remained neutral, but I detected a flicker of concern in her eyes.

"The Vraxeik instructed us to be selective about sharing this knowledge," I said. "It needs to be implemented with precision, not rushed into production."

Quen nodded slowly. "I understand. This will need to be handled at the highest levels of the Court, with appropriate discretion."

"We're not asking for permission," I clarified. "We're offering partnership. The Vraxeik selected us specifically because they believe humanity is ready for this responsibility."

Smith stood, smoothing his uniform. "I believe Carpisma can provide the necessary resources and expertise. With the Court's oversight, of course."

"Of course," Quen replied, though her tone suggested the matter wasn't settled. "We'll need to verify this information independently before proceeding."

"That's reasonable," Temper said. "But time is a factor. Thirteen billion years may seem distant, but establishing the initial resonance fields will take centuries."

Quen gathered her materials. "Captain Smith and I will take this information back to Earth immediately. I assure you; it will be handled with the utmost discretion."

Smith nodded to us. "We'll be in touch within the week with a preliminary assessment. Until then, I suggest you continue your research but take no further action."

As they prepared to leave, I caught Joan's consciousness brushing against mine through our hive mind connection. A subtle warning. Something about Quen's careful neutrality didn't sit right with either of us.

We shared a quantum thread back to Falfsun. The gravity pull activated, and I felt the familiar sensation of falling through space, my stomach lurching as reality bent around us. Joan remained perfectly still beside me, her diamond form reflecting fractured patterns of starlight. Temper, back in his dragon form, curled his tail around himself, eyes closed in contemplation.

We materialized on the stabilized crust of Falfsun, the star's energy currents flowing beneath our feet. Our villa stood before us, its structure shifting subtly to accommodate the stellar movements.

"I need to process these equations," Temper said, his voice rumbling. "The implications for the future are revolutionary."

I nodded. "Go. We'll talk tomorrow."

Temper turned and walked down the flame crest path toward his own home.

Inside our villa, Joan's form rippled and changed, black diamonds melting away to reveal her human appearance. She moved to the observation window, where Falfsun's plasma flows created a hypnotic display of reds and golds.

"You don't trust her," I said.

Joan's fingers traced patterns on the quantum glass. "Quen calculated every word, every gesture. She was performing, not responding."

"Smith seemed genuine enough."

"Smith follows protocols. The Court follows agendas."

I sank into a chair that adjusted its molecular structure to my body's contours. "What do you think they'll do?"

"They'll verify the equations. They'll recognize the potential. Then they'll debate endlessly about implementation while seeking ways to control the process." Joan turned to face me. "The Vraxeik didn't choose the Galactic Court. They chose us."

The realization settled over me. "We need allies we can trust. People who understand what's at stake without political considerations."

"Marcus and Bea," Joan said immediately.

I nodded. "They've been studying ancient civilizations for years. If anyone can appreciate the historical significance of this moment, it's them."

Joan moved to stand beside me, her consciousness brushing against mine through our hive mind connection. "They should hear it from us directly."

"I'll send a Quantum Thread."

The message was simple: *Need to see you both. Important discovery. Can we visit?*

Their response came almost immediately: *Always welcome. Come tomorrow.*

We arrived at Marcus and Bea's home the next day, materializing on the pearl-white beach of their moon. Twin suns cast dual shadows across the sand, one golden, one tinged with red. Their house stood on stilts above the turquoise water, bamboo walls filtering the sunlight into dappled patterns.

Marcus emerged onto the wraparound porch, his face lighting up when he saw us. Though physically he appeared no older than a young man, his eyes held the wisdom of someone far older.

"Papa! Joan!" He embraced us both, his enthusiasm unchanged by time. "Bea's inside finishing an analysis. Come up!"

We followed him up the woven reed steps. The interior was open and airy, scientific equipment sharing space with comfortable furniture in a seamless blend of laboratory and home.

Bea looked up from a holographic display, her face breaking into a warm smile. "What perfect timing. I just finished cataloging some artifacts from the Meridian system."

After greetings and refreshments, we settled on their porch overlooking the gentle waves. The serious nature of our visit must have been evident in our expressions.

"Something's happened," Marcus said, leaning forward. "Something significant."

Joan nodded, her form shifting briefly to reveal her diamond structure before settling back into human appearance. "I've made contact with an alpha civilization from beyond our galaxy. The Vraxeik."

Marcus's eyes widened. Bea set down her cup with a soft clink.

"They've given us knowledge," I continued. "About manipulating vacuum energy to slow universal expansion."

Joan projected the equations into the air between us, the symbols glowing against the backdrop of the twin suns. "The universe is flattening. In thirteen billion years, we'll reach a point of no return."

"Unless we implement these principles," Bea whispered, her scientific mind already grasping the implications. "This is... revolutionary."

Marcus stood, moving around the projection to study it from all angles. "The Court knows?"

"We informed them yesterday," I said. "Along with Smith and Carpisma. Their response was... measured."

"Political," Joan corrected.

Bea's fingers traced the equations, her expression thoughtful. "You don't trust them to handle this properly."

"We need people who understand what's at stake," I said. "Beyond politics or profit."

Marcus and Bea exchanged a glance, a silent communication born of their years together.

"You want our help," Marcus said.

"We need allies," Joan replied. "People who can see the bigger picture."

Bea stood, determination clear in her stance. "Our research can wait. This is about the future of everything."

Marcus nodded, his expression solemn yet excited. "Where do we start?"

"With verification," I said. "Then careful implementation of the first principles. The Vraxeik were clear: this must be done methodically, with precision."

"Our lab can run the initial simulations," Bea offered. "We have processors specifically designed for multidimensional calculations."

Marcus placed his hand on my shoulder, his touch a reminder of the bond we shared. "The four of us, saving the universe. Quite the adventure, Papa."

I smiled, feeling a weight lift from my shoulders. With Marcus and Bea on our side, the path forward seemed clearer, the future less uncertain.

"The greatest adventure yet," I agreed.

CHAPTER TEN

Celesticon Reunion

The quantum gardens shifted in response to our excitement, their luminous fronds pulsing with anticipation. Joan had transformed our living space for the occasion, extending the dimensional pockets to accommodate our friends. Marcus and Bea arrived first, materializing on our threshold with garment bags slung over their shoulders. Temper followed minutes later, his red dragon form lumbering through the door with a large trunk balanced precariously on his tail.

"Uncle Temper!" Marcus embraced him, careful to avoid dislodging the trunk. "What did you bring? Your entire wardrobe?"

"Just the essentials," Temper huffed, setting down his burden with surprising delicacy. "A proper costume requires accessories."

Joan appeared from one of the dimensional folds, carrying a tray of iridescent drinks that caught and refracted the ambient light.

The room adjusted to accommodate us all, the ceiling lifting and walls expanding. Our home on Falfsun existed in constant flux, responding to our needs and moods. Today it sensed celebration.

"Shall we reveal our costumes?" Marcus suggested, eyes bright with enthusiasm. "I've been planning mine for months."

We arranged ourselves in a circle, garment bags and trunks at our feet. The anticipation was palpable, reminding me of holidays long past when we gathered on Hellfire to exchange gifts.

"I'll start," Temper announced, opening his trunk to reveal a gold-trimmed flight jacket emblazoned with the insignia of the Solar Dominion Air Corps. He held it up proudly. "Colonel Jett Vortex, from the Vortex Chronicles. I even replicated the star-forged gauntlets."

"Perfect choice," Bea applauded. "Those radio broadcasts were legendary."

"Your turn, Marcus," Temper prompted.

Marcus unzipped his garment bag with theatrical slowness, revealing a sleek exo-suit of shifting nanoweave material. "Major Kael Vindex from the Vindex Protocol trilogy. The adaptive armor actually works, thanks to some modifications."

"You'll win the Quantum Battle Arena for sure," I nodded appreciatively.

Bea stood next, unfurling her costume with a flourish. A flight suit of deep red with gold insignias caught the light, complete with retractable energy blades mounted on gauntlets. "Nova Striker from Eclipse Vanguard. The action figure was my favorite toy growing up."

"The original or the Eclipse War Edition?" Temper asked, leaning forward with interest.

"Original, of course. My parents gave it to me for my tenth birthday."

Joan transformed beside me, her form shifting from her usual human appearance to something more fluid. Her skin rippled with a haunting, liquid-metal effect before settling into the unmistakable appearance of Nyx Hollow from HOLLOWVERSE. "You wouldn't even know it's a costume," she said, her voice altered to match the character's distinctive timbre.

Everyone stared in amazement. Joan's shape-shifting abilities allowed her a perfect recreation that no conventional costume could match.

"That's incredible," Marcus whispered. "You even got the eyes right."

All attention turned to me. I reached into satchel and withdrew my costume piece by piece. The graphite-black flight suit with neon-purple chronometric circuits. The modular shoulder rig. The signature chronoblade.

"Commander Zeth Radon," Temper identified immediately. "Chrono Rift was criminally underrated."

"Three seasons wasn't nearly enough," Bea agreed. "The cliffhanger still haunts me."

I fastened the chronoblade to my hip, feeling a nostalgic connection to the character. "I watched the original broadcast back in the '90s. Never thought I'd end up with a lifespan that makes his space-time manipulation look primitive."

"Let's try them on," Marcus urged. "I want to see the full effect."

One by one, we donned our costumes, transforming our gathering into a tableau of science fiction history. Temper's golden gauntlets gleamed as he struck a heroic pose. Marcus's exo-suit adjusted to his movements with fluid precision. Bea activated her energy blades, which hummed with convincing power. Joan shifted between forms, demonstrating Nyx Hollow's terrifying transformations.

I completed my ensemble by activating the chronometric circuits, which pulsed with purple light in perfect rhythm with my heartbeat.

"We look magnificent," Temper declared, his dragon features somehow enhancing rather than diminishing Colonel Vortex's dashing appearance.

The chronometric circuits on my suit pulsed in rhythm with the final toast of our pre-Celesticon gathering. We stood in our Mediterranean-ish villa on Falfsun, five figures pulled from different eras of science fiction, raising glasses that caught the ambient starlight.

"To Celesticon," Marcus proclaimed, his exo-suit shifting subtly as he moved. "May we find fellow travelers worthy of our costumes."

Joan established the quantum gravity focal point with elegant precision, her Nyx Hollow form rippling slightly as she manipulated the dimensional coordinates. The familiar sensation of free-falling seized me; a momentary weightlessness followed by the stomach-lurching plunge as we surrendered to the pull, our bodies plummeting through the void toward Requiem Prime.

Reality reassembled around us. The bustling central plaza of Requiem Prime materialized in a kaleidoscope of color and sound. We'd arrived directly at the heart of Celesticon, the largest science fiction celebration ever held in the settled galaxy.

"By the stars," Temper whispered, his dragon form garnering immediate attention in his Colonel Vortex costume. "It's magnificent."

The plaza stretched before us, a vast circular expanse ringed by towering obsidian spires that reflected the twin moons overhead. Holographic constellations danced between buildings, recreating famous star systems from beloved science fiction universes. The air vibrated with music from a dozen different performance stages, each featuring orchestras playing iconic soundtracks that blended into a surprisingly harmonious symphony.

Thousands of attendees filled every available space. Costumes from centuries of science fiction tradition created a living tapestry of imagination. A group of revelers dressed as the entire crew of the Nostromo passed us, followed by a family whose elaborate mechanical suits transformed them into convincing Mechanoids from the Quantum Crusade series.

"The Hyperlane Sprint is starting in twenty minutes," Bea pointed toward the eastern sky where illuminated racing lanes had been established between the tallest buildings. "We should find a good viewing spot."

We navigated through the crowd, passing vendor stalls selling everything from replicated props to actual artifacts from classic film sets. The scent of exotic foods filled the air. Spices from a hundred worlds mingled with the rich, heady aroma of freshly prepared beverages at the Nebula Feast pavilion.

"Commander Radon!" A young woman in an impeccable recreation of Dr. Elara Voss's uniform from the third season of Chrono Rift approached me. "Your costume is incredible. The chronometric circuits actually pulse!"

"Thank you," I replied, slipping into character with surprising ease. "The temporal fluctuations are particularly strong tonight."

She laughed with delight before rejoining her friends, all dressed as various characters from the same series. The encounter left me with an unexpected warmth. After centuries of existence, there was something profoundly comforting in this celebration of stories that had once captured my imagination.

We passed the entrance to the Dimensional Rift Challenge, where participants navigated a complex maze of shifting realities. Beyond it, the Quantum Battle Arena roared with the sound of simulated combat, energy gauntlets flashing as competitors engaged in elaborate duels.

"Look at that," Marcus pointed toward the central stage where the Celestial Symphony was preparing to perform. Cosmic costumed musicians adjusted their instruments that vibrated in unfamiliar frequencies, producing sounds that shimmered and twisted, defying ordinary perception.

The Alien Masquerade parade wound through the plaza, a serpentine procession of fantastical beings rendered in bioluminescent body paint and holographic overlays. Leading them was a figure whose costume seemed to bend light around it, creating the illusion of a being composed entirely of starlight.

"This is remarkable," Joan observed, her Nyx Hollow form drawing appreciative glances from passing attendees. "So many imagined futures converging in one place."

We found a viewing platform for the Hyperlane Sprint just as the announcer's voice boomed across the plaza. "Welcome, cosmic travelers, to the thirty-seventh annual Celesticon! The largest gathering of science fiction enthusiasts ever assembled awaits you!"

The crowd roared in response, a unified expression of joy that transcended origin and age. In that moment, surrounded by friends and strangers celebrating imagination itself, I felt a profound connection to something greater than myself.

We lingered at the edge of the viewing platform, letting the final moments of the Hyperlane Sprints wash over us. Streaks of light carved impossible paths across the sky, each racer a blur of color and velocity. The crowd surged with every twist and near-collision, their excitement contagious. For a while, we simply watched; no words, just the shared awe of motion and mastery. But as the last racer crossed the finish line and the cheers began to fade, a quiet settled between us. The spectacle had passed, and something more personal was calling.

The announcer's voice faded as we moved away from the viewing platform. The spectacle of Celesticon surrounded us, but my mind had already begun drifting elsewhere. Joan glanced at me, her Nyx Hollow form rippling slightly as she sensed the shift in my thoughts.

"They're here," she said simply.

I nodded, feeling a familiar tug of excitement and nostalgia. "The

Misfits confirmed their arrival coordinates. They should be at the Galactic Arcade by now."

We weaved through the crowd, past a group performing an elaborate reenactment of the Battle of Andromeda Gate. Temper bounded ahead, his dragon form creating a natural path as attendees stepped aside with looks of wonder. The Galactic Arcade pulsed with neon light, holographic game interfaces floating in mid-air while participants ducked and weaved through simulated space battles.

And there they were, clustered around a vintage gravity-race simulator. Shiloh spotted us first, her commander's uniform from some obscure series I couldn't place gleaming under the arcade lights. She abandoned her game mid-race and rushed forward.

"Captain!" Her embrace was fierce, genuine. "Or should I say, Commander Radon?"

The others turned at her exclamation. Tumbler emerged first, her sleek exosuit adorned with simulated gravity-modulators, suggesting a history of effortless aerial maneuvers. Wire greeted us next, his luminescent bodysuit threaded with energy filaments, mimicking the taut precision of a tightrope walker. Skyhook landed beside us, his winged mantle flaring outward, the design echoing the grace of someone accustomed to soaring arcs and daring swings. Jester was last to appear, stepping out from behind a holographic asteroid in a shape-shifting ensemble, its shifting patterns flickering unpredictably, perfectly suited to someone who thrived on misdirection and playfulness.

"The prodigal spacers return!" Jester proclaimed, confetti somehow materializing from his sleeves.

Joan stood at my side, her form perfectly still in a way that told me she was observing, cataloging, understanding.

We moved to a quieter corner of the arcade, claiming a circular booth that expanded to accommodate our growing group. The familiar banter resumed as if no time had passed, though it had been years since our last gathering.

"Tell us everything," Shiloh insisted, leaning forward. "The rumors about you living on a star can't possibly be true."

"Actually," Temper interjected, his dragon snout forming what passed for a smug smile, "that part is entirely accurate."

Their expressions of disbelief launched us into stories of our adventures since we'd last met. I found myself recounting tales of the Din crew, memories I hadn't revisited in decades.

"The Din were legendary," I explained, the chronometric circuits on my costume pulsing faster with my rising emotion. "Before the Paradise tragedy, they were the most cohesive team I'd ever seen."

"Captain Wither Drake led them," Temper added. "Tactical genius. Grave Digger kept them alive through impossible situations. Scratch could build anything from nothing. Tracer navigated paths no one else could find."

"And Go David was their photog," I said, feeling a strange disconnect as I spoke about myself in the third person. "They called him 'the lens.'"

Tumbler leaned forward. "Were they as good as the stories say?"

"Better," Temper and I answered simultaneously.

I pulled up archived footage from my planck toolkit, projecting it onto the table. The Din in action, moving with supernatural coordination through a Wilderness Channel challenge. The Misfits watched, transfixed by the fluid teamwork displayed.

"Their rivalry with Captain Blackmane was legendary," I continued. "Every season, they'd challenge him. Every season, they'd come close but fall short."

"We never defeated him," I admitted, an old frustration bubbling up unexpectedly. "Ten attempts. Ten failures. The Paradise tragedy happened before we got our eleventh chance."

Joan's consciousness brushed against mine through our shared hive mind connection, sensing the surprising depth of my frustration. I felt her curiosity as she explored this emotion, one she hadn't encountered in me before.

"It was just a game," Skyhook offered gently.

"It became more than that," I said. "Blackmane represented something we couldn't overcome. A perfect adversary. When Paradise was lost, so was our chance to finally beat him."

"The game preserved his character model," Wire noted. "He still exists in the Wilderness Channel."

"It wouldn't be the same," I shook my head. "The original crew is gone. Go David is gone. I'm... someone else now."

The table fell silent. Joan's mind intertwined more deeply with mine, understanding flowing between us. She felt my irrational attachment to this unresolved challenge, the symbolic weight it carried.

"What if you weren't alone?" Shiloh asked suddenly. "What if the Misfits stood with you?"

I studied the faces of my friends gathered around the table. The Misfits leaned forward with expressions ranging from curiosity to determination, their costumes catching the arcade's shifting lights.

"Captain Blackmane," Skyhook said, rolling the name around like a rare coin. "The big boss of the Wilderness Channel."

"The undefeated," Wire added, his fingers tapping a restless rhythm on the tabletop.

Tumbler's eyes lit up. "I've seen the archived footage. No team has ever beaten him, not even close."

"The Din came as close as anyone," I said quietly. The words felt strange in my mouth, distant yet personal. "We had strategies, countermoves for every trick in Blackmane's arsenal. We just needed one more attempt."

Shiloh straightened in her seat, commander's uniform gleaming under the arcade lights. "Then let's give you that attempt."

"The Misfits," she continued, gesturing around the table. "We take on Blackmane. For the Din."

Jester pulled a coin from thin air, walking it across his knuckles. "The ultimate tribute. Finish what they started."

My chronometric circuits pulsed faster, matching my quickening heartbeat. The proposition was absurd. I wasn't Go David anymore, not really. That life felt like someone else's memory.

"The original Din trained for years," I protested. "Captain Drake, Grave Digger, Scratch, Tracer. They were the best."

"And we're not exactly novices," Tumbler countered, flipping a coaster into the air and catching it behind her back. "The Misfits have taken down some legendary bosses."

Wire nodded. "Remember the Void Leviathan of Sector Nine? Everyone said it couldn't be beaten."

"Three attempts," Skyhook reminded us with a grin. "We took it down in three."

I felt Joan's consciousness brush against mine through our hive mind connection. Not intruding, just present. Her curiosity flowed between us as she explored this unexpected corner of my past. I sensed her surprise at the depth of my attachment to this unresolved challenge.

"It wouldn't be the same," I said, but my resolve was weakening.

"It's not meant to be the same," Shiloh replied. "It's meant to be a tribute. Honoring what the Din stood for."

Marcus leaned forward. "I was a Din too, for a little while, and I've heard you talk about Captain Drake and the others. You admired them."

"I did," I admitted. "They were more than teammates."

Joan's form shifted slightly beside me, her Nyx Hollow appearance rippling with subtle movement. "This matters to you," she observed, her voice carrying layers of understanding that only I could fully comprehend through our connection.

Through our shared consciousness, I felt something else from her. Not just understanding but offering. Her unique abilities, her perception of reality that transcended conventional dimensions. With Joan's help, perhaps...

"The Wilderness Channel operates under Breach Law," I said slowly, looking at Joan. "Reality bends there. Conventional strategies fall apart."

"Breach Law," Joan repeated, and I felt her interest spark through our connection. "Where reality refuses to obey its own rules."

Temper's dragon eyes widened as he followed my train of thought. "Joan's abilities would be... compatible."

"More than compatible," I said. "She naturally perceives reality in ways that align with Breach Law."

"So we have a secret weapon," Shiloh concluded with satisfaction.

Joan's consciousness pressed gently against mine, conveying without words: *I will help you close this circle. Together, we can face this undefeated adversary.*

I looked around at the expectant faces of the Misfits, then back to Joan. For decades, I'd carried this small, irrational frustration. This unfinished business. Now, surrounded by friends both old and new, I felt something unexpected. Hope.

"Alright," I said finally. "For the Din. We challenge Captain

Blackmane."

"When?" asked Temper.

"Now," I said, surprising myself with the conviction in my voice. "We challenge him now."

The Misfits exchanged glances, a silent conversation flowing between them before Shiloh nodded. "The Quantum Battle Arena. It's perfect."

"We'll need to reconfigure it for Wilderness Channel protocols," Temper said, his dragon form straightening with newfound purpose. "I'll check with the other arena competitors to make sure they don't mind."

"Let's invite everyone at Celesticon to witness it," Marcus suggested, his eyes bright with excitement behind Major Vindex's tactical neural HUD.

Joan's consciousness brushed against mine, her thoughts carrying both caution and support. *Are you certain about facing him now, before the team has time to prepare?* she asked through our connection. *This matters deeply to you.*

I nodded, feeling decades of unfinished business crystallize into a single moment of clarity. *I'm certain.*

The Quantum Battle Arena stood at the heart of Celesticon, a massive geodesic dome pulsing with energy fields and holographic interfaces. Inside, competitors wielding energy gauntlets and plasma swords had just finished their simulated galactic skirmishes and were filing out of the arena as we arrived. Outside, a crowd had already gathered, drawn by whispers spreading through the convention.

Shiloh stepped forward, accessing the arena's central control panel with practiced ease. "Reconfiguring for Wilderness Channel protocols," she announced, her fingers dancing across the interface. "Activating Breach Law parameters."

The arena's interior shimmered, reality wavering as conventional physics gave way to chaos. The familiar became strange, gravity shifted unpredictably, objects phased in and out of existence, and the very air seemed to breathe with sentient purpose.

Wire connected to the Celesticon announcement system. His voice boomed across the plaza, carrying to every corner of the convention. "Attention, cosmic travelers! History unfolds at the Quantum Battle Arena. The legendary Captain Blackmane faces a challenge from the

Misfits, in honor of the fallen Din crew."

The crowd's response was immediate. Thousands of attendees surged toward the arena, their costumes creating a river of color and light. Within minutes, every viewing platform surrounding the dome was packed with spectators.

"He's coming," Tumbler whispered, pointing to the arena's far entrance.

The air crackled. A storm gathered inside the dome, reality bending around a single point of distortion. Then he appeared.

Captain Silas Blackmane materialized in the arena, his crimson jacket and black sash rippling with spectral energy. Maelstrom's Fang hung at his hip, pulsating with an eerie light. His piercing storm-gray eyes swept across us, lingering on me with unnerving recognition.

"Well," he drawled, his voice carrying the weight of countless victories. "What have we here? New challengers for the Tempest's Wrath?"

His gaze shifted back to me, and his expression hardened. "I know you. You were with the Din." His eyes turned to Temper, narrowing. "And you, dragon... there's something familiar about you."

I stepped forward, the chronometric circuits on my Commander Radon costume pulsing faster. "We challenge you, Captain Blackmane. For the Din."

Blackmane's laugh echoed through the arena, deep and contemptuous. "The Din? That pathetic crew? Ten attempts, ten failures." He spat on the ground, the saliva evaporating into glittering motes of light. "Captain Drake was never worthy enough to challenge me. A pretender playing at piracy."

Pain shot through me at his callous words. To hear him dismissed so cruelly reopened wounds I hadn't realized still existed.

Through our connection, I felt Joan's protective anger rising. Her Nyx Hollow form rippled dangerously, the edges of her body becoming less distinct.

"And now you bring this... collection of outcasts?" Blackmane continued, gesturing dismissively toward my friends. "Children playing dress-up, thinking they can succeed where the Din failed?"

Shiloh stepped forward, her commander's uniform gleaming under the arena's shifting lights. "We are the Misfits. And we're here to finish what the Din started."

Blackmane's crew materialized behind him: Gideon with his massive Titanbreaker Maul, Elaria cradling her Voidpiercer Rifle, Malachai twirling his staff Tempestcall, Saria with her harp-like Siren's Lament, and Finn checking the chambers of Inferno's Grin.

"Very well," Blackmane said, drawing Maelstrom's Fang with a flourish. The blade hummed with power, sending ripples through the Breach Law reality. "Let's see if you can provide even a moment's entertainment before you fall."

Joan moved to my side, her form shifting subtly as she adjusted to the Breach Law environment. I felt her bristling through our connection, her ancient consciousness affronted by Blackmane's arrogance.

He underestimates us, she communicated silently. *He doesn't understand what we're capable of together.*

I nodded, feeling the weight of Commander Radon's identity settling over me. "For the Din," I whispered, as the Misfits formed a circle around me, ready to face the undefeated adversary at last.

The arena's reality twisted as Blackmane raised his hand. Fog poured from nowhere, swirling around our feet and climbing upward until it engulfed everything. When it cleared, we stood on what appeared to be the deck of a ship, but nothing about it followed natural law.

Through the fog, Blackmane's vessel, the Tempest's Wrath, materialized. Its hull shimmered with blending colors, simultaneously solid and liquid. The wooden deck grain shifted beneath our feet; patterns rewrote themselves with every step. Blackmane stood at the helm. His coat remained perfectly still while his hair thrashed in the wind like angry serpents.

"Welcome to my domain," Blackmane's voice came from everywhere at once. "Where reality obeys me."

The horizon blurred, colors bleeding from the edges of objects, smearing across my vision. Sounds arrived from contradictory directions, impossible to track. The water beneath us rippled, but not like water; at times it behaved like polished glass, reflecting twisted images of the sky. At others, it vanished completely, leaving us suspended over nothingness.

Shiloh stumbled, her footing uncertain on the shifting deck.

"Defensive stance!" she shouted, but her voice arrived after her lips had stopped moving.

Blackmane's crew materialized around us. Ironhide swung his Titanbreaker Maul in an arc that shattered the space around us. The blow landed before he'd even begun the swing, sending Skyhook flying backward.

"Wire, on your left!" I called, but "left" had no meaning here. Deadeye Thorn fired her Voidpiercer Rifle. Each bullet split into random possibilities, existing in multiple states until observed. Some hit before being fired. Others curved through dimensions we couldn't perceive.

Tumbler flipped to avoid a shot but found herself moving sideways instead of up. "This isn't possible!"

"Everything is possible under Breach Law," Blackmane laughed, the sound rippling through us like physical waves.

Stormcaster's magic merged with the chaos. The air itself became a weapon, molecules rearranging into patterns that attacked our senses directly. Jester fell to his knees, overwhelmed by sensory assault.

I watched Blackmane standing at the helm, reality bending around him. His black mane had become a living thing, each strand a thread of pure chaos. Maelstrom's Fang pulsed with power that fed on the impossible.

"This is why the Din failed," Blackmane called. "You cannot fight chaos with order."

I felt Joan's consciousness brush against mine. *But you can fight chaos with understanding.*

Joan stepped forward, her form shifting as she embraced her Nyx Hollow identity. The black diamond of her skin absorbed the chaotic light around her. She raised her hands, and frost crystallized in the air.

"Frostbite Strike," she whispered.

A concentrated burst of icy energy shot from her palms, not toward Blackmane but toward the distorted reality surrounding us. Where it touched, chaos slowed. Colors stopped bleeding. Sounds aligned with their sources.

Blackmane's confident smile faltered. "What is this?"

Joan moved with fluid grace, each step leaving frozen footprints that stabilized the deck beneath us. "Glacial Barrier," she intoned. A wall of unbreakable ice rose between Stormcaster and Tumbler, blocking his magical assault. The ice didn't just exist in physical space; it froze the probability waves of Breach Law itself.

"Impossible," Blackmane hissed, raising Maelstrom's Fang. The legendary sword howled as it cut through the air, reality splitting along its edge.

Joan countered with "Absolute Zero," briefly lowering the temperature around Blackmane to near absolute zero. His movements slowed as breach fluctuations ceased in the extreme cold.

I felt our hive mind connection pulse with power. Joan wasn't fighting Breach Law; she was working within it, using its own principles against it. Her ice magic didn't try to impose order on chaos; it simply slowed chaos to a manageable pace.

The Misfits rallied. Shiloh found her footing on the stabilized deck. Wire regained his sense of direction. Skyhook launched himself skyward, this time actually moving up instead of sideways.

Blackmane roared in frustration, swinging Maelstrom's Fang in a wide arc. The blade left trails of distortion, cutting through Joan's ice barriers. He advanced toward us, each step bending reality more severely.

"You think you understand Breach Law?" he snarled. "I am Breach Law!"

Joan met his gaze, unflinching. "No. You merely use it." She cast Ice Nova, releasing a shockwave of frost that rippled outward, countering the waves of distortion emanating from Blackmane.

For the first time in the battle, Captain Silas Blackmane looked uncertain. He raised Maelstrom's Fang high, gathering power for a devastating strike.

Blackmane's blade whistled down, unraveling space as it fell. I braced for impact, but Joan was faster. Her form blurred, shifting between states of matter as she stepped directly into the path of Maelstrom's Fang.

"Absolute Zero Cascade," she whispered.

The temperature plummeted. Frost crystals bloomed across the deck in fractal patterns. Blackmane's sword slowed mid-swing, entropy itself grinding to a halt around the blade. Ice crawled up the metal, encasing it in a glacial embrace that dulled the blade's hunger for power.

Blackmane struggled against the cold, his movements becoming sluggish. "What manner of magic is this?"

Joan didn't answer. Her consciousness brushed against mine through our hive mind, conveying more than words ever could. I understood immediately what she needed from me.

"Misfits! Convergence pattern!" I shouted.

They moved without hesitation. Shiloh circled to Blackmane's left flank. Marcus and Bea came from the right, hardening their armor for close combat. Temper's dragon form reared from the back, flames building in his throat. Jester fanned out to the right, ready to launch a counter attack against Blackmane's startled crew.

Joan's ice magic had created something unprecedented in the Wilderness Channel: stability within chaos. Small pockets of predictable physics amid the swirling Breach Law.

"Now!" I commanded.

We struck as one. Shiloh's tactical assault drove Blackmane backward. Marcus closed in with his Arcblade, the dark matter filaments cutting through Blackmane's defenses. Temper unleashed a concentrated burst of flame, creating a sudden temperature differential that shattered Blackmane's hold around Maelstrom's Fang.

The legendary sword fell from Blackmane's grasp, clattering to the deck.

Joan stepped forward. Her form shifted again, black diamond skin absorbing and reflecting the chaotic energies of Breach Law. She raised both hands, frost gathering around her fingertips.

"Permafrost Prison," she intoned.

Ice erupted from the deck beneath Blackmane's feet, encasing him up to his waist. More crystals formed around his arms, locking them in place. His crew rushed forward to aid him, but the Misfits intercepted them with practiced precision.

Tumbler and Wire engaged Ironhide, using his size against him. Skyhook dropped from above onto Stormcaster, disrupting his spellcasting. Jester's unpredictable movements kept Deadeye Thorn's aim scattered and ineffective.

Blackmane struggled against his icy bonds, his face contorted with rage and disbelief. "Impossible! No one masters Breach Law but me!"

Joan moved closer, each step leaving crystalline footprints that stabilized the deck. "You never mastered it. You only exploited it."

Through our connection, I felt the immense focus required for Joan to maintain control in this environment. Breach Law pulled at her consciousness, trying to scatter her thoughts across probabilities. She resisted with millennia of experience navigating quantum realities.

I stepped forward, picking up Maelstrom's Fang. The sword hummed in my grip, its chaos temporarily subdued by Joan's influence.

"For Captain Drake," I said quietly. "For the Din."

Blackmane's crew, seeing their captain immobilized and his legendary weapon in enemy hands, broke formation. Ironhide backed away, lowering his maul. Deadeye Thorn lowered her rifle. Stormcaster's magic fizzled out as his concentration faltered.

"Retreat!" Deadeye called, her melodic voice cracking with fear. "Back to the channel!"

They scattered across the deck, reality warping around them as they fled. Without Blackmane's focus, the Tempest's Wrath began to destabilize, its impossible architecture folding in on itself.

Blackmane watched his crew abandon him, his storm-gray eyes wide with shock. For the first time in countless battles, the feared captain faced defeat.

"The Din sends their regards," I told him, raising Maelstrom's Fang.

I brought Maelstrom's Fang down in a sweeping arc, not toward Blackmane, but into the deck beside him. The legendary blade sank deep into the wooden planks, severing the captain's connection to the Breach Law reality he had manipulated for so long.

The effect was immediate and spectacular. The chaotic environment collapsed around us, reality snapping back to conventional physics with such force that it threw us all backward. Colors reintegrated, sounds synchronized with their sources, and gravity resumed its predictable pull.

The Tempest's Wrath dissolved into mist, leaving us standing in the center of the Quantum Battle Arena. The holographic interfaces flickered back to life, displaying our victory in pulsing neon letters that stretched across the geodesic dome. The crowd erupted into deafening cheers.

Captain Silas Blackmane knelt where his ship had been, his crimson jacket now dull, his black mane hanging limp around his shoulders. Without Breach Law to empower him, he looked smaller, almost ordinary. The arena's conventional physics held him firmly in place.

"Impossible," he whispered, his voice no longer echoing from multiple directions at once. "No one has ever..."

Shiloh stepped forward, her commander's uniform still pristine despite the battle's chaos. She cast a solemn glance over the battlefield, where frost still clung to the ruins, the undeniable mark of Joan's victory. She exhaled, steady but reverent.

"The Misfits have succeeded where the Din could not. But it was ice—Joan's ice—that turned the tide. A force as unyielding as the warriors who came before us."

The crowd's roar intensified. Spectators pressed against the barriers, their costumes creating a kaleidoscope of color around the arena. Some wore replicas of Captain Drake's jacket. Others had painted their faces with the Din emblem. They chanted "Misfits" over and over, the sound rolling through the dome.

Joan moved to my side, her form shifting subtly as she readjusted to conventional physics. The black diamond of her skin caught the arena lights, fracturing them into tiny rainbows. Her expression remained impassive, but through our hive mind connection, I felt her satisfaction.

"A fitting tribute," she said quietly.

I nodded, feeling the weight of victory settle over me. We had done what Captain Drake could not. We had defeated the undefeatable foe, avenged the Din, and written a new chapter in the legend of the Wilderness Channel.

Joan leaned close, her lips near my ear. "Remember this moment, Go David," she whispered. "Treat me well, or you might find yourself in Blackmane's position someday."

Her tone was light, playful, but through our connection, I felt something else: a flicker of her true nature, ancient and powerful beyond human comprehension. For a brief moment, I glimpsed the vastness of her consciousness, spanning dimensions I could barely perceive.

I chuckled, both at her joke and at my own momentary unease. Joan was alien in ways I was still discovering, capable of wielding forces that defied conventional understanding. But beneath that power lay something else I could feel clearly through our connection: genuine affection, trust, and a deep-seated playfulness.

I would never risk losing you, I thought, knowing she would sense it through our bond.

Her response came not in words but in a wave of emotion: warmth, trust, and a complex tenderness that transcended human expression. Our hive mind connection hummed with harmony, two vastly different consciousnesses finding perfect resonance.

The crowd continued to cheer as we made our way toward the exit, leaving Captain Blackmane and the Wilderness Channel behind. Today, we had written legend. Tomorrow, we would return to our quantum villa on Falfsun, to the life we had built among the stars.

"I never imagined we'd actually pull it off," Marcus said, his Major Kael Vindex costume gleaming under the festival lights.

Shiloh punched his arm playfully. "Never doubted us for a second."

The celebration moved to a nearby cantina, its walls adorned with memorabilia from classic adventure games. A bartender slid drinks across the counter, each glass glowing with bioluminescent liquid that shifted colors with the ambient music.

"To Joan and the Misfits," Temper raised his glass, his dragon form drawing curious stares from other Celesticon attendees. "And to Captain Drake, wherever his spirit sails."

"To Joan and the Misfits," we echoed.

Bea leaned forward, her Nova Striker costume catching the light. "So what really happened in there? One moment Blackmane had us cornered, the next everything just... stabilized."

Joan's fingers brushed against mine under the table. Through our connection, I felt her amusement.

"Let's just say we found the pattern in the chaos," I replied.

Temper snorted. "Very cryptic, Captain."

Stories flowed as freely as the drinks. Marcus recounted his first disastrous attempt at navigating the Wilderness Channel. Shiloh told tales of near-victories against lesser bosses. Even Bea, usually reserved, shared her experience with the Dimensional Rift Challenge from last year's Celesticon.

I watched them, these remarkable people who had become my family. The Misfits weren't just a gaming clan. They were the connections that anchored us through time's relentless passage.

Joan leaned close. "They're happy," she whispered, her human form warm against my side.

"We gave them something rare," I replied. "A perfect moment."

Through our connection, I felt her understanding. We who measured our lives in centuries recognized the value of these fleeting celebrations.

The night deepened. Other Celesticon attendees approached our table, asking for details about our strategy, requesting photos with the team that defeated Blackmane. A group of Din cosplayers presented us with a replica of Captain Drake's jacket, modified with the Misfits emblem stitched alongside the original.

"He would have approved," I told them, running my fingers over the fabric.

As the festivities continued around us, Joan and I found a quiet corner. The sounds of celebration created a comfortable backdrop to our silence.

"You were magnificent," I said.

Her smile held secrets from a thousand worlds. "We were magnificent."

I nodded, feeling the truth of it through our connection. What we had accomplished wasn't just about gaming prowess. It represented something deeper: our ability to bridge vastly different perspectives, to find harmony in apparent chaos.

"I think it's time," she said after a while.

I knew what she meant without further explanation. The others had their own lives to return to, responsibilities that waited beyond this celebration.

We rejoined the group as the first hints of morning touched the horizon. The cantina had emptied except for our table, where empty glasses and shared stories had built a monument to our victory.

"Back to reality tomorrow," Marcus sighed, his arm around Bea.

Shiloh nodded. "Etherean patrol won't wait."

"And those star charts aren't going to study themselves," Bea added.

One by one, they stood to leave, exchanging embraces and promises to meet again soon.

As they departed, I felt Joan's consciousness brush against mine, sharing her contentment. We had given our friends this perfect moment of triumph and unity. Now they returned to their paths, carrying this victory with them.

Tomorrow, Joan and I would return to our villa on Falfsun. But tonight, we savored this rare convergence of paths, this celebration of what we had accomplished together.

CHAPTER ELEVEN

A Shared Destiny

The months following Celesticon settled into a comfortable rhythm. Joan and I found peace living next door to Temper on Falfsun, where the boundaries between ordinary existence and cosmic wonder blurred daily. Our home pulsed with the star's energy, walls shifting subtly to accommodate our needs.

Most mornings began with Joan materializing in the kitchen after one of her dimensional explorations. She'd appear with little warning, sometimes bearing strange-looking fruits from distant realms or simply carrying the faint scent of quantum tunnels.

"The corridor between the seventh and eighth dimensions was particularly beautiful today," she remarked one morning, her form settling into solidity as she reached for a cup of coffee. "Like swimming through liquid mathematics."

I nodded, having long stopped questioning the impossible nature of her journeys. "Temper's waiting on his lawn. Says Falfsun's corona is showing unusual patterns."

Temper's property remained our frequent destination. His patch of impossibly green grass, shielded from the worst of the star's heat, served as our meeting place. I often found the two of them there, Temper's dragon form casting a peculiar shadow as they pointed at phenomena invisible to ordinary perception.

"Falfsun's mass has increased nearly fourteen percent since last year," Temper announced as I approached, his tail swishing with excitement. "At this rate, its fusion reactions will settle into the steady burn typical of red dwarfs within three years."

Joan nodded, her eyes reflecting the star's deep crimson glow. "The magnetic field lines are stabilizing nicely. Feel that harmonic resonance?"

I couldn't, of course. Their perception extended far beyond mine, but I enjoyed their enthusiasm, nonetheless.

Between these peaceful moments came my duties. The Etherean patrols took me across dozens of systems weekly, hunting for unauthorized colonization attempts. The Weltnehmen corporations grew more creative with each passing month, developing stealth technologies and ecological workarounds to bypass Galactic Court restrictions.

Last Tuesday, I caught a Proxima Mining vessel deploying seed drones over a gas giant's moon. The drones would have transformed the delicate methane ecosystem into an industrial mining operation within months.

"Gravity pull initiated," I announced to their captain over the comm channel. His face paled as I activated my Planck toolkit.

The satisfaction never diminished, watching their vessel suddenly accelerate toward Earth, dragged by artificial gravity. Their protests cut off mid-sentence as the quantum corridor collapsed behind them, leaving only empty space where exploitation had been planned.

The Court's justice would be swift, if not particularly harsh. First offenses typically resulted in heavy fines. Second offenses meant vessel seizure. The system worked, mostly.

Evenings in our villa centered around cooking. The kitchen expanded or contracted according to our needs, sometimes opening to reveal the star's surface rolling beneath transparent floors, other times closing into a cozy space that might have belonged in any Earth home.

"You're using too much heat," Joan observed as I attempted to recreate Alice Tracker's Solar-Spiced Fusion Pasta. Her latest episode had featured ingredients from three different star systems.

"Alice says the quantum foam needs to reach exactly ninety-three degrees," I protested, adjusting the Planck toolkit's energy output.

Joan smiled, her outline flickering as she reached through a fold in space to retrieve a spice that I had forgotten. "Alice doesn't cook on a living star."

Joan had become a devoted follower of "Seasoned Table". Alice's enthusiasm for cosmic cuisine had inspired a whole segment on stellar cooking, though a lot of her viewers still didn't realize that she'd actually filmed on Falfsun's surface.

The pasta turned out perfectly, despite our concerns. We ate on the villa's observation deck, watching energy currents dance across Falfsun's horizon while discussing Marcus and Bea's progress with the Vraxeik technology.

"They've nearly completed the initial simulations," I said, reviewing the latest update. "Once the Court approves the project, we can begin the first practical field tests."

Joan nodded, her expression thoughtful. "The universe has time. We have time."

And we did. Our quiet life on Falfsun stretched before us, measured not in days or years but in stellar cycles and dimensional shifts. For now, this peace was enough.

Joan and I settled into comfortable patterns, punctuated by her dimensional excursions and my enforcement patrols. Sometimes we'd spend entire weeks exploring the quantum tunnels together, other times we'd simply watch Temper's experiments from the safety of our observation deck.

Marcus and Bea visited occasionally, bringing news of their research on the Vraxeik technology. Each simulation they ran brought us closer to understanding how vacuum energy manipulation might slow the universe's relentless expansion. The work was painstaking, requiring precision beyond anything humanity had attempted before.

"We can't rush this," Bea explained during their last visit. "One miscalculation could destabilize entire galactic sectors."

Joan nodded, her eyes reflecting the gravity of the moment. "The Vraxeik spent millennia refining these techniques for their native spacetime. We must honor their caution before adapting them to ours."

On the morning that Captain Smith contacted us, I was tending to our garden. The plants lived in several stages at once: blossoming, ripening, shedding. Joan had conjured this place for me, knowing how deeply I missed the fertile soil of Lucky Star Farm.

I felt her consciousness shift before I heard her voice. Our hive mind connection, forged during the time crystal crisis, allowed me to sense her emotions even when we weren't actively sharing thoughts.

"Go." Her voice carried an unusual tension. "Captain Smith is calling."

I found her in our communication room, her form flickering slightly as it sometimes did when she was unsettled. Smith's holographic image hovered above our table, his expression carefully neutral.

"Joan," Smith nodded respectfully. "The Galactic Court has formally requested your presence at a closed hearing regarding the Vraxeik technology."

Joan's skin rippled, black diamond patterns momentarily visible beneath her human appearance. "When?"

"Three days from now. Earth's governments and the united congregations want a firsthand account of what you learned. It's mostly procedural posturing, the final step before granting approval to begin practical implementation."

I felt Joan's unease pulse through our connection. Though she never said it aloud, I knew she distrusted bureaucracy. Her experiences spanned dimensions and civilizations far beyond human comprehension; sitting before a panel of officials felt confining.

"Will Marcus and Bea be there?" I asked.

Smith nodded. "They'll present the simulation results. But the Court specifically wants Joan's testimony about the Vraxeik themselves. They need assurance this isn't some cosmic trap."

Joan remained silent, her mind calculating possibilities I could only partly perceive.

"I'll accompany her," I said, reaching for her hand. Through our connection, I sent reassurance, memories of other challenges we'd overcome together.

"That would be appreciated," Smith replied. "The Court can be... intimidating, even when they're on your side."

After Smith's image faded, Joan turned to me. "They fear what they don't understand."

"They're being cautious," I countered. "Manipulating vacuum energy across galactic scales isn't exactly a minor undertaking."

Joan smiled, her form stabilizing. "You're right, of course. The Vraxeik themselves required consensus among sixteen elder councils before implementing their first test."

I squeezed her hand. "We'll face them together. Besides, I'm curious to see Earth again after all this time."

"Earth," Joan repeated, as if tasting the word. "So small, yet so significant."

We spent the next day preparing. Joan reviewed the Vraxeik knowledge she'd received, organizing it into terms humans might comprehend. I contacted Marcus and Bea, coordinating our approach. The technology's implementation would require unprecedented cooperation between Earth's governments, the congregations, and the Ethereans.

"Do you think they'll try to control it?" Joan asked that night as we watched Falfsun's corona dance above us.

"They'll try," I admitted. "But some things can't be controlled, only guided."

Joan nodded, her gaze distant. "Like the universe itself."

The day of the hearing arrived with the peculiar stillness that always seemed to accompany important moments. Joan and I traveled to Earth, the familiar sensation of falling through reality lasting only seconds before we materialized outside the Galactic Court complex in Geneva.

The building itself was a marvel of post-Weltnehmen architecture, constructed from materials gathered across seven star systems. Its translucent walls shifted subtly with the movements of those inside, a physical manifestation of justice's fluid nature.

Marcus and Bea waited for us at the entrance; both dressed in formal attire that seemed at odds with their usual research garb. Bea embraced Joan while Marcus gripped my shoulder.

"The simulation results are solid," he murmured. "Even the Court's scientists couldn't find fault with our methodology."

Joan nodded, her ant form perfectly maintained despite her obvious tension. "They'll question my interactions with the Vraxeik most intensely. Their fear centers on trust."

"We're scheduled after you," Bea added. "Our testimony is purely technical."

We approached the massive doors of the hearing chamber. Two Court officials stood guard, their uniforms bearing the insignia representing all major Earth governments and congregations.

"Only the witness may enter," one stated, gesturing toward Joan.

She turned to me, her eyes conveying more than words could. Through our connection, I felt her resolve strengthen.

"I'll be fine," she said simply.

"I know you will." I squeezed her hand, sending reassurance through our link.

The doors parted, revealing a semicircular chamber beyond. Joan stepped forward, her posture straight and confident. The doors sealed behind her with a soft hiss.

I turned to Marcus and Bea. "We have some time to kill. Are you hungry?"

Marcus grinned. "Starving."

"How about an early lunch at Selene?" I suggested. "Joan's testimony will take at least that long."

Bea's eyes lit up. "The restaurant on the Moon? I've been wanting to try it!"

We activated our Planck toolkits simultaneously, initiating gravity pulls to the coordinates of Selene atop the Moon's Sea of Rains. The universe compressed around us, stars blurring into streaks of light before resolving into the stark lunar landscape.

Selene materialized before us, its boundaries defined by shimmering streams of lunar dust suspended in midair. The restaurant had no walls, no ceiling, just elegant tables floating above the gray lunar surface with Earth hanging in the black sky above.

A host greeted us, leading us to a table positioned for an optimal view of both our home planet and the cratered lunar horizon. "The seven-course tasting menu is exceptional today," she suggested.

We unanimously agreed, settling in as our first course arrived.

"Crab with basil, heirloom tomato, and burrata cream," our server announced, placing delicate opaline plates before us.

The dish was a miniature work of art, the crab arranged in a spiral pattern with droplets of basil oil suspended above it, defying lunar gravity through some culinary trick.

"So," I began, savoring the sweet crab meat, "tell me more about your ghost ship."

Marcus's eyes lit up. "We finally have time to study it again. The ship's frescoes are unlike anything we've encountered. They line entire corridors, telling stories we're still deciphering."

"They used color differently than humans," Bea added as our second course arrived. "Sea bass with dashi broth, artichoke three ways, and platinum caviar."

The fish floated just above the surface of the broth, steam rising in perfect spirals.

"Their art depicts journeys between galaxies," Marcus continued. "Not just physical travel, but philosophical transitions. We think they saw expansion itself as a kind of migration."

I nodded, "And the artifacts?"

"Mostly ceremonial," Bea replied. "Though we found what might be personal logs, recorded in phaseglass structures that respond to touch."

I hesitated, then voiced the thought that had been circling my mind. "I've been considering contacting David and Amy."

They both looked up from their sea bass.

"You should," Marcus said immediately. "Why wouldn't you?"

I poked at a sphere of artichoke puree. "It's been decades. They've built their lives in Haven. I'm not sure I belong in that world anymore."

Bea reached across the table, her hand covering mine. "David is your Prime, Go. You share the same foundation, even if your experiences have diverged."

"And Amy loved both of you," Marcus added. "She always understood what your split meant better than anyone."

I lifted my gaze to Earth, suspended in the endless black of the lunar sky. Somewhere beneath its restless clouds, my other self walked beside the woman we had both loved. The longing had faded, no longer sharp as it once was, but love, quiet and enduring, remained in its own way, untouched by time.

"Perhaps you're right," I conceded.

Our peach dessert arrived, adorned with sorbet and honey

zéphyr. The sorbet melted slightly in the restaurant's warmth, creating rivers of sweetness that pooled around sugar filigree. I savored each bite, the tart-sweet flavors mingling on my tongue while my thoughts drifted toward Earth.

"I should get back," I said finally. "Joan's testimony will be finishing soon."

Marcus nodded, wiping his mouth with a napkin that shimmered like stardust. "We should head to the Court too. Our presentation slot is next."

We paid and activated our Planck toolkits, gravity-pulling back to Geneva. The Court building stood serene against the afternoon sky, its translucent walls reflecting sunlight in gentle waves. No sign of Joan yet.

"We'll see you after," Bea said, squeezing my arm before they headed inside.

I found a quiet bench in the adjacent garden and pulled out my planck pulse. The device hummed softly as I entered David and Amy's contact information, numbers I hadn't used in nearly seventy years but somehow never forgot.

My finger hovered over the activation button. What would I even say? *Hello, it's the copy of you who went to the stars while you stayed behind?* The thought made me chuckle nervously.

Before I could reconsider, I pressed connect. The communicator pulsed three times, then a holographic interface appeared above my palm. The connection symbol spun lazily as it searched across Haven for their signal.

"Hello?" David's voice came through first, followed by his image forming in the hologram. His face – my face – looked older than when I'd last seen him, but still remarkably youthful for someone well over two hundred.

His eyes widened. "Go?"

"Hello, David." My voice sounded steadier than I felt.

"Amy!" he called over his shoulder. "Amy, you need to see this."

Her face appeared beside his, and something in my chest tightened. Her hair was still the same warm brown with touches of silver, her eyes just as bright. Seventy years had passed, but medical advances on Earth had been kind to them both.

"Go David," she said softly. "Is it really you?"

I nodded, suddenly finding words difficult. "It's been a while."

"Only about seven decades," David said with a hint of a smile. "Nothing major."

The tension broke. We laughed, and suddenly it felt like no time had passed at all.

"Are you on Earth?" Amy asked, leaning closer to the hologram.

"Geneva. Just for the day. I'm waiting for..." I hesitated, then decided to keep it simple. "For a friend who's testifying at the Galactic Court."

"We're not far," David said. "Just outside London. We could be there in an hour."

I hadn't expected this, hadn't dared hope they'd want to see me so readily. "I'd like that. Very much."

We agreed to meet at a small pavilion in Parc Geisendorf, just outside the city. After ending the call, I sat back, my heart racing with a mixture of anxiety and anticipation. Joan was still inside, and Marcus and Bea would be presenting soon. I sent Joan a quick message through our link, explaining where I'd be.

An hour later, I stood beneath the pavilion's wooden beams, watching people stroll through the park. Families with children, elderly couples, teenagers sprawled on the grass. Ordinary life continuing as it had for centuries, oblivious to the cosmic scales being balanced in the Court building across the city.

Then I saw them approaching along the path. Amy looked exactly as she had in the hologram, dressed in a simple blue dress that caught the afternoon light. David walked beside her, his gait mirroring my own. I smiled, and she smiled pensively back.

David and I circled each other and then, almost in unison, we said, "You are one good-looking dude."

"Are you thinking what I'm thinking?" David asked.

I nodded. We turned to Amy.

"Which one of us is which?" we asked together.

This got a laugh out of her. She walked over and took both of us by the arm.

"I swear, you two are the best-looking men I've ever met!"

Then, more seriously, she said, "I wasn't sure you would ever want to see me again."

"I wasn't sure you would want to see me either."

I filled them in on everything: Marcus and Bea, the adventures I had been on, my relationship with Joan, Temper as a dragon living on Falfsun. They told me about their life, about Tom, Temper's Prime, who was currently off-world, working for the Giese congregation. I told them about the Paradise and the two million lives lost.

Emotion overwhelmed me. I hugged David. "Thank you for giving me my life."

Amy told me about her friendship with the Oracle, and how he had helped her finally beat her crippling thiamine deficiency illness for good. David had been her rock, as always. She dried her eyes and asked, "I'm glad to hear your stories... so everything is going well for you now?"

I beamed. It felt good to reconnect after all these years.

"Amy, I've had a remarkably awesome life. If there is anything that I can do for either of you, don't hesitate to call." We agreed to keep in touch from now on and meet occasionally whenever time permitted.

After saying goodbye to David and Amy, I found myself craving solitude. Their faces lingered in my mind, familiar yet strange, like looking at an old photograph of myself taken in a life I never fully lived. I activated my Planck toolkit and initiated a gravity pull back to the Moon, choosing coordinates away from Selene's elegant dining spaces.

I materialized on the vast plains of the Sea of Rains. My boots sank slightly into the fine regolith, leaving perfect impressions that would remain untouched by wind or rain for centuries to come. Each step I took etched a quiet permanence into the lunar surface. The thought made me smile. These footprints would outlast most human monuments.

I walked slowly, savoring the slight bounce in my step from the reduced gravity. Earth hung in the black sky; a perfect blue marble wrapped in swirling white clouds. Unlike the flat, distant image of the Moon in Earth's nighttime sky, Earth appeared gloriously round, like a polished gem suspended in the void. I imagined I could leap high enough to pluck it like an apple from one of my trees on Lucky Star Farm.

I jumped, testing my theory. The sensation of floating momentarily made me laugh out loud. The sound in the airless atmosphere stayed silent within me. I jumped again, higher this time. For a fleeting moment, as I glimpsed the slight curvature of the Moon's horizon, I felt as if I might tumble off its edge into the endless black. It was a strangely delightful sensation.

Finding the shadow of a crater wall, I materialized a simple lawn chair using my Planck toolkit. The absurdity of sitting in ordinary furniture on the lunar surface struck me, but that was my life now. The extraordinary had become commonplace, the impossible routine.

I created a drink next, a glass of iced tea that would have instantly frozen or boiled away without a shell of tempered reality protecting it. I sipped slowly, gazing up at Earth, thinking of all the lives continuing there, oblivious to the cosmic scales being balanced in the Court.

Through our hive mind connection, I gently reached toward Joan. She allowed me in, maintaining her focus on the Court proceedings. I could see through her eyes: the semicircular chamber, the panel of officials representing Earth's governments and the united congregations, their faces serious as they questioned her about the Vraxeik.

"And you're certain their intentions were benevolent?" a woman in congregation robes asked.

"The Vraxeik evolved beyond deception millions of years ago," Joan replied. "Their entire civilization was built on radical transparency. Dishonesty would have been as foreign to them as breathing water is to humans."

I sensed her frustration at having to translate concepts that transcended human understanding into terms these officials could grasp. Yet she remained patient, her ant form perfectly maintained despite the pressure.

A man in a business suit leaned forward. "But this technology, manipulating vacuum energy across galactic scales. The potential for weaponization is concerning."

"The technology cannot be weaponized," Joan stated flatly. "It functions on principles that require universal balance. Any attempt to concentrate or direct the effect would cause immediate collapse of the system."

I smiled at her directness. Joan never bothered with diplomatic niceties when facts would suffice.

As the questioning continued, I let my attention drift back to my surroundings. The stark beauty of the lunar landscape stretched in all directions; craters upon craters, some so ancient they had been partially erased by newer impacts. The horizon curved gently away, a reminder of how small this world was compared to Earth, yet how vast compared to human scale.

My life had become something I could never have imagined when I first split from David. I had been created for a thirteen-hundred-year journey that never happened, then forced to forge a new purpose. I had found love with Amy, lost her to time and distance, raised Marcus, befriended Temper, and now found connection with Joan, a being who had once seemed utterly alien.

Through our link, I felt Joan's attention shift briefly toward me. *It's going well,* she sent. *They're afraid, but they're listening.*

I sent back warmth and reassurance, then withdrew slightly to give her space to focus. The taste of iced tea lingered on my tongue as I gazed up at Earth, suspended in the void like a promise of home I no longer needed to keep.

I left the stark lunar surface behind, my gravity pull delivering me to the courthouse steps in Geneva. The Galactic Court building rose before me, its translucent walls capturing the late afternoon sunlight in gentle, undulating waves. Officials and representatives from across the known galaxy streamed through the main doors, their expressions ranging from thoughtful to concerned.

Joan was just stepping outside when I arrived. Her black diamond skin gleamed in the sunlight, catching the light in a thousand tiny facets. In this public setting, she had chosen to maintain her ant form rather than her human appearance. I wondered if her hardened, glimmering exterior was a protective shell, an attempt to fortify herself against whatever had shaped her past. Perhaps she saw herself as an insect, small and insignificant against the enormity of the universe. That thought brought a familiar unease to the pit of my stomach.

She turned toward me, her faceted head tilting slightly. No words passed between us, but I felt her presence in my mind through our hive connection.

They're considering the evidence, she projected, her thoughts precise and measured. *The Court remains skeptical, but they're not dismissing the Vraxeik findings outright.*

I nodded, moving closer to her side as a group of congregation representatives passed by, their formal robes rustling against the marble steps. *"And Marcus and Bea's presentation?"*

Compelling. Their analysis of the Vraxeik's technology provided tangible proof that supported my testimony. A ripple of something like pride moved through our connection. *The humans listened more attentively to data they could see and measure.*

"Of course they did," I said with a small smile. "We're stubborn that way."

Joan's form shifted slightly, the diamond planes of her body catching different angles of light. *Your species fears what it cannot understand.* The thought wasn't accusatory, merely observational. *Fear is a reasonable response to the unknown.*

A cool breeze swept across the courthouse plaza, carrying the scent of nearby gardens. I studied Joan's alien form, struck by how vulnerable she seemed despite her impenetrable exterior. She sensed my feelings and confirmed my impressions with gentle thoughts that felt like smiles.

You see me clearly, Go David.

"I try to." I gestured toward a quiet path leading away from the courthouse. "Shall we walk? I could use some movement after sitting still for so long."

We moved away from the crowd, following a tree-lined path that wound through carefully tended gardens. The path was empty; most court attendees having chosen more direct routes back to the city center.

You met with your Prime today, Joan observed, her mental voice soft with curiosity.

"Yes. And Amy." I let the memories of our reunion flow through our connection rather than trying to articulate them with words. Joan absorbed them silently, her ant form glittering as we passed through alternating patches of sunlight and shadow.

You feel... settled, she finally responded. *The meeting brought closure.*

"It did." I reached out, my fingers hovering near her diamond surface without touching. "Seeing them helped me understand that we've all found our paths. Different journeys, but equally valid."

Joan's form shifted again, this time more dramatically. The black diamond facets began to flow like liquid, restructuring themselves until she stood beside me in her human form, her dark skin warm in the fading light.

"The Court will reconvene tomorrow," she said aloud, her voice carrying the musical quality I'd grown to cherish. "They want to review the simulation data overnight."

I nodded, feeling a cautious optimism in her tone that mirrored my own. "Then we have the evening to ourselves."

As we walked through Geneva's gardens, away from the Galactic Court building, I felt a strange sense of full-circle completion.

"It occurs to me," I said, "that my entire existence has been about connection."

Joan glanced at me, curiosity rippling through our hive mind link. "How so?"

"I was created to connect Earth to the stars, to bridge the distance between here and Orion. When that purpose was taken from me, I felt lost."

We passed beneath an ancient oak, its branches casting dappled shadows across the path.

"Then I connected with Marcus, raising him from a confused young thruman into someone who could build his own relationships. I maintained my connection with Temper, keeping him tethered to humanity while he communed with his star."

Joan's consciousness brushed against mine, encouraging me to continue.

"And now, there's you. A connection that transcends conventional understanding." I smiled, feeling the truth of it settle within me. "And beyond us, this work with the Vraxeik technology. It's about connecting our efforts to the greater cosmic balance, ensuring life continues its journey."

"Connection across scales," Joan observed. "From personal to universal."

"Exactly." I stopped walking, turning to face her. "That's why seeing David and Amy today felt right. It closed a circle that needed closing. I'm not just a copy sent to the stars anymore. I'm Go David, who builds bridges between worlds."

Joan's form shimmered slightly, black diamond facets momentarily visible beneath her human appearance. "And what of the future? Once the Court approves the Vraxeik technology?"

"More connections," I said simply. "New understandings. The work never ends, it just changes form."

The setting sun caught the edges of the courthouse's translucent walls, sending rainbow fragments dancing across the garden. Tomorrow would bring decisions and responsibilities. But tonight, I understood my place in this vast, expanding universe more clearly than ever before.

We strolled through the gardens in comfortable silence, the evening light softening around us. Earth's ancient city sprawled beyond the courthouse grounds, its timeworn buildings standing shoulder to shoulder with modern architecture that seemed to defy gravity. After the intensity of the court proceedings and my unexpected reunion with David and Amy, this quiet moment felt precious.

Joan walked beside me, her human form moving with a grace that still fascinated me. Her eyes caught the fading sunlight, reflecting depths I'd only begun to explore through our hive mind connection.

"Are you hungry?" I asked suddenly.

She turned to me, her expression curious. "I could eat."

"I was thinking..." I paused, considering the absurdity of what I was about to suggest. After battling colonizer bots, containing time crystals, and testifying before the Galactic Court about the fate of the universe, my idea seemed almost childishly simple. But perhaps that was exactly what we needed. "I was wondering, would you like to go on a picnic? I know a great spot on the moon."

Joan's eyebrows rose slightly, and for a moment, I thought she might find the suggestion too frivolous. Then her lips curved into a smile that transformed her entire face.

"The moon," she repeated, as if testing the idea. "With real food? Not quantum-generated?"

"Absolutely real," I promised. "I spotted a little market near the courthouse. We could pick up some cheese, bread, maybe some of those Earth fruits you were curious about."

Her smile widened. "I'd like that."

Twenty minutes later, we'd assembled a modest feast in a wicker basket I'd found at the market. The shopkeeper had wrapped crusty bread in paper, adding a selection of local cheeses, plums, and a bottle of wine with two glasses. I'd added a checkered cloth on impulse, earning an amused look from Joan.

"Traditional," I'd explained with a shrug.

Now, with our purchases secure, we found a quiet alley away from curious eyes. I activated my Planck toolkit, feeling the familiar tingle as the quantum field enveloped us. Joan stepped closer, her shoulder brushing mine as I initiated the gravity pull.

The world blurred, then reformed around us. We stood once again on the Sea of Rains, but this time I'd chosen coordinates that offered a perfect view of both Earth and the rising sun just cresting the lunar horizon. The luminous glow of Earth hovered against the endless black, a brilliant blue-white beacon in the void. The Sun's stark radiance poured over the cratered terrain, casting long shadows that stretched toward infinity.

I spread the checkered cloth on the fine lunar dust, anchoring it with small rocks I gathered nearby. Joan watched me with that gentle curiosity that made me feel simultaneously ancient and newborn.

"You've done this before," she observed.

"Picnics, yes. Lunar picnics?" I laughed. "This is a first."

We settled on the cloth, a veil of borrowed Earth enclosing us in a perfect bubble of warmth and breath. I arranged our simple feast between us, pouring wine into the glasses with a flourish that made Joan's eyes crinkle at the corners.

"To new adventures," I said, raising my glass.

She mirrored my gesture, her dark eyes reflecting starlight. "To finding home in unexpected places."

As we clinked glasses, I felt something settle within me. The universe might be expanding toward entropy, and tomorrow we would continue our work to save it. But tonight, under Earth's watchful gaze, we had this moment of perfect simplicity.

Joan took a bite of cheese, her expression thoughtful. "It's strange," she said after a moment. "I've traversed dimensions, walked between universes, yet something as simple as this..." She gestured to our picnic, to the lunar landscape around us. "This feels more extraordinary."

I nodded, understanding completely. "Sometimes the ordinary becomes miraculous when shared with the right person."

She smiled at me, and in that moment, her ant form shimmered briefly through her human appearance, not a revelation, but a quiet gesture of trust. A glimpse of the many selves she carried, offered only to me. I smiled back, cherishing the intimacy of that flicker.

"The ant approves of our picnic," I said, warmth blooming in my chest.

She nodded, amused. "Ants are so cute."

We sat together in our borrowed bubble of Earth, surrounded by silence and stars, the universe vast and unknowable—and somehow, in this moment, entirely ours.

As Earth hung in the void above us, I realized how far I'd traveled from my original purpose. Created to journey to Orion, I had instead found my destiny in unexpected connections: with Marcus, with Temper, with Joan, and now potentially with the fate of the universe itself.

"What are you thinking?" Joan asked, her voice gentle in our shared atmosphere.

"About destiny," I replied. "How rarely it resembles what we imagine."

She nodded, understanding flowing between us through our connection. "The Vraxeik believe destiny isn't predetermined but emerges through relationship, with each other, with the cosmos itself."

I reached for her hand, feeling the warm solidity of her chosen form. "Like us."

"Like us," she agreed.

We sat together, a small bubble of life on the barren lunar surface, sharing bread and wine and possibility. Tomorrow we would return to the Court, would begin the work of implementing the Vraxeik technology, would take our place among the civilizations responsible for guiding universal forces.

But tonight, under Earth's watchful gaze, we had this perfect moment, this shared destiny that neither of us could have predicted but both had somehow found.

The universe might be expanding toward entropy, but here, between us, something was growing stronger, more connected, more resilient. And perhaps that was the true purpose all along: not to reach Orion, but to discover that the journey itself was home.

Leave a Review

Reviews help independent authors like me keep creating stories that matter. If you enjoyed this book, I'd be deeply grateful if you shared your thoughts. Even a sentence makes a difference.

Please consider leaving a review to help others discover this story.

About the Author. David Melde is a ceremonial literary science fiction author and founder of Bright Thread Books, a mythic imprint devoted to transformative, philosophical fiction. His work invites readers into moments of presence, reflection, and quiet disruption. Every book is a living ceremony.

Book Club Questions

Book Club Discussion Questions for "The Go David Chronicles: Book Three - Destiny"

Character and Identity

1. **Identity Exploration**: Go David struggles with his identity throughout the series. If you could create a "copy" of yourself for a specific purpose, what parts of your identity would you want that copy to preserve, and what parts might you hope would evolve differently?

2. **Character Growth**: Which character do you believe undergoes the most significant transformation in this book? What catalyzes their change, and does it resonate with any transformations you've experienced in your own life?

Relationships and Connection

1. **The Hive Mind Experience**: Joan and Go David share a hive mind connection that allows them to experience each other's thoughts and feelings directly. If such technology existed, would you want to connect with someone this way? What would be the benefits and drawbacks?

2. **Chosen Family**: The novel emphasizes connections formed through choice rather than biology. How does your own experience with "chosen family" compare to the relationships formed in the book? Has a friend ever become as important to you as a family member?

Philosophical Ponderings

1. **Time and Perspective**: Characters in the book live for centuries and view time very differently than humans with standard lifespans. How might your priorities and values change if you knew you would live for thousands of years? What would become more important or less important?
2. **Reality and Perception**: Joan tells Go, "Think in shapes, not lines." How do you interpret this advice about perception? Have you ever experienced a moment when shifting your perspective fundamentally changed your understanding of a situation?

Playful Questions

1. **Adventure Games**: If you could join any of the adventure games mentioned in the book (like the Din missions or Wilderness Channel), which would you choose and what role would you want to play in the team?
2. **Stellar Cooking**: Alice Tracker creates recipes that harness the power of stars. If you could cook one meal using cosmic energy, what would you prepare and how might it be enhanced by stellar power?

Personal Reflection

1. **Letting Go**: Go David struggles with letting go of his father's watch and the memory palace, symbols of his past. What object in your life carries similar emotional weight, and how would you feel if you had to part with it?
2. **Connection Across Differences**: The book portrays meaningful relationships between vastly different beings (humans, thrumans, dimensional entities). What's the most profound connection you've formed with someone very different from yourself, and what made it possible?

Big Picture

1. **Cosmic Responsibility**: The Vraxeik entrust humanity with helping to shape the universe's future evolution. Do you believe humans are ready for such responsibility? What evidence from our history suggests we could handle—or would misuse—such power?
2. **Finding Home**: Go David eventually finds home not in a physical place but in his connection with Joan. Where or with whom do you feel most "at home," and has that changed throughout your life?

www.ingramcontent.com/pod-product-compliance
Lightning Source LLC
Chambersburg PA
CBHW022035240626
47154CB00007B/2419